Dedication

Mickey's Revenge is dedicated to my mum, dad, brother Johnnie, sister Shirley, Aunt Mary and brother-in-law Vic who have all sadly passed away . . . memories that will always be with me.

I know they are all looking down, celebrating with me and saying, "Well done girl! Happy days, keep smiling"

Acknowledgements

Wendy Hearn, who has been with me since the beginning. Her passion, energy, and optimism keep me going, and her knack for business and marketing, get my books into readers hands.

Don McNab-Stark, my editor, whose endless support, invaluable feedback, suggestions, insights, and inspirations keep me writing.

For

My readers who have been there for me all the way, at book signings, on social media, and with Amazon reviews. A big, big "thank you" to you all for your encouragement and support. I wouldn't be Sandra Prior Author without each and every one of you.

I hope you enjoy reading Mickey's Revenge as much as I enjoyed writing and getting it out there to you!

Love has its place, as does hate.
Peace has its place, as does war.
Mercy has its place, as do cruelty and revenge.

Meir Kahane

Prologue

Tommy was fumbling with his zip as the girl pushed the door to the toilet stall open, both of them breathing hard. She lifted her short black dress, exposing a perfect, firm bum. "Fuck me!" was all she said.

Tommy needed no second invitation. With one hand he pulled his cock free from his trousers, and with the other he felt between her legs, pulled her wet thong to one side, spreading her moist lips. Within seconds he was deep inside her, the girl leaning against the back wall of the stall, pressing herself back towards him.

Their muffled grunts were the only sound, barely audible over the pounding music from the bar, as Tommy buried his face in her neck, kissing her, smelling the perfume of her fine blonde hair. Neither said a word, their bodies conveying everything they had to express as he thrust again and again against her lean, muscular frame.

All the anger, all the frustration, all the heartbreak of the past week poured out as Tommy reached his climax. With a gasp he pushed hard one more time, then sagged against the girl, his head on her back as he came inside her. One arm against the wall, one arm wrapped around her, he fought back the tears, the rising tide of despair.

He could feel her moving, ready to turn around now that they were done, but he had to hold still for a moment longer, compose himself, before finally standing up.

The girl turned around, a bright smile on her face and swept her wild hair back from her sweaty brow. "Think you needed that, eh Tommy?"

Tommy said nothing. Fucking hell, she was about half his age! He gave his trademark Taylor grin – that wicked, wolfish expression that he'd got from his dad. "You weren't exactly holding back!"

She smiled again. "Let's get you straightened up, shall we?"

While Tommy wiped his wet cock dry with some toilet paper and then zipped his trousers, the girl ran her fingers through his hair and straightened his tie. "That's a bit better."

Tommy tucked his shirt in his trousers, buttoned his black Armani suit.

The girl gave a nod of approval. "Sorted." She made one last adjustment. "There. It wouldn't do to look a mess at Mickey Taylor's funeral, would it?"

Tommy grinned, checked his watch. Time to go. The show started in half an hour. He gave her a quick peck on the cheek and headed out the stall past two startled middle aged women who were checking their make-up in the mirror.

The girl followed, pulling her short skirt back down as she went. "Do you even know my name?"

Tommy grinned. "Who needs to know your name? I'd recognise your arse anywhere!"

Sharon

If there was one thing the Taylors knew how to do, it was a funeral. It was a show, a production, a thing of beauty, and a chance to show the rest of the world just what the family were about. For Sharon, it was also the chance to finally step out of her brother's shadow.

Everything had to be immaculate, the best that money could buy, something that would leave an indelible impression in people's minds for years to come. The Taylors were all about power, and power was all about the impression you created.

Not just two black horses, not even four, but six, walking in a slow stately manner; their black feather plumes seeming to defy the bright sunshine that had dawned to greet Mickey's funeral day. Behind the horses came the carriage - glass, a frame of black wood and gold trim, perfect for showing off the coffin. It too was black, covered in more gold trim and had cost a fortune. That was power - a coffin that cost more than most people earned in a year.

And then there was the procession. The whole family walking at a suitably slow pace down the Heathway, bringing the town to a halt, making sure that anyone and everyone knew that although today was the funeral of Mickey Taylor, of Dangerous, the Taylors were still a force to be reckoned with. Dagenham was still their town, their manor, and they could bring the whole fucking place to a standstill when they wanted to.

Sharon stared straight ahead as she walked. Her heels were fucking killing her - they certainly weren't designed for walking like this - but not a trace of it showed in her face. She looked regal, imperious even, in a beautiful designer Dolce and Gabbana black dress, her hair teased into place, her make up perfect. She still looked like a beautiful woman in her 30s, always cool and very chic, cosmetic surgery had done the trick. She had the money so why not. She moved gracefully, with a walk that attracted the attention of many of the men who had come out to watch the procession. And they had come out.

Though Sharon looked neither right nor left, keeping her gaze straight ahead on the coffin, she couldn't help but be impressed by the number of people who had turned out. Forget the Royal Family in their castle at Windsor, the Taylors were Dagenham royalty, and Mickey had been their king, and their loyal servants had come out to see the king laid to rest, to gawp at the family, and to speculate about what might happen next.

The king was dead - but who would take his crown?

Sharon allowed her eyes to stray around her at her brothers and sisters. How would they all react? What would they do now that Mickey was gone?

Terri walked beside her. Sharon stifled a sigh. Terri, what have you let yourself become? She had cleaned up well - Sharon had made fucking sure of that - but she looked like what she was. Old and tired. Her dress fitted her well, but she had refused to wear heels, and despite the best efforts of the hair stylist and the make-up girl, she looked worn out, beaten down by life. If there was one thing that Sharon could guarantee it was that Terri was going to be hard work. Hard work helping her keep it together, hard work keeping her out of trouble, just fucking hard work however you looked at it. Mind you, she would be easy compared to her brother...

Georgie walked beside Terri, holding her hand like a kid on a trip to the playground.

He was way ahead of the crowd; he looked amazing in his tailored Hugo Boss suit, which fitted him perfectly. He had aged well, considering what he had been through, the years had been good to him. He was still a handsome and very attractive man. Since they were little Georgie had always looked immaculate, from his fingernails to his shoes. This perfect exterior hid the constant torment and turmoil that was going on inside.

First and foremost there had been his overwhelming grief at Mickey's death. Sharon had heard all about the stages of grief, but fuck, no one could tell you what to do when someone was completely stuck in denial. Georgie just wouldn't accept that Mickey was dead. Mickey was Mickey. Mickey was Dangerous. Mickey was his brother. Mickey was the most alive, vibrant, powerful person you could ever imagine. And therefore, for Georgie, Mickey could not be dead. End of story.

It had taken three days for Georgie to finally start to accept that people weren't lying to him. Three days of arguments and tantrums, of Terri crying her eyes out, of Georgie sulking then retreating into Samantha, his alter ego, before finally emerging on the fourth day with a cold eyed look and announcing, "We have to wipe out the fuckers who killed Mickey!"

Sharon had just given him a hug, and he had collapsed against her, all his grief and sadness pouring out in a torrent of tears that seemed like it would never end.

Once she had managed to stop him crying, he had snapped instantly into revenge mode, wanting to head right out the door there and then to kill whoever had murdered Mickey. He had only calmed down once she had convinced him that they didn't know who had killed Mickey, but once they did it would be taken care of.

If she had thought that was the end of her troubles with Georgie she was sorely mistaken. He appeared later in the day, dressed to the nines as Samantha in a slinky black dress and announced that this was what he was going to wear to the funeral. Fuck, that had sparked yet another row; Georgie insisting that he wanted to look his best, and Samantha was him looking his best, and Sharon screaming that he couldn't go to his brother's funeral dressed as a fucking transvestite queen!

Funnily enough it was Terri - drunk half the time, out of her head Terri - who had brought him round.

"Georgie," she said suddenly, in the middle of another row between Sharon and Georgie. Terri had been sober for years but she relapsed and went back on the booze when she killed that pig of a husband of hers.

He had paused, glared at her. "Samantha!" he hissed.

"Samantha," Terri corrected herself. "You have to go as Georgie, or Mickey might not recognise you."

Sharon started to say something caustic, about Mickey not being in a fit state to recognise any of them, when she noticed the expression on Georgie's face. Beneath the thick layer of make-up he always wore as Samantha she saw him stop, pause and think. There was a long moment of silence, then Georgie suddenly pulled off his wig, stomped off back to his room on his high heels; his graceful Samantha walk gone. "You're right," was all he said.

Sharon snuck another glance at Georgie. He seemed to be holding it together, his face a mask, hiding the turmoil of emotions that so often overflowed into wild outbursts. As long as he can keep it together for a couple more hours, she thought, he can go home and dress up as the Queen of fucking Sheba afterwards.

Finally she looked in front of her and saw the two men she didn't have to worry about - Martin and Tommy.

Martin was Martin. He never really changed, never seemed to vary his mood, was always there, always dependable, always Martin. She wondered how he did it - calmness was hardly a trait that the Taylors were usually noted for. Sharon laughed inside - she often wondered about Martin.   She was the adopted one, the one who should be different from the others, yet it was Martin who was least like the rest of them.   In a family noted for volcanic outbursts of temper, mercurial mood swings and unpredictable actions, Martin displayed none of that behaviour.   He was steady, predictable, calm, always in control, always the one to figure things out, act rationally, logically.   At times it was almost creepy.   Not that they didn't need it, of course.   Among a bunch of hot heads, a collected, rational person was worth his weight in gold, but it still didn't always sit well with Sharon. That was why she so often tried to ruffle his feathers and get a reaction out of him.   But Martin would just smile at her. "Sharon," he would say, and that one word would convey everything.   I know what you're doing, it would say.   It won't work.   I won't react.   And no matter how much Sharon glared and fumed, Martin wouldn't react.

Mickey had listened to him, though, and thank Christ for that.   For all his faults - and Mickey had many - he knew Martin's worth, knew when to shut up and listen to his brother rather than rushing into something full of blind rage.   But would his son be the same?   Sharon doubted it.

Tommy walked directly in front of Sharon.   He was a man now, of course, but Sharon had a hard time seeing past the tow-headed nipper of her memory.   He had been a cheeky little sod when he was a kid, and not much had changed.

Sure, he was fully grown, a big strong man, as big as Mickey, but to her he was still little Tommy – the little shit who had always tried to nick the mints or cigarettes out of her handbag when her back was turned.

But he took after his dad in more than just his looks. He also had his temperament, his hunger. Mickey had seen all this in his son, had done his best to keep a lid on it, but now, with Mickey gone, well, Sharon fancied that the genie would be well and truly out of the bottle. She could see it in the way Tommy walked. Despite the funereal pace of the hearse in front of them, Tommy still managed to walk with a swagger, looking around him, meeting people's gaze, noticing how many people had turned out, soaking up the adulation, the power. The carrot for the donkey had been held out for years, Tommy was ready to show them all how hard he could kick. There was no doubting it, Tommy was a Taylor, a Taylor in his prime, coming into his inheritance and ready to grasp it with both hands. She would need to keep an eye on him. He was a bright boy, always had been, but he had a reckless streak as wide as Mickey's and would get himself into trouble if he took on too much too soon.

She had already seen it with Jeanette. Tommy had a wife and kids at home, but he had embarked on an affair with Jeanette – fucking Frankie the gypsy's daughter – at a time when the two families were at war! And fuck me if the jammy little sod hadn't pulled it off too, manufacturing the fight between Mickey and Frankie Junior that had brought the families back together. So now he had a wife, two gorgeous little daughters, and Jeanette on the side, and everyone who was anyone in Dagenham knew it except Tommy's poor silly bitch of a wife, sitting at home with the kids!

That was Tommy all over that was, taking a chance, not thinking of the consequences, getting in the shit, yet somehow emerging from the manure with a flower in his teeth and a smile on his face, smelling of roses. Sometimes you have to take a chance, thought Sharon – luck is a fickle mistress, but if you're one of her favoured ones, it can take you a long way.

Sharon looked up as the procession slowed. They were at the gates of the cemetery, the crowds even thicker here, coppers too. Isn't that an irony, she thought, keeping back a smile. The cops here to protect the Taylors, help them out? I bet they drew straws for this duty today, short straws get to go to Mickey Taylor's funeral!

Fuck 'em. Fuck 'em all.

Sharon pulled herself up even taller, ignored the pain from her feet, walked with stately elegance past the staring faces, her face a mask of imperious disdain. They had come for a show, well they weren't going to get one. This was the family's day, Mickey's day, and Sharon was determined it was going to go off without a hitch, the Taylors united, dignified; Dagenham's very own royal family at their regal best.

She took a deep breath as they passed through the wrought iron gates, finally left the crowds behind, into the calm island of the cemetery. And for the first time that day Sharon found her thoughts turning to the one person who really mattered right there and then - Mickey. She felt a lump in her throat, had to gulp down hard to force it back, to keep her cool, haughty demeanour, while inside she was suddenly in turmoil, churning. Mickey, how could you? How could you die? And like that? On the floor of a filthy pub toilet, throttled and stabbed like some common, petty criminal?

Sharon felt the tears prick at the corner of her eyes. She had loved Mickey. Had loved the vicious, ruthless, bastard, and now that he was gone she had lost the best, strongest thing in her life. Fuck! Fuck! Pull yourself together woman!

She glanced to her side, saw Terri looking at her anxiously, her frail face showing her sadness and grief, her fear, her hurt. With a supreme effort of will Sharon suppressed her emotions once more, reached out and squeezed Terri's hand, gave her a comforting smile. "It's all right, Tel," she whispered, "We'll get through this together, love, OK?"

Terri

Terri glanced at Sharon. She made it look easy. How did she do that? How did she look calm and in control at all times, look glamorous even? Terri knew she looked like shit, she certainly felt like it. She ached all the time, was always tired, felt like she was about a hundred years old. The thought of getting dolled up like Sharon did every day was beyond her – she was happy just to make it out of bed before midday, and even then she had to suck down several cups of coffee and smoke a couple of fags to feel even half way alive.

Terri stepped inside into the cool, quiet interior, glanced around at the workers from the funeral home, standing with their hands clamped behind their backs, eyes staring straight ahead. Imagine working in a job like that, always having to look serious, sombre, calm. She wouldn't last a day. They all trooped into the church, filed into their seats; the siblings in the front row, Mickey's coffin on a stand in front of them. Terri sighed. She knew he was dead, thank you very much, did they really need to stare at his bleeding coffin through the whole ceremony? The organ was playing some funereal dirge, appropriate, but depressing nonetheless. This wasn't Mickey, not the way she remembered him – Mickey was full of life, full of energy. He would have taken one look at all the miserable faces and told them to all cheer up, stop looking like they were sucking on lemons and crack a smile. Let's face it, you could either be miserable and mournful that someone had died, or put a smile on your face and celebrate their life, their memories. Mickey had always tried to put a smile on Terri's face. Suddenly an image of a Mayesbrook Park, or Matchstick Island as they all called it, came into Terri's mind. Mickey with her, buying her favourite ice cream, a ninety nine with not just one flake but two, covered with crushed nuts and finished off with strawberry sauce. Mickey knew how to turn her frown upside side down. It brought back some of the rare good childhood memories of the pink flamingos, feeding the ducks, picnics by the paddling pool, the ice cream kiosk, the days of the park keeper and double swings; those were happy days.

It was after another of her endless rows with Jimmy, she had called Mickey up crying, and he, in typical fashion had showed up at her door twenty minutes later, with that infuriating, cocky smile on his face. But his smile faded when he saw her. "Fucking hell, Terri, look at the state of you," he had growled. Terri was still in her dressing gown, hair a mess, no makeup, eyes red and raw from crying. "Where's that prick, I'm going to kill him!"

"No, Mickey!" she had answered quickly, "It's not him." Terri could never tell Mickey the truth about Jimmy, she knew Mickey would kill him if he ever truly knew what went on.

Mickey stalked into the hallway, looking around. "Don't make excuses for that nasty cunt," he told her, "You can't put a flower in an arsehole and call it a vase." He turned and looked at her. "Where is he?"

"No, no, honestly Mickey, it's not Jimmy. I'm just a bit upset, emotional; you know the way it is with women."

He glared at her, his brows furrowed with concern. "You're not lying to me?"

"Course I'm not."

Mickey sighed. "Come 'ere." He put his arms around her, gave her a big hug. Terri had to hold back the tears as his strong arms wrapped around her. She felt so safe, so loved when Mickey held her. It was the only time in her life she felt that way.

Finally Mickey let her go, grinned at her. "Come on, shake a leg," he told her. "We've got a date. I'll give you ten minutes to get your act together."

Terri knew better than to argue with Mickey. She scrubbed at her tear stained face with the sleeve of her dressing gown. "OK, give me a minute to get myself together." She gestured to the messy living room. "Make yourself at home."

Mickey took one glance at the mess, headed for the door. "I'll wait outside."

It took Terri twenty minutes to make herself presentable, but Mickey was waiting for her, sitting on the bonnet of his black BMW. "About fucking time," he told her, giving her a peck on the cheek. "Jump in."

When Mickey stopped at the park, Terri gave him a funny look, but he said nothing, opened the door for her, and offered her his hand like a real gentleman taking a lady on a date. They strolled towards the pond, stopped and bought an ice cream on the way. Terri couldn't stop grinning. "You remembered," she said. "Mum always used to bring us here for an ice cream, and to feed the ducks when we were sad about something."

Mickey handed her an ice cream. "Magic stuff, ice cream," he said. "It's hard to be too miserable when you're eating an ice cream and watching the ducks."

Terri smiled, despite herself.

"That's more like it." Mickey looked at her. "So what has that fat cunt been up to this time?"

Terri didn't like talking about Jimmy to Mickey. Mickey hated Jimmy, thought he was an absolute low life. He wouldn't have thought twice about tearing him apart. Terri knew she had to be careful what she said to Mickey. If she ever told him just how badly Jimmy treated her, Mickey would have killed him.

But before Terri could say anything, their attention was caught by a little boy, about three years old, toddling towards them and crying his eyes out.

Mickey stopped, crouched down in front of the kid. "What's a matter with you, all them tears?"

The little boy said nothing, his face red, just continued to cry, a miserable, wailing sound of pure despair.

"I know him," said Terri. "He's Betsy's little boy."

Mickey glanced up at her. "Betsy Bottle?"

Terri nodded. Betsy was well known in the area, an alcoholic with an abusive husband, she spent more time inside a bottle than outside one.

Mickey looked at the little kid, suddenly held his ice cream out to him. "Like ice cream, do you?"

The little boy stopped, mid cry, peered at the ice cream. For a moment he seemed to be considering, then he simply held out his hand. Mickey grinned and handed the ice cream over. The boy carefully took hold of the cone, began to happily slurp on the ice cream. Mickey glanced up at Terri. "Told you it was magic stuff."

He stood up. "Have you lost your mum?"

The boy nodded, still licking happily on the ice cream.

Mickey held out his hand to him. "Let's find your mum, shall we?"

The little boy took Mickey's big hand. "OK."

It didn't take long to find Betsy Bottle – she was sprawled out, drunk, asleep, on a park bench, an empty bottle clutched to her chest.

Mickey took the boy, Ryan, off with him to get a coffee for Betsy while Terri tried to wake her up. But it was what happened next that was pure Mickey. Once Betsy was awake, he had Terri take her home in a taxi and help her get sobered up and cleaned up while Mickey took Ryan to the playground. By the time he showed up with the boy an hour later, Betsy was somewhat presentable, able to scoop Ryan up in her arms and look after him. "Thanks so much," she told them, "I don't know what happened, I was just feeling…" Her words trailed off. There was no need for further explanation. Her battered face told its own story.

Mickey took Terri out for lunch at a local café, then dropped her back home, but his happy mood had been tarnished. She could see something was on his mind. She didn't add two and two together until a couple of days later when she heard that Mickey had tracked down Betsy's husband and beaten the shit out of him; told him that if he ever saw another mark on Betsy's face, he would kill him.

Terri gazed at the coffin. That was Mickey in a nutshell. Look after a kid. Protect an abused woman. Beat the shit out of an abusive husband. Dagenham was his manor, and even if he couldn't control everything that happened there, when something did come to his attention, when he heard about something that wasn't right by his way of looking at the world, then he would deal with it in his own way. Betsy's husband left her not long after that, and Mickey helped her find a job at a local supermarket. And you could bet that every year since, an envelope had appeared through her doorway just before Christmas, a little something to make sure that Ryan and his mum had a good Christmas.

Terri took a deep breath, tried to pay attention to what the priest was saying. He'd been rattling on for a while, but none of it was getting through to her. She should probably be listening, he was saying something about Mickey, but what the hell would the priest know about Mickey, the real Mickey? They each needed to mark Mickey's passing in their own way, and she could think of no better way than to think about him when he was alive. And was he ever alive! Mickey had been a force of nature, more alive than anyone she had ever known. He never stopped, never rested, never seemed to get tired. Yes, he could be a hard, cruel bastard, but for those he loved, those he took care of, he was always there. And always did what was necessary, even if it wasn't what you might have chosen for yourself.

She glanced around the church, full of sad faces. It held so many memories for her. This church had always been a big part of the Taylor family lives. Terri was sure that's where her Mum Lizzie had found her strength, hope and courage throughout her life.

They had all been baptized there, had their communion and confirmation – Lizzie had insisted on all of that – Terri had even got married there. What a farce that had turned out to be, with the scruffy dregs of Jimmy's low life family huddled in two pews on one side, and the Taylors and all their relatives done up to the nines filling the other side of the church. It was embarrassing then, and had gone downhill from there. Bobby's funeral had been there, of course, and now they were back again for Mickey's funeral. She had thought the fuss when Bobby had been buried was excessive, but Mickey's funeral outdid even that. What with the crowds and the press, there seemed to be reporters and TV cameras everywhere. All Terri wanted was to be left alone to grieve in her own way, without a thousand pairs of eyes on her.

She looked around at her siblings. Martin, his face as implacable, as unreadable as ever. The Kid, the youngster. She still thought of him that way, even though he was a grown man, had been running the business alongside Mickey for over a decade. Then Sharon. Terri loved Sharon as you can only love a sister, but she was a hard faced bitch, presented a controlled face to the outside world whatever was going on – but Terri knew what it cost her, what demons lurked beneath the surface. And finally Georgie. Georgie was grinning, a peaceful smile on his face as though he were looking at a beautiful sunset, or listening to a favourite piece of music, not at his brother's funeral. What the hell was Georgie thinking about?

Georgie

Mickey.

Mickey, Mickey, Mickey.

You silly sod.

Fancy getting knifed and murdered in a dirty pub toilet! Just the thought of it made Georgie's skin crawl – rolling around on the floor of a nasty public toilet, amidst the piss and dirt and blood. That was no way to go. Not that Georgie hadn't spent some time hanging out in men's toilets – but that was another story – and he had never actually rolled around on the floor…

Georgie still didn't really believe that Mickey was dead. He knew Terri had told him, Sharon had told him, they had all told him, but it still didn't make sense. How could Mickey be dead? He was the biggest, the strongest, the bravest, the most alive person Georgie had ever known. It just didn't make sense. If Mickey was dead, how was it possible that any of them could still be alive?

He looked around. Where are you Mickey? Where are you hiding? Mickey was always one for practical jokes, had always been able to make Georgie laugh, even when things were really rough. So wouldn't it make sense that that was what Mickey was doing now?

Playing a practical joke? Georgie started looking for hiding places – behind the massive array of flowers, or perhaps crouched behind the purple velvet curtains. Then his eyes fell on the coffin. Ah! That was it! What better place to hide than in the coffin, then jump out and surprise everyone at the end! The ultimate practical joke! That would top everything.

He stared at the coffin, imagining Mickey hiding in there, a grin on his face as he waited for his big moment. Georgie found himself willing the coffin to pop open, for Mickey to leap out. He stared at it intently to be sure that he didn't miss it.

He risked a quick look around the room. No one else was looking at the coffin in the same way, they were singing along to some dreary hymn. It was their secret, Mickey and Georgie, they were the only ones who knew about it. And wouldn't the others be surprised when Mickey appeared? The shocked looks, the wide eyes. But Georgie would not be shocked. He and Mickey would share a look; Mickey would wink at him, because he, Mickey's brother, he knew all along that it was a joke, that Mickey couldn't possibly be dead.

He stared and stared at the black coffin, so ornate, so big, so final... And then Georgie suddenly felt cold, as though the icy wind of death had brushed over him. Mickey was in that coffin, but he wasn't coming out. He was really dead. Georgie felt numb as the reality intruded into his mind. All the sad faces around him, they all knew the truth. Georgie's fantasy was just that. He was foolish, deluded. Mickey wasn't coming back.

Georgie looked down at his sharp suit, felt naked, exposed. Surely everyone could see through this thin material, past his shirt, through his skin, deep into his very soul. He needed his shield, his protection. He needed Samantha. Samantha looked after him, kept the world away. If Samantha was with him, everything would be all right, he could cope, he could face up to a life without Mickey...

Georgie began to squirm, his skin crawled as though a thousand ants were creeping across it, their tiny feet scratching, pinching, pulling at his skin. He wanted to rip his clothes off, tear at his skin, rid himself of his tiny tormentors. Why couldn't he? Why hadn't he been allowed to bring Samantha? If she had been here he wouldn't feel like this, he would be safe, comfortable.

He glanced at Terri, who noticed his look, smiled at him, squeezed his hand. Her touch felt good, soothed him. Gradually he began to calm down, remembered why Samantha couldn't be there. It was for Mickey, so Mickey would recognise him, would know him as he left this world for another.

But where? Where was Mickey going? Straight to hell, that's what a lot of people would say! But that didn't seem right to Georgie, that wasn't the Mickey he knew. Mickey was tough, brutal of course, but he was also loving, caring and funny. Georgie fought to stifle a laugh, and Terri gave him a curious look. What could he say? He had just remembered the blow up doll...

They were teenagers, Mickey and Georgie, two tearaways who loved getting into mischief. Or rather, one tearaway – Mickey – who was never out of trouble, and another – Georgie – who tried to curb his brother's worst excesses. But there were times when Georgie just had to go along.

The blow up doll was Mickey's idea, of course. Georgie had no clue where he'd found it, but he had learned that with Mickey it was better not to ask. They'd just had another rough night with their dad, Bobby, who had come home drunk again, shoved them around, threatened to kill them both. In most households that would have been a night that stuck in the memory forever, but in their house, well, it was just another night with their cunt of a dad.

But early the next morning, Mickey pulled the blow up doll out from under his bed, started inflating it. Georgie looked at him curiously. "What are you doing with that?"

Mickey grinned. "A present for the old man."

Georgie was still mystified. "Why would you…"

Mickey cut him off. "Course, I won't give it to him direct." He winked at Georgie. "I was thinking I'd leave it in his car…"

And then Georgie understood. Bobby always parked his car out back when he came home from a night boozing and whoring, then slept late. But Lizzie, their mum, she was up early, making breakfast, cleaning the kitchen, taking the rubbish out, and she would see Bobby's car…

Lizzie was a small woman, and she had suffered some fearful abuse from Bobby over the years, but despite all the horrors he had inflicted on her, there was one thing she wouldn't tolerate – public humiliation. What happened in the Taylor home was one thing, but take it outside, where the neighbours could see it and you would feel Lizzie's wrath.

The two boys crept downstairs, barely making a sound. After years of trying to stay away from their dad's violent temper they knew which boards to step on and which to avoid. Mickey had the doll clutched under his arm, Georgie following behind, scared out of his wits, but determined to be a part of it.

Georgie crept ahead and gave Mickey the all clear – there was no sign of Lizzie in the kitchen yet. They stole through the empty house and out into the back alley. As expected, Bobby's convertible was sitting there, unlocked as usual. Bobby was arrogant enough to think that no one would be stupid enough to steal his car; it would be a death sentence.

Mickey glanced around, then stepped round the rubbish bins to the car, eased the passenger door open and slid the doll into the front seat.

Softly, softly he shut the front door, turned and grinned at Georgie. "What do you think?"

Georgie was standing by the gate, keeping an eye and an ear out for Lizzie. He peered at the car. "You can't really see it."

Mickey scowled. "What do you mean?"

"Come take a look."

Mickey hurried over to stand beside Georgie, at the back gate, where Lizzie would come out to put the rubbish in the bins. Georgie was right, the morning sun was putting a glare on the windscreen, so you couldn't see inside.

"Fuck!" He hurried back to the car. "Keep an eye out for mum!"

While Georgie kept watch, Mickey fumbled with the catches, opened the soft top of the car and folded it down. He stood back, grinning. "Now tell me you can't see it!"

They hurried back inside. Georgie was in a hurry to get back to their room, but Mickey stopped him and pointed. Lying on the kitchen table were Bobby's car keys and wallet.

Georgie shook his head. "No, Mickey!" he whispered. "We're going to be in enough trouble already."

Mickey grinned. "You saw him last night," he reminded Georgie. "Pissed as a fart he was, could barely make it up the stairs. He won't remember where he left them." He picked up the wallet, peered inside, smiled. "There you go." He pulled out a handful of notes, giving Georgie a twenty. Georgie started to hesitate, but what the heck, where else was he going to get twenty quid?

Mickey thumbed through the other notes, slipped a few in the pocket of his pyjamas, then reached up onto the kitchen shelf for an old biscuit tin. He pulled the lid off and peered inside – their mum's grocery money. Mickey shoved the rest of the notes in and put the tin back.

"What about his keys?" whispered Georgie.

Mickey glanced at him. "What you got in mind?"

Emboldened by Mickey's bravery, Georgie grabbed the keys off the table, went to the back door and hurled them as hard as he could. They sailed over the back fence, disappearing into the alleyway. Trying hard not to laugh, the boys crept back up the stairs into their room and settled down to wait.

It wasn't long before they heard Lizzie on the stairs, but it seemed like ages before they heard anything more. They sat on the floor by their door, which was open a crack, listening.

"What's she doing?" hissed Mickey, as impatient as ever.

"Making herself a cuppa," Georgie told him.

Then two minutes later. "Now what?"

"Looking at the paper and having a fag."

And then again. "What the bleeding hell is she doing now?"

But this time Georgie didn't need to answer.

"Bobby Taylor!" They could hear her storming up the stairs, sounding like she was about to blow a gasket. "You get rid of that thing right now," she yelled, "or this will be the last night you ever sleep under this roof!"

Her angry footsteps stomped past the boys' bedroom door, and they heard Bobby grumbling and moaning as Lizzie rousted him from his bed. Despite his protestations of innocence, he had to drag himself downstairs and deal with the doll before Lizzie would give him any peace.

The boys expected a beating as a result of the prank – they got one most nights anyway – but Bobby never figured it to be them. Instead he blamed his mates, said it had to be some of them winding him up.

Georgie smiled cheekily. That was Mickey all over. Coming up with an audacious plan, somehow pulling it off, and coming up smelling of roses. Except that last time, in that nasty, stinking toilet. Bet he didn't smell of roses then, thought Georgie. Bet he smelt of piss and shit and blood and sweat. And the bastards who did this are still out there.

He glanced up at the big coffin one last time, shivering as he did, feeling as dead, cold and empty as Mickey was. Mickey had played his last prank, Georgie knew that he wasn't going to pop out - not now, not ever. Then he closed his eyes and began softly crying.

Sharon

Sharon held herself upright, very straight, very proper. Even though it was all friends and family in the chapel, she never let her guard down, not for anyone. She had lived inside her shell for too long to let it slip now, especially at a time like this. Outside she looked like what she was – the glamorous, successful professional woman. Professional indeed! If any of them had known what her profession had been for the last thirty years they would have shit themselves. High class hooker and dominatrix. That's what it would have said on her business card, if she'd had one. She rolled her eyes. Thank fuck she'd kept that from Mickey. Fuck knows what he would have done if he'd got wind of that; he would have done his nut!

Sharon paused mid-thought. If Mickey had found out… the more she thought of it, the less likely it seemed that Mickey never knew. How could he not? He knew everything that went on. And while it was true that his world was Dagenham, the manor, he had tentacles, eyes and ears, all over London, through the gypsies and various other connections. And if there was one thing that Sharon knew about Mickey, it was that he looked after her, kept an eye on her.

She smiled. Did he ever look after her! Her mind suddenly flashed back, forty years or more, and the faces of two boys appeared before her, as fresh as if she had just seen them yesterday. Freddie Walker and, fuck, what was the other bloke's name?   Matt Simmons, that was it. Freddie was tall and skinny, with a mop of blonde hair and a cheeky grin. Matt was more stocky, muscular, with dark, brooding good looks; the captain of the football team.

She'd really fancied both of them, and both of them had been sniffing around her. That wasn't unusual in those days, Sharon had the look, boys couldn't take their eyes off her. Sixteen years old she was, already with a woman's figure; big firm tits, long legs, and like a lot of the girls in those days she wore her skirt so short it was more like a belt. Thing was, she couldn't choose between the two of them. It was doing her head in, and as a teenage girl, she was moping around because of it. Well, that and something else that was playing on her mind.

Mickey found her in her room one day looking miserable, and being Mickey he started asking her what was going on, with that mixture of concern and control that he had, badgering away until she told him everything.

The truth was she was upset about Paul and the abortion, how he had made her go through with it. The thought of that so called doctor with his crooked tobacco stained teeth and dirty hands still haunted her, the feeling as her insides, her baby, were scraped out of her still played in her mind over and over again - but she couldn't tell Mickey about that.

You always had to be careful what you told Mickey, he had an opinion on everything, and a strong one at that. So just to shut him up, she told him she had these two boys at school after her, and how she couldn't choose between them. Mickey put an arm round her shoulders, gave her a hug and that grin of his. "Don't worry, Shal. It will all work out, I'm sure." Course it was going to work out, thought Sharon, Mickey was going to bloody well make sure it worked out...

"All right, Shal."

It was her mate Tracey, one of the girls that Sharon hung around with, another who, like Sharon, was much more interested in boys than anything the teachers had to offer. Sharon gave Tracey a nod, noticing the big grin on her face. "What's got you so excited?"

Tracey was breathless and had obviously been running – not something she normally ever did through choice. "Your brother, Mickey, he's quite a dish, isn't he?"

Sharon scowled. "What do you care about my brother? And why have you got that silly grin on your face?"

Tracey nodded back behind her. "He's over there, behind the sports field."

"Mickey? What the fuck's he doing there?"

Tracey's expression changed. "I thought you knew? Thought you'd, you know, that you'd asked him to –"

Sharon didn't wait for Tracey to finish, turned and hurried off across the field, Tracey scampering along in her wake.

It wasn't hard to find Mickey, he had attracted quite a crowd. Thirty or so teenagers, boys and girls, all gathered round to watch him and see what he was doing. Mickey already had quite a reputation in the area, most people either knew him by sight, or knew of him. The boys all wanted to be him, and the girls; they all just wanted him.

Sharon pushed through the crowd. "What the fuck is going on!"

The crowd parted, and Sharon found Mickey with his back to her, two boys pushed up against the fence – Freddie Walker and Matt Simmons. Mickey turned and glanced at her. "All right, Shal?"

The two boys looked terrified, Mickey held them about three feet apart, one big hand holding each one by the shirt front.

"Just 'aving a little question time," Mickey told her.

Sharon was confused. "Question time? What the fuck do you mean?"

Mickey explained it as though he was talking to a simpleton. "These wankers fancy you, right?"

Sharon felt suddenly embarrassed. "I guess so," she mumbled.

"So if they want to be your boyfriend, I need to know whose gonna be with you, taking you out, snogging you, all that business."

Sharon was speechless.

"So, I figured a little question time would help us make the right decision."

Sharon finally found her voice. "Us!"

"Yeah, well it's your decision, but I figured you could do with a little help."

There were some sniggers from the crowd.

"So you thought you'd bowl up here and beat the shit out of them? Is that your idea of helping?"

Mickey frowned. "No! Why would you even think that?"

Sharon just rolled her eyes.

"I just want to ask them one question each."

Despite herself, Sharon was intrigued. "One question?"

Mickey nodded. "Yeah."

"You reckon you can figure out which of these tossers should be my boyfriend from one question?" Sharon shook her head. "This I have to hear. Go on then, what's your one question?"

Mickey turned back to the boys, still held in his big paws, nervous, excited and as confused as everyone else. "You, what's your name?"

"Freddie," mumbled the first one.

"And you?"

"Matt," answered the other.

"All right, Freddie, tell me about Matt. What's he like?"

When he heard the question, Freddie gave a cheeky grin. "He's a wanker. He shagged Stacey Parker in the playground at school, then brought the condom into class to show everyone."

There was a murmur from the crowd, and a girl peeled away, hands covering her face – Stacey Parker.

"Thinks he is Mr. Golden Bollocks," he added. "Gives all his shags a score out of ten."

Mickey glared at Matt. "Is that right? Anything else?"

"Oh, he's a dirty bastard, he picks his nose in class and wipes his snot under his desk."

Several other boys nodded.

Mickey gave Matt a dirty look. "All right then, what can you tell me about this wanker?"

Matt frowned. "He's a wanker."

"Yeah, I said that. What else."

"Well, he's, y'know, a tosser."

Mickey rolled his eyes, glanced at Sharon, then back at Matt. "Anything else?"

Matt was clearly struggling. Suddenly his face brightened. "He's shit at football!"

Mickey shook his head, released his grip on both the boys and turned back to Sharon. "You wasted my time over this?"

"I didn't – " Sharon started to protest, but Mickey cut her off. "If I ever see you with any of them fucking arseholes I will fucking disown you!"

The crowd laughed as Mickey turned to them, suddenly right in their faces. "And as for you fucking two, if I ever hear one dodgy word about you, that you tried to get in my sister's knickers, or you've been mouthing off, anything, I will find you, and I will rip your fucking faces off! You hear me?"

They both nodded vigorously. "Yes, sir!"

Mickey scowled at them. "And don't ever call me sir! It makes me feel fucking old!"

Sharon smiled to herself. That was Mickey, always looking out for people. Smart, too. Sharon would never have thought of that, asking them to talk about the other one. She was going to miss Mickey, his laugh, his wicked sense of humour, but most of all his love. Throughout her life, through all the heartbreak and turmoil, there was one person who had always been there for her, one person who she always knew deep in her heart, loved her more than any other – Mickey. And for the first and only time that day, a solitary tear forced its way between her eyelids, even clamped shut as they were, and trickled down Sharon's cheek.

Martin

Martin's face was as impassive as ever. He knew what people thought of him, that he was a cold bastard, didn't smile, didn't laugh, never gave anything away, but he had to be, had to be the ice to Mickey's fire, the calm one to offset Mickey's spontaneous approach to everything. That's not to say Mickey wasn't a thinker, it was more that he did his processing subconsciously; answers and solutions just seemed to come to him spontaneously, which often hid how smart he was.

It also suited Mickey to have people think that way. If they thought of him as violent, quick to anger, vicious – in a word, Dangerous – he figured they would underestimate him. But he also knew that fear only got you so far, and violence was only one of many responses, and often not the best one.

As he got older, his reputation did most of the work for him – who in their right mind would fuck with Dangerous? – but especially in the early days, he had to be careful where and when he threw his weight around. Although the Taylors had a reputation, they were always quite a small crew and didn't have a ton of muscle at their beck and call. Fuck, if people had only known, they were often surprisingly vulnerable, with little back up and protection, sliding along on fast talk and confidence, taking advantage of people's fears and misconceptions.

The Jewel; that was a classic example of Mickey's style, his cleverness, and of course his balls. Trevor McKnight, the owner, was a real piece of work, Martin hated the whiny bastard, but for better or worse that club was a good source of income.

Mickey and Martin supplied them with cheap booze, gave them protection from the other predators out there, and in exchange they got a weekly cut, a right good earner when McKnight was playing the game. Trouble was, this arsehole hadn't paid the full amount for weeks, kept giving Martin the same old chestnut, that business was bad and that he'd definitely sort it out and pay them back next week. It just wasn't happening, he was really taking the piss out of them. Martin brought it to Mickey's attention one afternoon.

"McKnight's playing us for a pair of cunts," he told him.

They were sitting in the local, Mickey sipping on his Pernod and eyeing up a local slag in the corner whose tits were threatening to come all the way out of her dress. Mickey glanced over at Martin. "Still hasn't paid up?"

Martin shook his head. "Six weeks behind now."

"And you reckon he's taking the piss?"

"He says business has been bad and can certainly show me a set of books that suggest that."

"But…"

"I've gone by a few times recently, just stood outside on a Friday, Saturday night. The place is buzzing, plenty of bodies through the doors."

"So what do you want to do?"

"Send a few of the boys in, have them rough him up a bit, tell him to get his shit together."

"Who?"

The shortness of Mickey's question took Martin by surprise.

Mickey had stopped eyeing up the tart and was staring straight at Martin. "Who you want to send in?"

"I don't know, Wally –"

"He's run off with that bird he was shagging. Wales, Bristol, somewhere like that."

"Lucas?"

"On parole. Keeping his nose clean."

"Big Sammy?"

"Got himself sliced up by some spics last week."

"Shit, yeah, I forgot that."

Mickey stood up, drained his glass. "We'll go."

Martin looked surprised. "McKnight always keeps a few big boys around, we'll need some back up."

Mickey paused, eyeballed Martin. "I don't need no fucking back up!"

He wandered over to the tart, who was staring up at him, eyes full of lust. "All right, Mickey?" she slurred. She was well pissed. Mickey leaned over, slid his hand inside her dress and squeezed her tits. She didn't complain, reached up and squeezed his cock through his trousers. "You just sit right there," he told her, "get yourself another drink on me, I'll be back in about half an hour and we'll go somewhere fun, all right?"

She smiled, gave him another squeeze. "Whatever you say, Mickey."

Mickey turned back to Martin, who was finishing up his pint. "Ready?"

It was late afternoon, so when they arrived the club was just opening up. Mickey pushed in and was met by a big bouncer, eighteen stone if he weighed a pound, with a flattened nose and short cropped blonde hair. "Club's closed," he grunted, rumbling across the floor towards them. Mickey didn't break stride, marched straight up to the geezer and smacked him right on the nose before he could move.

He was a big bloke, so the punch didn't put him down, but Mickey was just getting started. He followed immediately with a vicious knee right in the bloke's nuts, and as he started to fold, smashed his rock hard forehead into the bouncer's already bleeding nose.

The big fellow crumpled to the ground, hands trying to hold both his nose and his nuts at the same time. A couple of big kicks into the ribs followed, and Martin swore he heard bones crack.

Mickey knelt down by the bloke and turned his head so that he could see him. "I'm Mickey Taylor," he said softly. "Heard of me?"

The bouncer nodded, peering through his watering eyes, dabbing at his bloody nose.

"So if you're smart you'll stay down, follow?"

Another nod.

"What's your name?"

"Pete. Pete Cole," he gasped.

Mickey looked at him for a moment, nodded. "All right, Pete. This will be our little secret, OK? I won't tell anyone, you can say you fell off a motorbike or something."

Pete nodded.

Mickey stood up, followed Martin's gaze as two more lairy looking blokes appeared from behind the bar, one of them carrying a baseball bat. Again Mickey didn't hesitate, strode forward to meet them. They stopped, facing each other. "I'm Mickey Taylor," he told them. "Heard of me?"

They exchanged a quick glance. "Yeah," said the bloke with the baseball bat, "So what?"

Mickey took a step closer. "So I'm your boss's boss. I'm the bloke he reports to. So either you can fuck off for thirty minutes while I talk to your boss, or I can take that baseball bat and shove it up your arse."

They hesitated for a moment.

Mickey glanced back at Pete, still struggling to get to his feet. "I went easy on Pete, he seems like a nice bloke. But you look like a pair of cunts, and my patience is running low. So which will it be?"

Again he took a step closer, now just inches from their faces, right in their personal space.

They glanced at each other, both took a step back. "Yeah, well I guess we could do with a quick break."

They stepped round Mickey, headed towards the door.

"Bat!" said Mickey. "Leave it here."

The geezer with the bat handed it to Martin and hurried out the door.

Mickey grinned at him. "Shall we go see that cunt McKnight?"

McKnight was in his mid-40s, with a bad comb-over and a belly that bulged over the top of his polyester trousers. He didn't glance up from his paperwork as the door opened. "What was that ruckus I just heard," he grumbled.

"Just your friendly neighbourhood watch come to check on how you're doing," said Mickey softly.

McKnight looked up, and his face froze when he saw Mickey and Martin standing in the doorway. He quickly plastered a slimy grin on his face. "Mickey, Martin, lovely to see you!" He licked his lips, glanced past them. "Where are my lads?"

"Pete's on his way to the hospital," Mickey told him, "and the others thought it would be a good time to go get themselves a cuppa and a sandwich."

Martin sat in a chair facing McKnight's desk, set the baseball bat on the edge of the desk. Mickey walked around behind the desk, perched on the edge, very close to McKnight. "Got a sheet of paper?" asked Mickey.

McKnight frowned. "Sheet of…"

"Paper," said Mickey. "A sheet of paper."

McKnight rustled around on his desk and handed Mickey a sheet of A4 paper.

"And a pen – nice thick felt pen if you've got one."

Confused, but smart enough not to question Mickey, McKnight handed him a black felt pen. Without a word, Mickey gave them both to Martin. Martin wrote in clear, black letters:

Club closed for refurbishment until further notice.

He grabbed a roll of tape off the desk, stood up and headed for the door.

"Wait! Wait!" squeaked McKnight. "What are you doing?"

Mickey glanced at Martin, who had paused in the doorway, then back at McKnight. "Martin tells me that your takings are down, business is bad, so you haven't been able to pay up properly for a while?"

Again McKnight licked his lips. "Well, yeah, but you know, peaks and troughs, peaks and troughs. We'll bounce back soon, I'm sure."

"Here's what I'm thinking," said Mickey. "I'm thinking your takings are down because the place is drab, dull, boring. It needs a freshen up, a new coat of paint. Don't you agree, Marty?"

Martin nodded. "It's a bit of a tip to be honest."

"So here's what we'll do. We will redecorate, at our expense. That's a very generous offer, isn't it Martin?"

Martin nodded. "Very generous."

"We reckon it shouldn't take more than six months to get it done."

"Six months!" squeaked McKnight.

"Well. Six or seven." Mickey stared at McKnight. "You don't think that's a generous offer?"

McKnight gulped. "It's very generous, Mickey, but I really don't think – "

"What? You don't think it's drab? You don't think it needs a freshen up?"

McKnight squirmed. "No, it's just that – "

"Ah! You think business will pick up without the refurbishment?"

"Exactly!"

Mickey nodded. "That's what we were thinking too, Trevor." He stood up, looked around. "We were thinking that business is just fine, and there's no reason for you to stiff us, to short us, is there Martin?"

Martin shook his head.

Mickey gave a big smile. "So it's agreed. You go back to paying us what we agreed, and the club stays open."

McKnight nodded, grinned nervously. "Yes, yes, that's great thank you Mickey."

"So that just leaves the matter of the money you owe us." Mickey picked up a set of keys from the desk. "That Porsche 911 outside. Yours, isn't it?"

McKnight's eyes went wide. "It – I mean – "

In a flash, Mickey picked up the baseball bat, slammed it down on the phone, disintegrating it. His dark, murderous eyes bored into McKnight.

"I, I..." He gulped, wiped his brow with a dirty handkerchief. "Please, take the car as a symbol of our relationship."

Mickey smiled. "Lovely. Where are the papers?"

For a second it looked as though McKnight might protest, then his eyes went back to the remains of the phone, the baseball bat still resting on the desk, Mickey's huge hand wrapped around the handle.

He scurried over to an old fashioned safe in the corner, rummaged for a moment, then held out the papers for the car.   Mickey reached out for them, then as McKnight closed the safe door and began to stand up, he shoved his foot into the door of the safe before it closed.

McKnight tumbled back onto his rear as Mickey stepped forward, opened the safe, knelt down and peered inside. He grinned as he looked inside. "Well look here, Marty, look what I've found!" He held up a big wodge of cash. "It looks like our missing money." He handed the cash to Martin and stood up.

McKnight looked up at him, his face a picture of despair. "But you've already got the car?" he whined.

Mickey still stood over him. "Of course. But the car is, what did you say? A symbol of our relationship. A gift freely given. The money – well that's a debt, isn't it?" He suddenly leaned over, got right in McKnight's face. "And believe me," he hissed, "you don't ever want to be in debt to us again! Are we clear?"

McKnight nodded.

Mickey stood up. "Lovely!" He grinned as he tossed and caught the car keys. "I think I'll go for a drive in my new Porsche!"

"You knew, didn't you?" said Martin, when they met up the next day.

Mickey gave him a look of pure innocence. "Knew?"

"Knew that he'd have to open the safe to get the papers for the car? That he'd have some cash in there?"

Mickey grinned. "Goes like stink," he said.

Martin laughed. "What? The car, or that blonde slag with the big tits that you picked up at the pub last night?"

Mickey took a long drag on his cigarette, dropped it and ground it under the heel of his shiny black boots, gave Martin a wink. "Both of them."

And that was the thing about Mickey. He was hard to pin down, often couldn't tell you his plan in advance, but he had one, knew what he wanted, had a pretty good idea of how to get it, and wasn't afraid to go with the flow once things started to unfold. Martin had never met a more decisive person, and ninety nine percent of the time, his plans, his hunches, call them what you like, they paid off. McKnight, for example, was never a problem again, ran the club for years, always paid on time, in full.

So how come, thought Martin, how come Mickey never saw this coming? How come someone – or more likely a few someones – were able to catch him unawares in the pub toilet? Did he know them? Were they strangers? Rivals? Was it random or planned? And how did they take you off guard enough to stab you and garrote you without you even having time to shout, to fight back?

It just wasn't like Mickey, and certainly wasn't a fitting way for his life to end. And now Martin had to figure out who the fuck did it, and keep a lid on all of those who were crying out for revenge, wanting to lash out at anyone and everyone who might have been involved.

He glanced around the room.   Like Tommy. Tommy was all fired up, ready to step up, ready for power, ready to revenge his dad's death. Martin sighed softly to himself. Tommy was going to be a tough one to handle.

Tommy

Tommy moved uneasily from one foot to the other, hands clasped in front of him, staring straight ahead. He hated anything like this; funerals, weddings, christenings, you name it, he didn't like it. The formality of it all, people all over-dressed, some of them you barely recognised they looked so different from their normal, everyday selves. Then you had to do certain things – stand here, walk there, look like this. It did his head in. This wasn't his dad, all stiff and formal and miserable. Even though he and Mickey often hadn't seen eye to eye, when Tommy remembered Mickey he was always, always full of life – whether it was laughing and joking, giving Tommy a bollocking about something, or kicking some geezer's head in; His Dad was just one diamond geezer.

Mickey had spent all Tommy's lifetime protecting him from what he did, but really, how much can you keep from your son when you are the most notorious gangster in the area, when everyone knows you're a crook, a hard man, when you've done fourteen years for murder? However hard Mickey tried to keep Tommy out of his business, there was no way he could completely isolate him from it without sending him away to grow up in another bleeding country!

Tommy understood all the reasons why – he had girls of his own now, completely understood that parental need to protect them, but he still resented it. He still held a lingering feeling that deep down, Mickey hadn't thought Tommy was good enough. Not smart enough, not hard enough, not ready to be part of the Taylor family.

Maybe it was his mum? Maybe Mickey thought that her genes somehow tainted him? Mickey and his mum had been separated for years now and Mickey had been with Miranda, so maybe that was part of it?

It wasn't for lack of trying on Tommy's part. He had always done everything that Mickey had asked of him. Kept his mouth shut when he should, always been there when he thought Mickey might need him, when he heard that the shit was hitting the fan, but Mickey had always pushed him away. He never brought him into the inner circle.

And what was the bone that he got, the family job? Running the fucking dry cleaning shops! It was embarrassing, that's what it was. Not that the money wasn't good – there was no way he could earn a quarter of what he made any other way – but still, Tommy Taylor, son of the notorious Dangerous, running a chain of fucking dry cleaning shops!

And the worst of it was, he had to be there, had to do a good job – he had Marty, Uncle Martin, always looking over his shoulder to make sure he was doing it right, making money for the family. He hated every minute of it, hated the smell, hated dealing with the customers. The only part he ever enjoyed was when he could hire a cute assistant for one of the shops. He'd lost track of how many of them he'd shagged in the last ten years, shagging away in his office, or getting a blowjob among the racks of clothes, but it still wasn't enough. He still wanted to work with his dad. That was all he'd ever wanted.

For a long time he had only had a vague notion of what his dad did – people talked, of course, kids at school whispered stuff that they had heard from their parents – but it wasn't like he ever saw Mickey doing anything dodgy. Then one day that all changed.

Tommy was a mischievous kid, never liked being at home, spent time wandering all over the neighbourhood, anything to be out of the house. He knew every little alleyway, every short cut, every derelict site, every piece of wasteland in the area. They were his haunts, his world, hanging out with his mates, fighting, smoking, all the things restless kids did.

That night he was out as usual, by himself, killing time and trying to find another reason not to go home. It was almost dark, dinner would be ready soon, and he knew his mum would be fussing around wondering where he was. But if he went home she would make him do his homework, have a bath, all those things he hated doing. So he wandered round in the dusk, looking for one more piece of mischief to get into, one more reason to stay out for just a little longer. And that's when he saw it – his dad's car, parked up the side of an abandoned warehouse.

Tommy knew the building well, he and his mates had often scavenged around in it, picking over the rubbish, playing out their battles and war games and adventures. Tommy moved cautiously towards the building – there was a geezer standing outside, one of his dad's mates, Derek, or something like that – so Tommy moved stealthily through the dusk, creeping in among the bushes and the long grass, circling round and staying hidden till he reached the back door.

He had played hide and seek there often enough that he knew how to open the back door without making a sound; lifting it slightly, then inching it outwards, little by little, until he could slip his slim body through the crack.

He tiptoed across the floor of the old office, over the rain soaked newspapers, past the remains of a fire left by the local tramps and hid himself behind a rusting filing cabinet. He could hear voices, angry and harsh, as he slowly peered out into the gloom.

It took a minute for his eyes to adjust, but there were huge holes in the roof, and there was just enough light coming in, past the roosting pigeons, for Tommy to make out what was happening.

There were three blokes. His Dad, another bloke, Bill something or other, he'd come to the house a few times, and a big blonde geezer. They were shouting, so Tommy could hear every word.

"I told you," shouted the blonde geezer. "I don't know nothing about it!"

Mickey glanced at Bill, then back at the blonde bloke. "I wish I could believe you, Sammy," he said softly.

Tommy had to strain his ears to hear him. Mickey looked around as though considering something. "And normally I would, but there's something nagging at me see..."

"What? Tell me what it is? Whatever it is I can explain it!" Sammy was eager, pleading.

Mickey turned to Bill. "Why don't you tell him, Bill? Tell him what you saw?"

Bill was an older geezer, in his 60s, with thin, silver hair, drooping puppy dog eyes. "I happened to walk past the shop that night," Bill said slowly. "I saw you – saw your car parked outside." He nodded slowly, thoughtfully. "You was there."

Silence.

Tommy held his breath. He had no idea what was going on, but it felt important, it felt dangerous. Even a kid could sense that something was in the air, something was about to happen.

Bill turned to Mickey. "Can I go now, Dangerous?"

Mickey nodded, his eyes never leaving Sammy. "Yes mate, thanks."

Bill turned and shuffled out, leaving Mickey alone with Sammy.

Tommy could feel his guts tightening. This was his dad he was watching. He could feel the tension in the air, knew something was about to go down. He was half scared, half excited as he peered into the gloom, desperate to miss nothing.

"So here's the problem we've got Sammy," explained Mickey quietly. "I know you were there. I know you were involved. But I also know you're too stupid to have planned something like that yourself."

"Fuck you!" growled Sammy. He was a big geezer, at least six inches taller than Mickey.

"You already did fuck me, when you turned over that shop," answered Mickey. Without warning Sammy lashed out at Mickey, a wild swing that would have taken his head off if it had connected – but Mickey was ready, was waiting for exactly that. As the flailing punch swung towards him, Mickey stepped lightly to one side, clubbed Sammy on the side of the head, sending him reeling away.

Before he could recover, Mickey was after him, moving, jabbing, hooking, a relentless flurry of blows that drove Sammy to his knees.

Tommy leaned out from behind the filing cabinet to watch – he had heard stories of what a great boxer his dad had been, how well he handled himself in a fight, but this, this was different. To actually see it…

As Sammy dropped to his knees Mickey moved in – he snatched up a bit of old packing case from the floor of the warehouse, whaled on Sammy's cowering back. There was a big nail in the packing case, Tommy saw it glint in the moonlight as Mickey battered Sammy over and over until he lay bleeding on the ground, his arms up for protection, begging Mickey to stop.

Tommy stood up, peering over the top of the filing cabinet. He could see the blood soaking Sammy's back and arms.

"Please, Mickey, please!" he screamed.

Finally Mickey stopped, tossed his weapon away. He took a moment to compose himself, adjust his tie, catch his breath. He stood over Sammy, his dark eyes boring into him. "Who was there? Who done the job with you?"

"No one!" wailed Sammy. "It was just me!"

Bam! Bam! Bam! Three times Mickey kicked Sammy in the ribs.

Sammy grunted in pain, curled into a ball, whimpering. "Last time Sammy, before I get nasty. Who else was there?"

For a moment Tommy thought Sammy wasn't going to answer, wondered what else his dad would do to him, but then he gasped, forced some words out past his pain. "OK, OK," he gasped, struggling to breathe. "It was Corky, Corky Black – it was his idea."

"I should have known!" growled Mickey. "And who else?"

"That fat geezer, the one they call Sausage."

Mickey nodded. "Yeah, I know him."

It was almost completely dark, Tommy was struggling to see the expression on his dad's face. "You hear that, Del?" Mickey threw over his shoulder.

"Yeah, I heard," came the reply. "Pair of cunts!"

"Soon as we're done here, I want you to track down those two, bring 'em to see me."

"Got it."

Mickey looked down at Sammy. It was hard to tell but it looked to Tommy as though the expression on his face was one of pity. "You're a stupid fucker, Sammy," said Mickey. "You'll never work for me again, and who's going to hire a bouncer with a face like that?"

"A face like – "

But Sammy never finished his question before Mickey's heavy Dealer boot stomped down on his upturned face, two vicious, crushing stamps that would have broken half the bones in his face.

Mickey looked down at Sammy's crushed face. "Better get yourself cleaned up."   And without a backward glance he was gone.

Tommy hardly dared to breathe. His heart was beating so fast he thought it would burst out of his chest, he could hear the blood rushing in his ears. For several minutes he didn't dare to move, not until he heard his dad's car start, reverse over the gravel, then slowly disappear into the night. Then finally he crept out from his hiding place – not out of the building, but into the warehouse, out to where Sammy still lay, groaning softly.

Tommy approached cautiously, one frightened step at a time. It was dark now, he was guided mostly by the sound of Sammy's laboured breathing. Finally he stood where his dad had stood just minutes before, looking down at the bleeding man. He was big, really big, but now he was broken, destroyed.

Suddenly he groaned, looked up. Tommy could see his eyes glinting in the moonlight as it crept through the broken roof. "Who's there?"

Tommy's first instinct was to turn and run, but something held him – this man was no threat. His dad had crushed him. He was nothing.

Tommy looked down at him, loathing in his eyes. "You stole from my dad?" he said softly.   "Are you fucking mental?"

Sammy peered up at him. "Who the fuck are you?" he groaned.

Tommy's eyes narrowed. "I'm Tommy, Tommy fucking Taylor," came the reply, "and don't you ever fuck with my family again!" And with that he kicked him, hard, in the face, just like his dad had done, before turning and running off into the night.

Tommy had never felt so exhilarated, so alive. The cold air burned in his lungs, but he barely noticed. What he had seen had thrilled him, scared him, excited him, but as he ran home, one thing was certain in his mind. When he grew up, he wanted to be just like his dad.

Tommy gazed at the coffin. Just like his dad. That was the idea. Yet here he was, years later, and what did he do? He worked in a fucking dry cleaning shop. Well fuck that. No more. His dad was gone, and it was time to take the handbrake off. Tommy had waited long enough, and now he was done waiting. There was no one now who could stand in Tommy's way – he had paid his dues, and now, now it was his time.

Family

They stood for a long moment, watching as the earth landed on Mickey's coffin. Gradually it vanished; the black box, the gold embellishments, the hopes and dreams, the love and the violence, the laughs and tears, all of it disappearing beneath the dry ground as the gravediggers shovelled the earth on with a slow, regular rhythm. Finally, all that was left was the family - the family and Mickey's legacy, his fearsome reputation, the memories preserved amongst the onlookers.

"I could do with a cup of tea," whispered Georgie.

Terri, stood beside him clutching his hand, stifled a giggle.

Sharon gave them a sharp look, but Martin looked at his siblings with kind eyes. "I think we could all do with a cup of tea." He glanced over towards the gates. The crowd had thinned considerably now that the main part of the show had finished. A fleet of black limousines were lined up outside the gates, ready to whisk them all away.

One by one they turned away, each with their own thoughts and memories playing in their heads, each with their own ideas about what the future might hold now that Mickey, Dangerous, the king of the Dagenham underworld, was gone.

Tommy was the last to leave, letting the others get a few steps ahead of him while he stared down at the rapidly filling hole, the casket now completely hidden, the sound of the dirt being shoveled now soft and rhythmic. "Bye you old bastard," he muttered under his breath, and turned to follow the others.

His wife, Sarah, was walking with the girls, Molly and Lucy each holding a hand. In a few short strides he caught up to them. Sarah looked up at him with her bright blue eyes and gave Tommy a searching look. "You all right?" she whispered.

Tommy nodded. "I'll be a whole lot better when today's over and done with."

Sarah gave him a wink. Though they weren't close any more - she knew he played away from home, just like his old man - she had been supportive through this. Tommy could see the concern in her eyes, the strain; he could read her like a book. He knew what she was thinking – she was hoping that the tragedy, the family coming together, might bring them closer once more, might make things the way they used to be, when they were younger. When they were in love. Tommy's eyes softened as he smiled back at her. "I'm fine, honest."

But before Sarah could reply there was a commotion up ahead, some pushing and shoving. Tommy glanced past his wife and kids to see what the fuss was about. A young woman, in her twenties, with a mane of blonde curls and a slim figure, was pushing past the other family members, trying to get to Tommy.

Ralph, a family friend who acted as a runner, bouncer, bodyguard, whatever was needed, had put his considerable frame between the girl and Tommy. There was no way she was getting past him. "This is a private funeral!" Ralph told her. "Can't you show a bit of bleeding respect for the family?"

The girl was having none of it. She had a look of defiance in her fiery eyes and was pointing at Tommy. "It's him I want to talk to - Tommy Taylor!"

Sharon scowled, glancing back at Tommy.

He heard a sigh beside him as Sarah muttered under her breath. "Who's this? Another of your bloody girlfriends?"

Tommy scowled. "Leave it out. I've never seen her before in my life!"

Ralph tried to lever her out of the way as the family passed, but she was sly. As he ushered her backwards, she slipped round the side of a large headstone and got ahead of him. Reluctant to tackle her in public, he had to let her go. She stormed up to Tommy, planting herself in front of him. "I want a word with you!"

At any other time Tommy would have been glad to give her a word, and a lot more besides. She had a strong jaw, a wild look in her eyes, and the black dress she wore showed a lean figure with full, swelling breasts. But now was not the time.

Tommy stopped and met her strong gaze. "All right. You got my attention. Now what the fuck do you want?"

For a moment it seemed that succeeding in her goal had taken the wind out of the girl's sails, but she quickly recovered. "You and I have something in common," she began.

Tommy eyed her up and down. "Apart from a being a cocky fucker, I don't see much we share."

The girl's eyes never left Tommy. She took a deep breath. "How about a dad?"

There was a stunned silence. Even Sharon, not one to normally be lost for words, just stared open mouthed.

Tommy scowled. "What the fuck you talking about?"

She glared back at him. "Mickey Taylor, that's what I'm talking about. I'm his daughter!"

The mention of Mickey's name was like a spell snapping. Sharon nodded to Ralph. "Get her out of here."

Ralph moved forwards, but the girl dodged out of his way. "I'm serious! You can't just ignore me!"

Sharon snorted derisively. "We can and we will. If we listened to every little slapper who claimed that Mickey was her dad it would be nightfall before we got out of this fucking cemetery." She turned and walked slowly away as Ralph grabbed the girl's arm, pulling her back. "Come on you lot," snapped Sharon. "If I don't get out of these bleeding heels soon I'm going to start getting really nasty."

"That will make a change!" giggled Georgie.

The family moved away as one, towards the gates, towards the peace and sanctuary of the waiting limousines, ready to swallow them up and whisk them away.

But as they did, Tommy couldn't resist looking back at the girl. She was no longer struggling - Ralph had a tight grip on her arm and wasn't letting her escape him again - but her look of defiance hadn't dimmed. She saw Tommy looking at her and called out. "This isn't the last you'll see of me! You mark my words, Tommy Taylor. I'll see you again!"

Sarah grabbed Tommy's hand and pulled him away, her angry eyes flashing as she looked at the girl. "There's always one, isn't there? One low life who thinks they can intrude at a time like this?"

Tommy said nothing. The girl had caught him off guard, and he didn't know what to think. Everyone knew that Mickey had spent a lifetime sleeping with anyone and everyone who took his fancy, so surely there had to be a bunch of little bastards out there of all shapes and sizes? But thinking it, knowing it and proving it were three different things, so why did this girl bother him so much?

They reached the gates, passed the much smaller group of friends and well-wishers who had waited patiently outside to say a few kind words and offer a hug or a kiss of consolation. Finally they were able to slip into the cars and escape.

Tommy slumped into the deep leather seats beside his wife and kids. His siblings were all in another car, the uncles, aunts, nieces and nephews spread out in the fleet of cars that lined the street behind them.

As the car pulled away, Tommy glanced out the window and saw the girl standing just inside the gates. She hadn't lost her defiant pose, and her eyes followed the cars as they left. Tommy tore his eyes away from her, letting out a deep sigh. "Thank fuck that's over with!"

In the second car, Martin and Sharon had their heads together, deep in conversation. "I thought she would be the problem!" hissed Sharon as the car pulled away.

Martin followed her gaze. It was Mandy, Mickey's ex-wife that Sharon was looking at. To be honest, Martin had shared her concerns, but to his surprise they had heard nothing from Mandy. She hadn't asked to be included with the family, hadn't fussed when her kids went without her. And now she was the model of decorum, standing outside in an elegant black dress, holding some white lilies, waiting patiently for the chance to go into the cemetery and pay her final respects to her dead husband.

Martin nodded. "Funny, isn't it? I mean, she had the right to be there, had virtually stalked Mickey during the final few months of his life, yet she didn't even want to come to the funeral. I mean, we could hardly have said no, could we?"

Sharon eased her shoes off and rubbed her tired feet. "Tommy said he asked her a dozen times, but she always said no. Said she wasn't a part of the family no more, why the fuck would she come to the bastard's funeral?"

"And you believe her?"

Sharon grimaced as she massaged some life back into her aching feet. "That bitch? No fucking way! She's up to something!"

"What can she do now?" wondered Martin. "Mickey's dead, and according to Sol his will is stitched up tighter than a witch's kootch. Mandy will be taken care of, she'll have no cause for complaint, especially with Miranda dead too."

Sharon said nothing. Amidst the fuss and palaver of Mickey's death and funeral it was easy to forget that Miranda had died too. Sharon had gone to her funeral two days before, though it was quite clear that Miranda's family didn't want her there.

They blamed Sharon for getting her involved with the Taylors in the first place. No one spoke to her, they barely even glanced her way. It was one of the most miserable experiences of Sharon's life - and she had several candidates - she couldn't wait to get away. But she had paid her respects to her friend, and that was what mattered.

And now, before the wake, they were all going to Sol's for the reading of the will. And if Sharon knew Mickey, even there he would somehow find a way to pull a rabbit out of a hat and have the last laugh. She smiled to herself. Fuck, Mickey, why did you have to go and get yourself killed? Couldn't you see we all still need you?

Mickey

It was a squeeze getting them all into Sol's office. He wasn't the sort of lawyer who regularly had conferences or big meetings. Sol worked in the shadows, in the margins, so any public show of affectation was out of the question. He was good and he knew it, so if you wanted his services, you came to his tiny office above the chip shop, and if there were several of you, well, you just squeezed in and made the best of it.

Sol sat behind his desk, hunched over some papers; his cheap suit crumpled and stained, a huge cigar smoking in an ashtray on the corner of his desk.

Martin watched him carefully. He was like a big lizard, eyes that blinked slowly, always calculating, always looking for the angle, the approach that would snare him a juicy fly with the minimum of effort.

Martin and Mickey had often speculated about how old he was, though neither of them really had any clue. Through the years they had known him his receding comb over had got thinner and thinner, his flabby jowls and paunch had hung lower and lower, but his eyes had never dimmed - nor his caustic wit when provoked - and he still had the sharpness to deal with any hot shot young lawyer who was foolish enough to take him on.

Sol peered at them through the smoke haze as they all took their seats, his eyes scanning each of them in turn. "So let me see," he mumbled. "Martin, Sharon, Georgie, and Terri..." His eyes finally settled on Tommy. "And you're his first born, Tommy?"

Tommy nodded. His aunts and uncles had all found chairs of various shapes and sizes, but there were only four of them, so Tommy was forced to stand.

Sol waved at the haze of smoke that hovered over his head. "Let's keep this simple. The will is ironclad, no room for arguments. Mickey takes care of all of you, and many more besides." He glanced towards Martin. "And of course, there are various assets that belong to the family that I am sure you are managing between all of you."

Martin gave a quick nod. He liked Sol. Sol understood the game, the way it was played, knew that there were certain rules and proprieties that had to be followed - that was his job - and certain areas that he stayed completely clear of.

"I'll give you all time to peruse the will before you leave," continued Sol, "though it cannot leave this office."

Sharon looked up, surprised.

"There is too much privileged information contained in it to risk it ever becoming public."

Martin glanced across at Sharon, who nodded. She settled back in her seat, not intending to contest that condition.

"What is of real interest, however, is this." Sol held up something in his shaking hand, and they all leaned forwards to peer at it.

"A DVD?" said Sharon.

Sol nodded. "Mickey gave it to me a few months ago. Said I should play it at this time, and not before." His small, slithery eyes looked at it suspiciously. "I have no idea what is on it."

There was a moment's silence as they all gazed at the DVD shaking in Sol's liver-spotted hand, its shiny surface catching the light and sending sparkling rainbows dancing across the smoke-stained ceiling. Sol nodded towards a TV and DVD player on a stand in the corner of the room. "Tommy, you are the youngest, can you make this thing play?"

Tommy squeezed past the others, took the DVD from Sol, squatted down and turned on the TV and DVD player. He slipped the DVD in, adjusted the volume on the TV player and stood back.

There was a moment of silence, then Mickey's face appeared. He was sitting in his office at the gym, a big grin on his face. "Bloody hell!" he began, "look at the miserable faces on you lot! I've seen cows at an abattoir looking happier than you! Cheer up! You're all about to become very rich!" He paused for a minute, sipped at a glass of scotch, the amber liquid glowing as the light caught it. "Pretty clever of me to make this, isn't it?" Mickey thought for a moment. "Course, if I was that fucking clever, I'd still be alive, so you wouldn't be watching this."

Martin couldn't stifle a grin. This was so bloody Mickey, running things to the last. Even when he was in the ground he had them all waiting on his every word, wondering what he would do next. No surprise there - Martin had spent a lifetime wondering what Mickey would do next.

Mickey's face turned serious as he set his glass down. "So, seein' as you are all watching this, it can only mean one thing. I bought the fucking farm!" He shook his head. "Not part of my plan, really, but what can you do? When your number's up, your number's up." For a moment he looked pensive, but quickly continued. "So here's the thing. There are certain facts I want you to know that I can't put in the will, things that even Sol doesn't want to know. So Sol, if you're listening, you crafty old crow, now is the time to stick your fingers in your ears!"

They all glanced across at Sol. He had turned his chair around, wasn't watching the video and gave every indication that he was engrossed in reading a file that was in his lap.

Mickey's fierce eyes and firm jaw stared out at them from the TV screen. Martin gulped back a rising wave of sadness. He had been fine all the way through the funeral, but this, coming right after, seeing Mickey alive, vibrant, in control, the way they had all known him, this was much harder to deal with. How could he be dead when he was there with them, the same old Mickey they had always known?

He glanced around. The others were all staring at the screen, each locked away with their own thoughts, their own feelings. Georgie had a melancholy look, almost wistful, while Terri's face was pure sadness, wringing her hands together as she gazed at Mickey's face. Sharon - she was unreadable as usual. Night and day was Sharon. Most of the time she was guarded, giving you nothing, holding all her emotions deep inside, until the moment they burst out, usually to give someone a right bollocking. And finally there was Tommy. He looked calm, but Martin knew him too well to be taken in by that, could see the tightness around his eyes, the clenching of his jaw muscles, the way he held himself, stiff and unyielding. Mickey had always held Tommy back, tried to protect him, but Martin could see so much of Mickey in him, waiting for the chance to break free. Waiting for this moment.

"So here's the big news," said Mickey, staring straight into the camera, straight down the barrel, the way he had always approached life. "I've got two other families." He paused for a moment to let it sink in. Terri gasped, Tommy's face grew even tighter. "One's in London, the other's in Ipswich." He gave another Mickey grin. "These things happen, right? Especially when you're as irresistible to women as me!" Again he turned serious. "Both of 'ems taken care of in the will - don't say nothing Shal, it's all legit." Sharon stared at the screen, looking as though she would like to bore holes in it with the intensity of her gaze. "Sol will explain it all, so don't worry about the details right now. It happened, I've dealt with it. So shut the fuck up and move on. Now, to the fun part. As you all know, not everything we did was totally legit, so there were times when we needed to hide certain things from the Old Bill or the tax man. So here, freely and willingly, are the keys to Mickey's magic kingdom. First, our old man's diamonds."

Sharon gasped, sat forward. "I knew he'd held some of those back!"

"You never know when tough times might come around, so I held a handful in reserve. You can find them…"

Martin sat back as Mickey detailed where he had hidden little pockets of cash, valuables, secrets and surprises. Tommy was taking all of it in, Sharon too, and she had a memory like an elephant when money was involved.

As for Martin, he just wanted to enjoy seeing Mickey one last time. There were other videos of Mickey, he could always watch those, but they were memories, pure reminiscence. But this, this felt like Mickey was there in the room with them, in the flesh, for the last time, and for Martin that was something to be savoured. Because of the age gap between them Mickey had always been there for Martin, had looked out for him when he was little, had been like the dad he never had, the dad who protected him from their evil bastard of a dad, Bobby Taylor. Mickey had kept him sane and alive when he was little, Mickey was the reason that Martin had stayed after coming back for Lizzie's funeral, Mickey had pretty much been his life for as long as Martin could remember. And now he was gone. Martin felt a lone tear prick the corner of his eye, hold for a moment, then trickle down his cheek. He reflexively reached up to wipe it away, focusing on Mickey's face and voice on the TV. "Goodbye you old bastard," he whispered to himself.

"That's about it," said Mickey. "All me dirty little secrets, all me hidden pots of cash - they're all yours now." He paused again, lifted his glass, drained it, and stared back at the camera. "Listen you lot! This is the serious bit! One piece of advice for all of you that's going to be really important right now, when emotions are all stirred up – forget what hurt you, but never forget what it taught you. One day you'll look back and realize it changed your life for the better. And finally, don't you ever forget who you are - who we are! We're the fucking Taylors, and Dagenham is our manor! Remember that!" For a long moment he held their gaze, then he leaned forward to switch off the camera, leaving them with the words, "Happy days, keep smiling," and the screen went black.

There was a long silence, broken only by the sound of Sol puffing on his cigar and the murmur of traffic from the street outside. Martin looked around the room, wondering who would be the first to respond. Right now they all looked stunned, overwhelmed, but that would soon pass as they got past the emotion of seeing Mickey and started to think about what he had said.

Sharon was the first to react. "What the fuck!" She looked around the room, as though searching for a target. Mickey was clearly who she wanted to blame, but he wasn't there. She finally settled her gazer on Sol. "You're telling me that because that fucking rabbit of a brother couldn't keep his dick in his pants, we have to pay for his bastard fucking families!"

Sol said nothing.

Sharon looked round at all of them. "It's fucking outrageous, that's what it is!"

Her glare turned back on Sol. "We're not going to pay these leaches are we?"

Sol's expression never changed. "Of course you are."

Sharon blinked in surprise. When she was on a rant, people usually avoided her. They certainly didn't contradict her. "What do you mean we're going to pay them?"

"It's quite simple. It's fully detailed in the will." He tapped his cigar on the ashtray, peering at Sharon through a thick haze of smoke. "And it's also the simplest course of action."

"Simplest! What do we pay you for? To take the simplest course of action, or to protect our assets."

"Sometimes they are one and the same. Believe me, following the will - one hundred percent - is undoubtedly the best course of action in this case." He waved his cigar towards them. "And in the overall scheme of things, it's not a lot of money."

Sharon sat back in her seat and looked around at the others. "What about you lot? Am I the only one who thinks we're throwing away money like confetti here?"

Martin started to say something, but it was Tommy who jumped in first. "It's what Mickey wants, Aunt Sharon, and Sol says it's for the best. There's really nothing to discuss, is there?"

Sharon looked up at him in surprise and glanced at Martin, who nodded in agreement. And just like that the wind went out of her sails. "Well, I suppose if you all think it's for the best…" Her words trailed off.

Sol gave a small smile. "So that's settled then."

Georgie looked from one to the other, then climbed to his feet, Terri beside him. "Well that was exciting!"

Terri giggled.

One by one the others rose to their feet.

Martin shook Sol's hand. "Thanks."

Terri looked at each of them, a lost expression on her face. "So what happens now?"

"We carry on," said Tommy quickly. "Business as usual." He looked over at Martin. "I'll take over Mickey's work, right Marty?"

Martin said nothing, looking thoughtful.

Sharon grinned. "The apple didn't fall far from the tree!"

Sharon

Sharon walked out of Sol's office, pleased with how the meeting had gone. There was plenty of money for all of them, all she had to do was make sure everyone stayed in line. There were two potential problem areas that she could see - Terri and Georgie, and Martin and Tommy. The first two were a pair of nut jobs who needed to be contained and looked after. The other two, well, Martin was the heir to the throne, but Sharon didn't see Tommy lying down quietly and just accepting that.

As Sharon walked to her car she passed two young guys, late twenties probably, city types in smart suits, and she couldn't help but notice that they gave her the eye as they passed. She grinned. Why wouldn't they? She looked very professional in her black suit, tight fitting white blouse, and black stiletto heels. Her outfit was set off nicely with a black hat and Ray-Ban sunglasses. With her briefcase and black leather gloves, she was quite a sight.

It reminded her of the day she had bumped into Paul, it was a year and a half now, she couldn't believe how the time had gone so quickly and how much had happened. She had just come out of a meeting in the city, walking back to her car, she suddenly found herself shoved to the side, landing flat on the floor next to her briefcase.

"I'm so sorry, are you ok?" A hand reached out towards her. "Let me help you up."

Still slightly disoriented, Sharon grasped the hand, looking up at a powerful man, over six foot tall, with thick dark hair and a deeply tanned face. The moment their eyes locked, they looked at each other in shock and disbelief. She recognised him straight away - it was Paul. Her Paul, her first and only true love. He gently pulled Sharon to her feet, their eyes never leaving each other.

"Paul."

"Sharon."

They spoke at the same time, both staring, smiling, not quite believing what they were seeing. And then they were in each other's arms.

The love Sharon had felt for him returned instantly, she felt young and alive again. The sparkle was back in her eyes. At that moment she was the happiest person alive. It felt like only yesterday that she had last seen him. He still had that tough and rugged look, so hot and horny, as handsome as ever. The love she had felt for him was back instantly, she realised that it had never left her, she had just buried those feelings so deep that she didn't think they would ever resurface.

She clung tight to him, reluctant to part, to break the spell. What had brought him back into her life? Was it was fate, coincidence? All she knew was that it was meant to be, that she was there at that time. If she hadn't been at the reading of Mickey's will, she would never have bumped into him. Why had this happened? She could feel his body against her, tall, lean, agile, and oh so handsome.

Finally they broke the embrace and looked at each other with excited eyes, both slightly breathless.

"Sharon."

She smiled back.

"I've just finished work for the day," said Paul quickly, "I'm in London for a few days. Do you fancy a coffee or a glass of wine? My hotel is a two-minute walk from here. That's if you're not busy and have got to get off somewhere." His words spilled out, a rapid stream that caught her off guard, keeping her there.

Her heart missed a beat. She wanted to jump up and down, scream and shout out how happy she felt, but she took a deep breath and managed to stay in control. She had a couple of hours till the wake started, but everything was sorted and arranged. Why not? When she replied her voice was slow and calm though her nerves were jangling.

"That will be lovely," she said. "We have a lot to catch up on."

"Come on then," he replied, flashing his gorgeous smile at her and taking her hand.

She walked hand in hand with him to his hotel in a complete and utter daze. My god, what she was doing, was she going mad? This couldn't really be happening, she must be dreaming. She couldn't believe he had come back into her life, that he was here next to her, holding her hand. It had to be fate, it was meant to be.

"You ok, Sharon?" he said, squeezing her hand.

"Yes, yes." She squeezed his hand back. "I'm just in a bit of shock that's all."

She couldn't believe her luck, why was he sent back into her life? She felt like a little love sick kid going on her first date, couldn't remember being this nervous in her life, and she'd been in some real predicaments at times.

"Me too." He pecked her on the lips. "I'm really happy we bumped into each other." Paul turned his million-kilowatt smile on her. "You haven't changed, have you? Still as clumsy as ever, bumping into things, knocking things over and spilling stuff."

"You still remember then?"

"Remember? I will never forget."

Sharon looked up at him. And you've managed to knock me off my feet again she thought as she gripped tight to his hand.

When they reached the hotel, there was no question of going to the bar for a drink, there was only one place they were ever going - Paul's room. As soon as they were in the lift he turned to her, traced his fingertips around her face, her eyes, her nose, her cheek, her forehead. Their eyes met, she felt she couldn't move, he was even more handsome than she remembered.

"You're so beautiful," he whispered as he took her in his arms and began kissing her. A shiver of pleasure went through her. The kiss began soft and slow, then quickly became hard and fast.

He was an amazing kisser, no one had ever kissed her like him. She felt like she was melting inside as his long hot kisses covered her face.

The bell interrupted them, they burst out of the lift as soon as it stopped and hurried to his room like two giddy young lovers. As soon as the door closed he began undoing his shirt, Sharon's hands exploring him as she helped peel his shirt off.

She was desperate to feel his skin against hers, his kiss was like nothing she had ever known. She wanted to relive every magical moment with him again, the touch of him, the taste of him, just being in his arms again. He made her feel good, feel alive. He was exciting. His arms slipped around her waist, encircling her and pulled her soft body close against him, then lifted her and lay her down on the bed.

She closed her eyes and surrendered to him as he began caressing her body, her thighs, her buttocks, his lips trailing kisses around her neck, down her spine, across her stomach, his hand on her inner thigh, Sharon's body tingling at his skilful touch. "Kiss me, Paul," she whispered, his mouth on hers, his tongue invading her mouth as she ran her fingers over his firm body

He ran his hands down her legs, kissing every inch of her body, touching and holding her so intimately, planting tender kisses and running his tongue all over her. She could feel his soft face against her thighs, his tongue searching, seeking, and her hips moved in rhythm, wanting him. She sighed contently, hungry for the pleasure he could give her, the texture of his soft silky hands massaging the smooth curves of her body.

Sharon began gasping and moaning, digging her nails into him, skin to skin, as he gently licked her, satisfying her every need. She was falling, spinning. She reached down, wrapped her fingers in his hair, pulled him closer, her hips moving in time to the thrust of his tongue, her eyes glowing with love. It didn't take long before she came, wriggling and squirming against his mouth, gasping and moaning.

He slid up beside her. Sharon gave him a wicked smile, kissed his mouth, tasting her salty juices on his face, then pressed her body against him, hard and firm, as he lay back and waited for her smooth mouth to kiss him all over, stroke and suck him. He felt the shiver of his skin exploding in a savage impulse. The spasms ran through him as she moved down his body until she reached his hard penis. She gently stroked him for a moment, feeling the anticipation build, then slowly reached out with her tongue, teased the tip, licked around the top, then suddenly engulfed him in her mouth, feeling him gasp and stiffen in sheer pleasure as she began working on him with her mouth.

She stroked and sucked, licked and teased until she could feel him getting close, then abruptly stopped, eased herself on top of him, feeling his full length inside her. "Oh Paul," she gasped, "It feels so good, you deep inside me. I've missed you so much." She thrust deeper and deeper, harder and harder, watching his handsome face, his sparkling eyes staring up at her in wonder and delight.

He pulled her towards him, kissed her throat, her neck, and her ears as she ran her hands over his firm arms and muscular chest, feeling the warmth and tightness inside her.

She kept repeating his name between thrusts as he moaned and groaned below her, Sharon pushing harder and faster. She paused. "Is it nice, does it feel good, Paul?"

"God yes, yes!"

She watched his face screw up with pleasure, listened to his soft moaning. She loved him so much, needed him, wanted him, now, tomorrow, forever.

Faster and faster she rode him, wanting it to last forever, but also wanting him to come, wanting every piece of him. With a sudden gasp he came, filling her deep inside, his kisses so hot, burning through her skin as she locked her mouth onto his warm inviting lips.

When it was done they lay there in each other's arms, Sharon talking, telling him her life story while he stroked her hair, her face, her soft skin. Her hand strayed down, felt his penis, felt it begin to stiffen in her hand. God he really turned her on, he did something to her. She smiled. "I think you're ready for more?"

He laughed, a sound that made her skin tingle. "With you? Always?"

She slowly examined his body, stroking his chest, breathing in the smell of his aftershave and began kissing - his neck, his chest, her hands on his stomach, her fingers tickling him as her mouth and tongue explored his body. This time was much quicker, Sharon hungrily taking him in her mouth, greedily sucking him into a violent orgasm.

Once more they lay back, and this time Paul finally and completely relaxed, his breathing slow and soft as he fell asleep. Sharon lay next to him, watched him as he slept. She couldn't take her eyes off his face, couldn't stop staring at him.

Suddenly his eyes opened, he found her staring at him. "What are you thinking," he whispered.

"At last we have found each other," she said softly. "Do you know how long I have waited for this day?"

He nodded. "I love you."

"And I love you, Paul," she whispered as he closed his arms around her. It gave her so much happiness just saying those words and meaning them, feeling them. She felt like a teenager drunk on his love.

"You're the only woman I have wanted to hold in my arms all through the night, the only woman I have ever loved," he told her.

Sharon looked into his eyes and knew what he said was true, knew his love would always be there, supporting her, loving her, cherishing her, fulfilling her.

She traced the shape of his lips with her finger and kissed him, murmured against his mouth, "I am never going to let you go again. You're mine, Paul."

She smiled at him, the smile of a satisfied and sophisticated woman, but it was with the eyes of a child she looked at him, the child who had felt so much rejection and pain. He had hurt her before, and for years she swore she would never forgive him, but now, against all the odds he had returned, and the past no longer mattered. After so many years of torment, her life was complete.

Tommy and Bernie

Tommy hated hospitals. Hated the smell, the look, the feeling of depression that sat over him like a heavy cloud as soon as he walked in the door. The only time he'd come to a hospital for something good was for the birth of his girls. Every other time was miserable; dealing with sickness, pain, death. Like now.

Tommy wandered down the row of beds, checking names, looking at faces. There were eight beds in the ward, four on each side. Each contained the shrunken shell of an old man, worn grey faces lined with pain and misery, the desiccated remains of once vibrant people, now just lying in a bed waiting to die. Welcome to the cancer ward.

"Tommy Taylor!" The voice was a thin croak, barely above a whisper, but in the deathly silence of the room it was enough. Tommy looked towards the far end and saw a thin hand waving at him. He trudged towards the waiting face, reluctant to meet Big Bernie, reluctant to even be there in the first place. But Sharon had insisted - family loyalties were family loyalties. That was the real world, the price Tommy had to pay if he wanted to really be part of the family business. "Bernie?"

The old man looked up at him. He'd been a big geezer once, heavy bones, big frame, but now his flesh hung off him. He looked like a small kid trying on his dad's suit. "I'd recognise Mickey Taylor's son anywhere!" he gasped through blue lips. "Fuck, you look just like Mickey when I first met him!" He reached out a withered hand and Tommy took it. His grip was surprisingly strong, and he held tight to Tommy's hand for a moment. "Thanks for coming, son. I know you don't want to be here." He wheezed, caught his breath. "Fuck knows I don't!"

He released Tommy's hand and flapped towards a seat by the bed.

Tommy suddenly remembered the fruit basket he had bought in the gift shop. "Here, brought you these mate," he offered.

Bernie gave a tired smile. "Stick 'em on the bedside." He looked longingly at the fruit as Tommy set the basket. The vibrant colours were the only bright things in the monochrome greys and whites of the ward.

Tommy dropped into the low chair and noticed Bernie's longing gaze. "Can I get you some?"

Bernie gave a toothless grin. "Fruit's a bit tough for me…" But still he looked longingly at the fruit. "Tell you what, give us an orange."

Tommy grabbed an orange, handed it to him. He grasped it in his claw of a hand, held it up to his nose, inhaled deeply. For a second his face was transformed, eyes closed, lost in a distant memory. Finally he opened his eyes and handed the orange back to Tommy.

"Wouldn't mind peeling it for me, would you? I can chew the pieces."

Tommy nodded, dug his strong thumb into the skin, releasing the sweet aroma.

"I love that smell," began Bernie. "Me and the misses used to go down to the south of Spain every year, you could pick the oranges right off the trees, so juicy they was, it used to just dribble down your chin while you ate. Gorgeous!" He reached out as Tommy handed him a piece, popped it in his mouth and slowly savoured it for a moment, his jaws working. Finally he swallowed, grinning. "Lovely."

Tommy handed him another piece, sat back, waiting.

Bernie gave him a sly grin. "Your Dad saved my life you know, in the Big House."

Tommy nodded. "Done CPR on you, right?"

Bernie shook his head. "That's not what I was referring to." He shifted slightly, groaned at the movement and settled back on his pillows. "He done that too - make no mistake, I wouldn't be here if he hadn't done that. But there was another time, when he was first starting his sentence." He paused to catch his breath and leaned in closer towards Tommy. "I know he never would have said it, but it was rough for Mickey when he first come inside. He was a target, had a reputation, but prison is different, it has its own rules, its own structure, and no matter what Mickey might have done on the outside, he had to start over when he was inside."

While Bernie caught his breath, Tommy took a banana from the fruit basket, slowly peeled it and chomped it down in three big bites.

"Course I knew of Mickey," continued Bernie. "He was from Dagenham, I was from Shoreditch, you hear things, but our paths had never crossed."

"What were you in for?"

Bernie grinned. "Armed robbery." He glanced down at his withered frame. "Hard to believe, ain't it? But I was a big lad, pretty lairy, liked to put myself about. But in prison, well, I was too cocky, didn't take time to learn the rules, pissed off the wrong person..." His voice and his thoughts trailed off for a moment, eyes closed as he fought for breath.

Tommy watched as his sunken chest rose and fell, struggling for air, barely moving the sheets so shallow was his breathing.

Bernie opened his eyes and saw Tommy watching him. "Lung cancer," he gasped. He leaned closer. "It's a real cunt, if you want my honest, medical opinion!"

Tommy grinned.

Bernie sat back. "So anyway, my number was up. I was running scared, knew they was coming for me, but when you're inside, there's nowhere to hide." He paused, breathed deeply, trying to slow the flow of the words as they tumbled out. "The showers, that was where they did it. No one to see it, and the blood washes away so the screws don't complain. You know it's coming when the place suddenly clears out. If you're smart you know it's time to leave, to see nothing, know nothing. So then it's just me and these three big blokes, one of them with a vicious looking shiv in his hand." He fought for breath, meeting Tommy's eyes.

"They was just about to do me when they noticed one geezer hadn't left, was still enjoying his shower like nothing was going on."

"Mickey?"

Bernie nodded. "Stark bollock naked he was, and he was a strong looking geezer too, all muscle, no fat. So one of these fuckers shouted out to him to get out, but Mickey just carried on washing his hair and ignored the fucker."

Tommy grinned. "That sounds like Mickey."

"Yeah, your dad never done anything just cause someone told him to." He breathed deeply. "So one of these geezers goes over to him, gets in his face, get the fuck out of here if you know what's good for you, that kind of shit." Bernie paused, grinned. "Well if you know Mickey, you know what comes next. Fucker didn't know what had hit him - three punches and he was out cold on the shower floor, the blood from his face running towards me."

Tommy couldn't help but grin. He loved hearing tales of his old man, the shit he'd done. "So what happened next?"

Bernie gave a hoarse cackle. "Well now the fuckers didn't know what to do. Kill me or deal with Mickey!" His smile broadened, and for a moment there was some real life, some colour in his face. "Mickey didn't give them the chance to make a decision. Just strode over, balls dangling, and took them both down, fast as anything you've ever seen. Nasty it was, a nasty thing of beauty." He coughed, reached for a tissue, spat something hard and grey into it, and wiped his mouth. "Before you know it here's three of 'em lying on the floor bleeding and groaning, and Mickey Taylor sticking out his big hand for a hand shake. 'I'm Mickey Taylor,' he said, 'and it looks like we now have some common enemies.'

Tommy couldn't keep the smile from his face. The story was so Mickey, everything he had loved about his old man. Direct, decisive, fearless - everything Tommy wanted to be.

Bernie lay back, tired from all the talking, and for a moment they sat in silence; Tommy thinking about his dad, Bernie recovering. Slowly but surely he got some strength back. He glanced over at Tommy. "I thought there would be hell to pay. The geezer he'd crossed, Mal, Mally, something like that his name was, he was a big shot up north, Newcastle, fancied himself as a top geezer. I explained to Mickey what he'd done, that he was now in a heap of shit with me, but Mickey just grinned. 'Follow me,' was all he said."

"So you did?"

Bernie nodded. "That's what you did with Mickey, you followed him, got swept along behind him. So we got dressed, headed back onto the wing, and Mickey marches straight up to this geezer Mal's cell. He had one of his boys in with him, Mickey broke his jaw with one punch." Bernie laughed at the memory. "Fuck, the expression on Mal's face when he saw Mickey standing there, me right behind him. Big, fat tattooed geezer he was, his face was red with fucking outrage when Mickey busted in, started shouting, do you know who the fuck I am, all that guff."

Tommy laughed. "Mickey didn't give a toss, right?"

Bernie nodded. "Mickey knew exactly who he was, knew exactly what he was doing. He busted the bloke's nose, fucked him up real bad, fucking blood flying everywhere, then dragged him out onto the balcony where everyone could see him, tossed him over onto the top of the cage below. The other fucking cons were all out watching, not believing what they were seeing." Bernie shook his head. "Fuck, your dad had bollocks." Another cough, more grey matter into a tissue. "So your dad knows he's got everyone's attention, right, including the screws - who were staying totally out of it, mind you." He closed his eyes, thinking. "What was it he said? 'That cunt is finished!' That was it! That cunt is finished, he said. You want anything on this wing, you come to me. My name is Mickey fucking Taylor, and this is my wing."

Bernie sank back onto the pillow, exhausted.

Tommy shook his head in admiration of his old man and gazed at Bernie. "And the screws, they didn't do nothing?"

Bernie shook his head. "They didn't care who was on top. They just wanted a strong man in place. Mickey was perfect for them."

"But what if–"

Bernie cut him off. "No what ifs, son. That was your father's thinking. No what ifs…"

Tommy sat back, thoughtful.

Bernie opened a death-shrouded eye and looked at him. "Mickey always decided what he wanted to do, then just did it. But he never wondered about what if, not before, not after…"

Tommy scratched his head and scowled. He loved the stories about Mickey, but at the same time, each one he heard added another layer, another stone on the pile, built his reputation up more and more, until it felt like a huge shadow towering over him, a shadow he could never climb out from beneath.

"I'd do anything for Mickey," said Bernie in a quiet voice.

Tommy nodded. "Wouldn't we all."

Bernie forced himself upright, leaned on his elbow so he could get closer to Tommy. "You tell me who killed him, I'll fucking kill them!" he hissed.

Tommy looked at the shrunken shell of a man, barely able to hold a conversation so wasted was he, and resisted the urge to smile. "That's the problem, it's been a fucking nightmare," he said after a moment. "We still ain't got a clue who killed him."

Bernie met his gaze for a moment, then slumped back on his pillows. "It's not fucking right," he gasped. "A man like that deserves to be revenged." He turned away from Tommy and rummaged in the bedside for a moment. When he sat up he had a photograph in his hand. "You probably think my stories are all made up, a bunch of bullshit from an old man," he wheezed. He handed Tommy the photo. "There's the proof."

Tommy looked at the photo. It showed Mickey in his prime, handsome, powerful, gazing fearlessly into the camera, and beside him a middle aged man in a suit, looking very pleased with himself. Tommy looked closer. The photograph had been taken in prison. "Who's the suit?"

Bernie grinned. "That's the governor."

Tommy couldn't help but laugh. "You're shitting me!"

Bernie shook his head. "That's how powerful your ol' man was. Even the governor wanted to be in a photo with him!"

Tommy looked at the photo for a moment longer, then handed it back to Bernie. He waved him away. "You keep it."

"No, I can't, it's yours."

Bernie lay back, closed his eyes. "I'll not be around much longer. You should have it."

"Cheers, Bernie."

Bernie opened one eye, peered at him. "One condition. Promise you'll come see me again. And you'll tell me if you find out who killed your dad."

Tommy nodded solemnly. "I promise."

Bernie closed his eyes once more, took a deep breath. "That's good then. Now fuck off and let an old man sleep!"

Tommy

It seemed strange seeing Sol outside his office. Tommy pictured him like some kind of hermit crab that carried its home around on its back. Sol without his smoke filled office just seemed strange, but there they all were in a meeting room at a fancy hotel. Very professional, very clean, very boring. Still, there was no way they would have got all the Taylors, plus the other two families into Sol's office. They would have had to sit in each other's laps.

Mind you, that might thaw the atmosphere - it was downright frosty right now, with Sharon setting the tone. She had dressed in all black, not too subtle - and her face hadn't cracked even the merest hint of cordiality as Sol's assistant, Marie - who looked almost as old as Sol - had introduced them all.

Tommy, Martin and Sharon were there representing the family - no point bringing Terri and Georgie, the pair of them were in la la land most of the time - plus the London crew and the Ipswich crew, as Tommy had named them.

The London crew consisted of a woman in her 40s - Tommy could see why Mickey had banged her, she was quite a looker - with a son and daughter, both in their teens. Though he hated to admit it, there was something of Mickey in both the kids. The boy was solidly built, had Mickey's strong jaw and wavy brown hair. And the girl - she was only about thirteen - had Mickey's eyes, the ability to look at you in a hard, flat way that left no doubt what she was thinking. She was doing it right now, giving everyone, including Sharon, the evils. He had to admire the girl's nerve; she wasn't intimidated at all by the setting, the legal talk, the tense atmosphere, the Taylors.

But even though he could see a bit of Mickey in the kids, Tommy found it hard to really think that they were related to him; his half brothers and sisters for fuck's sake! How could it be? Brothers and sisters were the ones you grew up with, your flesh and blood, part of your life. How could these youngsters be related to him? Mind you, Tommy wasn't really that close to his own siblings. Mickey had done everything he could to keep them at arm's length, away from the business, away from the dodgy side of what he did. The funeral was the first time Tommy had seen them in ages, and even then it had only been a quick hug and a kiss, a friendly greeting and two minutes small talk at the wake.

So this lot were just strangers to him, he didn't feel the blood bond that had tied him to his dad, and still bound him to Sharon and Martin, Georgie and Terri. They were Taylors, he was a Taylor, and that meant they lived and died for each other.

Tommy glanced over at the others, the Ipswich crew. Now that was a different story. Not that he regarded them as family, no, the same rules still applied to them, but the girl Melissa, the one who had come up to him at the funeral, well, she was something to look at. She was here with her mum, a tall, elegant woman in her early fifties, and she very much took after her mother.

Melissa was wearing an elegant black dress. She had a slim figure, long blonde hair, flashing eyes, horny as fuck; she was everything Tommy liked in a woman. And to make matters worse, every time he looked over towards her she seemed to be looking at him, giving him a little smile that under any other circumstances he would have considered an invitation.

Tommy shook his head and tried to focus on what Sol was saying.

He was trying to be responsible, take in the details, but he didn't really have the head for things like that. He could keep up if he really put himself to it, but he preferred getting on and doing things to sitting around and gabbing all day long. Just like his dad, that's what Sharon kept saying. He liked Sharon, she understood the way things were, understood Tommy. Martin was different, was more cautious, kept himself tightly wrapped up, you never knew what was going on in his head. Martin liked planning, strategy, was careful, didn't like exposure to any kind of risk.

Tommy glanced at Melissa again - once more she was looking his way - then turned his attention back to Sol. The conversation was stuck on the same point they had been debating for the past twenty minutes - the signing of an NDA, a Non-Disclosure Agreement.

Basically it said that if the London crew or the Ipswich crew wanted to get their hands on the money that Mickey had left them, they had to sign something saying that they would never talk about Mickey, never say anything about the Taylors.

Both the other families had brought their own lawyers, of course, so the three of them were haggling over wording, caveats and restrictions, stuff that just sent Tommy right off to sleep.

He stifled a yawn. He had to get some fresh air. Tommy gave Sharon a gentle nudge. "I need a fag, five minutes fresh air," he whispered.

Sharon nodded.

Tommy slipped quietly out of his chair and made his way to the door. He couldn't get outside quick enough.

He slipped out of a fire exit and onto a quiet alleyway behind the hotel. The fresh air felt good. He took several deep breaths, glancing upwards. It was a beautiful sunny day, the sky, where it showed through between the buildings, was a beautiful light blue, promising a warm day.

Tommy tapped his pocket - crap, he'd left his ciggies in the car. No problem, he was parked just twenty yards up the alleyway.

He admired his car as he walked towards it. It was his pride and joy, his new baby; a convertible Bentley, black, with rich, creamy leather seats. Tommy pressed the remote, and the car chirped as the doors unlocked. He opened the door, reached inside and grabbed his cigarettes. As he straightened up he heard a voice.

"Got one of those to spare?"

Tommy turned and found Melissa smiling at him. He held the packet out to her and she walked over to him, elegantly swaying in her heels, her hips moving seductively.

Her long fingers reached out to take a cigarette, close enough that he could smell her perfume. She gently placed the cigarette between her full, ruby lips and waited for Tommy to light it.

He pulled his gold lighter from his pocket and softly held her hand as he opened the lighter. Their eyes met, and they both held the look for a long time as he lit her cigarette. Finally she pulled away, letting out a breath of smoke and a tinkling laugh. "Will they ever stop talking and arguing?"

Tommy lit his own cigarette and grinned. "Not as long as my Aunt Sharon has anything to do with it. She'll delay things as long as possible, make everyone bleed blood before she finally signs those papers. Until everyone signs them, she'll still feel like there's a chance we won't have to give up any money."

Melissa nodded, her look far away, dreamy. "It doesn't matter, does it? I mean it's just money." She turned back to look at Tommy. "I mean, two weeks ago we didn't even know that money existed, and now here we are arguing over it."

Tommy nodded. But then, he would say anything to keep talking to Melissa. She was intoxicating. Her eyes just seemed to pull him in, and he found it hard not to look at her mouth. Sometimes when he met a girl, someone attractive, Tommy found himself possessed by an irresistible urge to kiss them. Melissa was having that effect on him.

"Don't you think so?"

Tommy shook himself out of his reverie.

"I said, it's only money. We should all just sign the papers and go out for dinner."

"I'd vote for that."

Melissa glanced past him at the car. "Yours?"

Tommy nodded, trying to keep the pride out of his voice. "Yeah. Like it?"

Melissa finished her cigarette, dropped it beneath her foot and ground it out. She ran her hand along the wing of the car. "It's gorgeous." She glanced at him, her eyes sparkling. "I've never actually sat in one."

Tommy grinned. "Want to?"

She nodded.

Tommy needed no second invitation. He hurried round to the passenger door and held it open for her. Melissa slid gracefully into the seat, rewarding him with a flash of thigh as she tucked her legs in. Fuck, not just great legs, but stockings too!

Tommy closed the door and quickly ran around the car to jump into the driver's seat beside her. He closed the heavy door, sealing them both into the luxurious interior. Melissa ran her hand across the leather seats, her dress still dangerously high on her legs. Tommy couldn't take his eyes off her.

"I have a confession to make," she began.

Tommy croaked out a reply. "Go ahead."

"Sitting in a car like this always gets me horny."

Tommy didn't reply. His eyes were on Melissa, her wicked grin, her full red lips. Without a word he leaned over and kissed her.

Their mouths met, tentative for a second, their lips barely brushing, then suddenly they were locked together, tongues intertwined, breathing hard, Tommy's hand on the back of her neck, then stroking her soft, silky hair.

Just as quickly they broke apart, both stung by the sudden eruption of passion.

Tommy looked away, wiped his hand across his mouth, tasting her lipstick. When he looked back she was staring at him, her eyes challenging.

"We shouldn't," he croaked.

Melissa nodded. "And yet here we are…"

Tommy couldn't find any words. He just stared at her.

Melissa leaned closer towards him. "Don't you ever like to do things you shouldn't?"

Tommy nodded.

Her hand reached out, caressing his thigh. He felt himself harden and wanted to grab her hand, slide it across onto his stiff cock.

She glanced around the car. "Have you ever, you know, done it in this car?"

Tommy shook his head.

"It seems such a waste…"

Her hand slid further up his leg. Tommy needed no further invitation. He reached across, pulling her towards him, kissed her hard, his hand starting on her shoulder, but quickly sliding down across her black dress to feel her firm breasts through the silky material.

Their mouths were locked together, eager, hungry, one kiss merging into the next with barely the time to catch their breath in between.

Tommy's hand slid down Melissa's body, felt her slim hips, her long, elegant legs. His hand quickly found its way inside her dress, felt her stockings, stroking the soft flesh at the top.

Melissa still had her hand on Tommy's thigh, but soon reached across and found his erect cock. As she squeezed him hard he gasped. Melissa broke free from the kiss. "I'll make you gasp!" she whispered.

Before Tommy could reply, she pushed him back in his seat, deftly unzipped his trousers, reached inside and wrapped her long, cool fingers around his cock.

Their eyes met for a moment, and Tommy felt a tingle run down his spine. He gulped. "Do you think–"

She cut him off. "Don't think - enjoy!" She glanced quickly around them to make sure no one was watching, then dropped her head into his lap.

If Tommy had gasped before, this was a groan of sheer pleasure as her mouth wrapped around him, instantly sucking his cock deep into her throat.

Tommy closed his eyes, leaned back, his mind free of all thoughts, all worries, just focusing on the intense pleasure Melissa was giving him.

Her mouth slid up and down on him; long, full strokes that drove him crazy. He reached down, grabbed her hair, starting to guide her up and down.

As he thrust up against her mouth she started sucking faster, her soft lips caressing him with each stroke. It didn't take long, Tommy quickly exploded in a hot torrent, gasping and moaning in sheer lust and delight.

Melissa kissed him softly, then sat up, smiling. She licked her lips, leaned her head on Tommy's shoulder, her hand still gently stroking him.   "Still think we shouldn't?"

Tommy let out a deep breath.   "Fuck, girl!"   He firmly moved her hand away.

She looked up at him, pretending to pout.

Tommy grinned.   "You don't leave it alone you're going to have to do it all over again!"

Smiling, Melissa sat back in her seat.   She checked her makeup in the mirror.   "My lipstick seems to have disappeared."   Still grinning she reached into her purse, pulled out her lipstick and carefully reapplied it.

Tommy just gazed at her.

She finished fixing her makeup and looked across at him.   "We'd better get back inside.   People might wonder what we've been up to."

"I don't think any of them would imagine us doing that!"

Melissa threw the door open.   "Probably not!"

They both climbed out, stared at each other across the long black bonnet of the car.   "Will we see each other again?" wondered Tommy.

Melissa sashayed towards the door of the hotel. "I'd imagine so. You owe me!"

Tommy stood admiring her for a moment, wondering where the fuck this was heading. "I'll be back in in a minute!" he called out to her.

Melissa said nothing as she slipped back into the hotel.

Tommy leaned against the wall, pulled out another cigarette. What the hell was he getting himself into?

Sharon

The wind seemed to blow straight in from the North Sea. Even in the summer it felt cold, reminding you that warmth and sunshine were temporary things. Sharon stood and stared past the house to the flat coastal land beyond, the sea less than a mile away. The wind brought a scent of it, so alien to her after a life in the city.

When they were kids Lizzie had sometimes taken them down to Southend on the train to scrabble in the rough sand with cheap buckets and spades. They had loved it. A day away from home, away from Bobby, playing on the beach, eating fish and chips, spending a few quid in the arcade, then riding back home on the train, covered in sand and vinegar, sunburned and happy, bringing the scent of the sea with them.

When they were older, teenagers, it had still been a place to escape to, but this time with mates. Leigh-on-Sea was where they had usually gone, to drink at the pubs - the Peterhouse and Ye Olde Smack were the ones she remembered - eating fresh shell fish from the cockle sheds, then spending the train ride back snogging or worse.

What was that bloke's name? Billy Farrell, that was it! She'd shagged him in the toilet on the train one time, a real knee trembler that was, with the rhythm of the train rocking on the tracks helping them as she rested on the little washbasin while Billy ploughed a hurried track in Sharon.

She smiled at the memory, but her smile faded as she gazed out eastward. This was not the cozy seaside she remembered, this was raw coastal Essex, a land of muddy estuaries, biting winds, home to smugglers and worse for hundreds of years.

Sharon turned her gaze to the house. It was sweet in a nauseating way. A pretty little three bedroom place at the end of a quiet street, painted primrose, backing onto open land. A perfect place to hide the two loonies away. That was how she thought of them now, Georgie and Terri. They were both as bonkers as each other in their own ways, both damaged by years of abuse, by the people they had killed, and by those who had died around them.

What better plan than putting them together somewhere quiet where they couldn't get into trouble? That was how Martin had put it. Sharon wasn't certain at first - she would have preferred to have them closer at hand, but that had even greater perils. Georgie - or Samantha - would be tempted to go back out on the pull, and Terri wouldn't be able to stay away from the booze and drugs. So Martin had found them this little house, and today was moving day. Sharon stubbed out her cigarette, took one last look at the bleak landscape, and headed into the house.

"Floral wallpaper? What were you thinking?" Georgie's voice greeted her as she stepped inside.

Sharon couldn't help but grin. She had wanted to get the decorators in before they moved Terri and Georgie in, but Martin reckoned that it would be better not to - give them something to do, he reckoned, keep them busy and distracted. Idle hands and all that stuff. He wasn't wrong.

Georgie was standing in the narrow hallway gazing at the flowery wallpaper that started by the front door and continued all the way up the stairs. "How very nineteen seventies." He met Sharon's eyes as she stepped inside. "That will have to go, tout suite!"

Sharon stifled a smile. Martin was a wise bird at times. Georgie was so preoccupied with the 'hideous' décor that he had stopped moaning about being dumped out in the back of beyond. Now if only Sharon could get Terri to relax and accept it.

Sharon left Georgie in the hallway bending Martin's ear about how long it was going to take him to redecorate, and went off in search of Terri.

She wasn't in the kitchen or living room, so Sharon went upstairs. It was a three bedroom place - one each for Terri and Georgie, one for family or guests when they came to stay - and Sharon finally found her in the back bedroom gazing out at the same bleak view she had recently been looking at. But Terri's eyes were miles away, not really seeing the windblown grass stretching to the horizon, the pale grey sky washed with tattered ribbons of cloud from a storm earlier that day, like the cobwebs clinging to the ceiling above their heads.

"I know why you're doing it," said Terri suddenly.

Sharon came and stood beside her and gently touched her shoulder. "It will be OK."

Terri shrugged her shoulder to shuck Sharon's hand off. Sharon dropped her hand by her side and stood mutely waiting for Terri to continue.

"I would probably do the same. Get us out of harm's way, let us look after each other." She turned and glanced at Sharon for a second. "Martin's idea was it?"

Sharon said nothing.

Terri turned back to her sightless gaze out the window. "I keep thinking back to that night." She paused, a catch in her voice, then forced herself to go on, the words spilling out. "I don't regret it, don't regret killing that fat, ugly bastard! He had it coming, I'd thought about it for years, but never had the balls, could never summon up the courage. Funny thing is, it was Mickey got me to do it in the end."

Sharon gave her a sharp look.

"Oh, he didn't know, didn't say nothing. But it was thinking about Mickey, what he would do if he knew the way the cunt treated me. And that got me thinking. Mickey never stood for no nonsense, always knew exactly what needed doing and just got on and did it. So I told myself, I'm a fucking Taylor, and no fucking Taylor should let a low life like him walk all over her." She paused, thinking, remembering. "I really don't regret it. I think of it almost every day, and most of the time it puts a smile on my face. If anyone deserved something like that it was him; the parasite of a man, low life scum. Fucking glad, that's what I am!" She turned back to Sharon. "Don't worry, I'll look after Georgie, keep him out of trouble."

Sharon gave her a sad smile. "I know you will. It's you I worry about."

Before Terri could reply, Georgie's voice came to them from down the hall. "Oh my God! Have you seen this bathroom! They must have killed at least a thousand avocados to make this bathroom suite! Tel? Tel? Have you seen it?"

Terri gave Sharon a quick smile. "Someone to look after, to mother? What more could I want?" She turned and headed towards the sound of Georgie's voice. "Avocados are a fruit you dozy twat! You don't have to kill them!"

"I know that!" replied Georgie testily. "I was trying to be funny!"

"You don't have to try, just be yourself."

"Who turned up your bitch meter today."

Sharon stood alone, smiling. Martin was indeed a wise old bird…

Sharon

Sharon walked in the door, kicked off her Armani shoes and threw her suede knee length jacket onto the coat stand. She was running late, and Sharon hated being late - she was always punctual, people who were late irritated her. Time wasn't for wasting. She would have to have a quick shower, change and go. She had less than an hour to get herself ready before her cab arrived.

The day hadn't started well, her first meeting went over schedule, so she missed her appointment at the hairdressers. They managed to fit her in eventually, but then she couldn't find her car keys - fortunately someone had handed them into lost property. Then to top it all, she got stuck in traffic for half an hour. It had to happen to her today, today of all days, when she had her special date with Paul, the man she loved with all her being.

From the moment they met, they just clicked, they were comfortable with each other, as though they had known each other all their lives. They didn't have to pretend to be anyone or anything different, they just fitted together perfectly.

She had become so attached to him, it scared her. She wanted him more and more every single day. He was her dream partner, every time she thought about him her heart would race and her body tingle. Together they had something very special, a chemistry like Venus and Mars, she called it. When they made love it wasn't just sex - Sharon knew the difference between the two. She had more than enough experience to know the difference between a fuck and making love.

All the little things he said made her smile inside. She was consumed by him, didn't have one single thought in the day that didn't include Paul in some way.

She loved everything about him; the way he talked, the way he laughed, how he drank his coffee, how tolerant he was with other people - even those who irritated the life out of him. How he would give her that look that said come on, I want to make love with you. The way he threw his head back when he laughed. She just loved every bit of him, even his stupid imperfections.

It was so easy being together - they could talk for hours and hours about absolutely anything, and even if they didn't talk it was not an uncomfortable silence, neither of them felt uneasy or ever had to find a topic of conversation. They found happiness in the simple things, things that didn't cost a penny, like watching a film, taking photos, holding hands, singing along to oldies on the radio, watching the sunset. Or choosing a poem a day for each other, or a song of the day, skimming stones, feeding the ducks, walking in the rain. Everything with him was magical. He was her beginning and her end.

Sharon didn't feel the need to go out and about when they were together. The time they had together was short, she wanted him to herself, didn't want to share him with anyone. They had lost so much time already. She didn't need to be out and about with him socialising, drinking, chatting bollocks with people.

She loved that man so much, he was her world, was everything she wanted, everything she needed. Never in her life had she wanted to get married, but they had talked about it, where they would like to get married, where they would live, it was all a fairy tale come true for Sharon. There was one big, complication however - he was married.

Alongside the love, the excitement, the dizziness, Sharon also felt mixed up, empty and confused. A part of her didn't like the effect he was having on her, the loss of control. Her worst fear every single day was that he was going to disappear from her life.

He had said he would leave his wife, he just needed the right time, the right opportunity to talk to her about it, but Sharon couldn't pin him down on a date. She didn't like the uncertainty of it all. She just couldn't cope with it, she needed to be in control of things, to know where she was heading and what she was doing. She couldn't make any plans with him, she couldn't send him cards or gifts, she couldn't book a holiday, couldn't organise anything.

And yet every day she was falling deeper and deeper for him, was totally and utterly consumed by him twenty-four seven. If her friends knew how she was with him they would be in total shock, it was so not the Sharon they knew. Her close friend Laura was the only person she had said anything to. Laura was a real down to earth friend and told Sharon she was a soppy mare. "What's the matter with you?" she would say, then tut and roll her eyes at Sharon. "You're sitting indoors on a Friday night and he's indoors all snuggled up with his old lady." She gave Sharon a look. "You're mugging yourself off girl," she continued, "you don't deserve this, you're worth more than that." She moved closer to Sharon, put her arm around her. "You should give him the boot, let him see what it's like without you. He will realise what he's lost when you're gone, then he'll get rid of his old lady and come crawling back to you." Sharon said nothing. "You can have any man you want, Sharon, what the fuck is wrong with you? I don't get it."

Why would she get it? Nobody would get it, Sharon didn't get it herself, the why's and when's constantly on her mind. She had tried analysing it all, she didn't know what he did to her. Maybe it was that first kiss? Or perhaps he had put some love potion in her drink? He was her first thought every morning and last thought every night.

Sharon was just undressing when the phone rang. As soon as she answered she recognised his soft, sultry voice. "Hi, sexy."

A smile instantly appeared on her face. "Hello Baby," she cooed. "How are you?"

"I'm missing you so much, I haven't seen you for a week." She could hear him smile as they spoke. She sat on the edge of the bed in just her lingerie. "I've missed you too, I can't wait to hold you in my arms, kiss your beautiful face. We have a lot of time to make up for. I've lost count how many kisses you owe me."

"You're going to get every kiss," he promised. "I'm going to kiss your beautiful body all over."

Sharon shivered. "Mmmmm, sounds good. I can't wait."

"I'm going start at your feet and kiss and lick my way up your beautiful body. Calves, shins, thighs, stomach, breasts, and then I'm going to spend hours kissing between your legs…"

Sharon giggled. "Ooh, you're driving me crazy, and I've got to get ready."

"I thought you liked it?" he teased.

"Like it? I love it! I'm soaking wet just thinking about it, that's what you do to me."

"What are you wearing tonight?"

Sharon glanced over at the black cocktail dress hanging on the wardrobe door. "It's a surprise. You'll have to wait and see."

"Will it look good on the bedroom floor?"

"Oh yes." She smiled to herself, reached between her legs and stroked herself through the thin material of her panties. "Why aren't you here now? I want you."

She could hear him breathing.

"I want you too," he whispered. "I want your legs wrapped tightly round my neck, my tongue licking you, tasting you, your hips wriggling against my face. You're wet now, aren't you?"

"Very," she gasped, rubbing herself faster.

"I'm kissing your pussy, my fingers inside you. Do you want it hard or soft, baby?"

"I don't care, just keep talking," she gasped.

"You're touching yourself, aren't you?"

"Uh-huh." Her fingers moved faster and faster across her clitoris, her breathing increasing.

"I'm licking your clitoris, then driving my tongue inside you."

Her hand moved quicker and quicker, her head back in ecstasy as she reached her climax.

"I'm tasting you, teasing you, devouring every inch of you…"

With a gasp she came, her body shivering and shaking as she fought to bring her breathing back under control. Finally she was able to speak. "Do you know what you do to me?" she whispered. "How much I love you?"

"Yes I do," he assured her, "I feel every bit of it. I love you too."

"I love you more than yesterday but not as much as tomorrow," she crooned.

"I love you too. See you soon babe, and don't be late."

"If I am it's your fault," she laughed. "I will get you back for this!"

"I'm looking forward to it."

"I'll see you soon Mr. Super Sexy."

"Ok babe, bye."

Sharon put the phone down. God she loved that man so much, he made her feel happy inside and out. He brought magic and sunshine into her life. That dull throb of loneliness that had been with her every single day before, it had vanished when she found him. She had found someone who loved her for who she was, understood her, and made her smile.

Sharon glanced over at her bedside table, at the photo that stood there - Mickey and Miranda on their wedding day. She traced her finger over the pair of them. It was so sad, they were gone too soon. She didn't realise how much she missed them both. But then she smiled. It had worked for them – Mickey was married when they had got back together, but he had divorced Mandy and he and Miranda had been blissfully happy.

Of course, Mickey had Miranda had a long history. Sharon gazed at the photo, thinking of the first time she had realized that Miranda was in love with her brother. They must have been sixteen, seventeen…

The school bell rang signifying the end of the school day. Sharon and Miranda walked arm in arm towards the school gate, chatting, waiting for their respective lifts home. Miranda had a chauffeur, while Sharon was waiting for Fat Jack, a good friend of her dad's. Fat Jack was like a bodyguard to her, watching her every move, so her dad knew who her friends were, where she was. He dropped her off at school every day, picked her up and took her home afterwards. It was the only way they could keep her from bunking off school.

Miranda, by contrast, was one of the most popular girls in the school. Everyone liked her, even the teachers.

She studied hard and got excellent exam results, all A's. Miranda had always been a good girl, had never been led astray. She'd never tried smoking, said the smell of it repulsed her. Drugs were not for her either, and she didn't even drink – though she had been offered both of them many times, she said she needed to be in control of herself, what she was doing. She studied hard at school and never brought any trouble home to her door - unlike Sharon!

Sharon was impulsive and loud, said things as they were, you had to take her or leave her on her terms. Miranda, on the other hand, was Miss Prim and Proper, but they somehow complemented each other. And now Miranda had started using the f word – it sounded so weird to Sharon when Miranda swore, she was too posh, it just didn't sound right, but it made Sharon smile.

She leaned against the wall, pulled out a pack of ciggies, lit one up, savouring the smoke. "I can't wait for your engagement party on Saturday," she began. "A big marquee and everything, very posh, very nice." She squeezed Miranda's arm. "I'm so happy for you and Charles, getting engaged and all. You know everyone in school is jealous?"

Miranda didn't say anything.

Sharon peered at her. "What's a matter with you? You ain't been right for ages, haven't been yourself."

Miranda bit her lip, looking away.

"Come on then, what is it? We never keep secrets. We tell each other everything." Sharon peered at her. "You're not pregnant are you? Have you and Charlie boy been doing the nasty?"

"No!" Miranda glared at her. "You know I haven't slept with him yet!"

Sharon shrugged. "So tell me why you are being so fucking miserable, then. You should be jumping through hoops with a big smile on your face." Sharon grinned. "You've either got PMT or there's something you're not telling me."

Miranda sighed. "I know I'm meant to feel so happy. Like you say, I should be grinning from ear to ear, right, jumping with excitement?" She looked away, then back at Sharon. "Everyone is happy with this fucking engagement - everyone except me. I don't feel anything for him. He does nothing for me, Sharon." She looked at her, her eyes pleading with Sharon. "What am I going to do?"

Sharon looked at her like she was crazy. "Are you mad? He's good looking, got a great body, one of the hottest blokes around, and he's loaded. With his filthy rich family you'll never want for nothing. He's over you like a rash and he don't do anything for ya? You're off your rocker." Sharon grinned. "I'll take Charlie boy off your hands for ya, put him through his paces, no problem!"

Miranda sighed, exasperated. "I wish you would."

Sharon looked at her more closely. "You're serious, aren't you?"

Miranda nodded.

"Well if it's that bad, you've got to tell him. Cancel this big fuck off party, give back the diamond ring. If you don't want to get married, break it off, sorted, done. Better now than after the party, right?"

"I wish it was that simple."

"It is. Just tell him."

Miranda shook her head. "I can't."

Sharon scowled. "Why not?"

"It's complicated."

"Go on…"

"I don't like him or love him, Sharon. He repulses me. And the thought of his spoilt, arrogant, selfish pig's his body on mine makes me want to gag."

"Ok, so if it's not right, it just isn't. Don't do it."

"The whole relationship is a big lie, a charade, a marriage of convenience, but I have no choice."

Sharon was puzzled. "What do you mean, no choice?"

"This engagement and marriage were planned between the families before I was even born," Miranda explained. "I have to marry him. The contract has been signed and sealed and I am the delivery. I was a baby made for payment."

Sharon listened to her in shock, stared at her wide eyed. "Fucking hell, Miranda, that's sick."

There were tears in Miranda's eyes. "Everyone is happy with the news except me. Love is meant to be a magical feeling and all I feel is sick when I think of Charles. I don't love him one single bit."

Sharon took her arm, forced Miranda to look at her. "You need to talk to your mum and dad! You can't marry him, there's got to be a way out. How can you get engaged to someone you hardly know, and what you do know you don't like?"

"I've tried, but they won't listen," Miranda replied quickly. "All I get from my mother is 'he's a nice boy, from a good family. Charles is a man with upstanding values, we are so proud of you, we just want the best for you you're a very lucky young lady, Miranda, blah blah blah."

"What about your dad?"

"He's even worse. He's a renowned sports man, he tells me, an excellent rugby player, his dad is one of the richest men in London. You're marrying into a fine family Miranda."

Sharon didn't know what to say.

"Sharon, I hate them, hate him," sobbed Miranda. "It's not the best for me, it's the best for them – I've spent my whole life watching them sucking up to his family, it makes me feel sick, I feel like a piece of meat. How could they do this to me? They are happy and proud because I'm marrying Charles Stock, but I'm in love with someone else."

Sharon nearly chocked. "What? Who?"

But before Miranda could reply they saw Charles sauntering towards them looking cool, calm and collected. He was built like a brick shit house with short cropped hair, deep, dazzling blue eyes. He was well aware he could get any girl he wanted at any time; Charles always got what he wanted. He was full of himself, with a massive ego, and didn't seem to care who knew it. As Charles approached there was the roar of a car and

Mickey pulled up in his Triumph Stag. He jumped out grinning. "All right Shal, Miranda. Fat Jack's out on a job, so you got me today!"

And there it was, that moment, the moment when Sharon realised who Miranda was in love with. She took a quick glance at Mickey as Charles wandered up, but there was no doubt, no question. Miranda had fallen in love with Sharon's brother.

Sharon had been gazing at their wedding photo, holding it in her lap. Still smiling she set the photo back on the bedside, finished undressing and got in the shower. If it could work for Mickey and Miranda after all those years, it could work for her and Paul. She couldn't wait to be in Paul's arms. She was deliriously happy that they were going to be spending the whole weekend together, she felt like a little kid at Christmas. It was going to be perfect, and nothing could spoil it.

Tommy

Tommy had missed the gym. With everything else that was going on, it had been a couple of weeks since he'd been there, and he'd forgotten how much he loved the place. But as soon as he walked in the door, and the smell of sweat and liniment washed over him, the sound of fists pounding, weights crashing, music blasting assailed him, he instantly felt better, like he was home.

Taylors had always been Mickey's place. Everyone knew that. It was his home, his castle, the centre of his world. But now, without Mickey, what was it? Whose was it? Martin had never really cared for it. Sharon certainly didn't feel at home there. That left Tommy. Tommy, the heir apparent, the chip off the old block, the apple that had fallen close to the tree. Tommy looked around. Why not? Why shouldn't he take possession of the gym, make it his, his domain? Someone had to care for it, love it, and it had to be a Taylor. Right there and then Tommy made the decision. From now on, this was his, his gym, his passion, his home.

"Tommy? Can I have a word?"

Tommy turned towards the soft voice, almost out of place in the hurly burly of the gym. But the speaker wasn't out of place. It was Kenny, the fastest, best fighter Tommy had ever seen up close, and Mickey's protégé, his great hope for the upcoming London Olympics. "What's up, Kenny?"

Kenny looked nervous. As powerful and certain as he was in the ring, he was shy and nervous when talking to people. "I...I was thinking," began Kenny.

Tommy glanced over. He could see Martin and Sharon sitting in the office, waiting for him, ready to begin their first official business meeting since Mickey's death. "Yeah, what's up?"

"Your, dad, Mickey? Well he was training me..." Kenny's words trailed off.

Tommy was distracted. Sharon and Martin were talking, he didn't want them starting without him, didn't want them making decisions without him there. Who knows what they were discussing?

"Well, I was wondering. Would you train me?"

Tommy turned suddenly back to Kenny. "What?"

Kenny almost seemed to flinch as Tommy stared at him. "I'm sorry, I didn't mean to - "

" - you want me to train you?" He looked around the gym. There were several other fighters being put through their paces by their trainers. "There's loads of other trainers here, better and more experienced than me. What about The Lip?" They both turned and looked at a grizzled man in his 50s with a hard body and a fierce face. He was working with a young fighter in the far corner of the gym.

Kenny shrugged. "I dunno. He's a good trainer but..."

"But what?" Tommy gazed at Kenny.

Kenny looked embarrassed.   "Well…he's not a Taylor…"

Tommy stared back at him. "And that matters?"

"That's everything! Your dad, it wasn't just that he was a great trainer - he was good, don't get me wrong - but he was a Taylor. And you, you're just like him, and you know the game, and…"

Tommy had never heard Kenny say that much - ever. "And you want me to train you?"

Kenny nodded.

Tommy looked around the gym. Big shoes to fill. But if it was going to be his club, what better way to make his mark than train the best fucking fighter in the whole pace? He turned back to Kenny. "You work with me, you do it my way, right?"

Kenny nodded eagerly, his face wreathed in a smile.

Tommy was thoughtful for a moment. "All right, write down your training program, everything you've been doing. And list your strengths and weaknesses, what you're good at, where you think you can improve. Got it?"

Kenny looked like he'd won the lottery. "Yes, sir!"

"You meet me here six o'clock sharp tomorrow, ready to work, got it?"

Kenny nodded again.

"Now go shower up, make sure have a good meal tonight. As of tomorrow you're going to need all your strength!"

Martin looked up as Tommy strutted in. "About bloody time." He glanced up at the clock on the wall. "Seven o'clock we said."

Tommy glanced at the clock. Five past seven. He started to say something, then bit his tongue. There were going to be battles ahead, and Martin's demeanour told him that he was expecting a fight. He'd let him win this one, save his power for the important issues. "Sorry 'bout that." He settled into a chair opposite Martin's desk and glanced at Sharon, who rewarded him with a quick smile. "So where do we begin?"

Martin shuffled some papers on his desk, clearing his throat. "Mickey's death is a timely reminder to us of the realities we face."

Fuck, thought Tommy, this is the death of his brother, and he's talking about it like a fucking stockholders' report or something.

"We've been sailing close to the wind for a long time, sooner or later it was going to cost us." He leaned forward. "The world has changed, some big players have moved in, and we can't compete."

Again Tommy bit his tongue, choosing to bide his time. "So what's on your mind? You've got a plan, right? I mean, you've always got a plan, don't you." He tried to keep the edge out of his voice, but it was impossible. Both Sharon and Martin knew him too well.

Martin sat up straighter.

Sharon looked back and forth between the two of them, saying nothing. Watching, waiting. That was Sharon's way.

"OK, I'll get straight to it. I think we should go legit. 100%. I've been pushing Mickey in that direction for years, and the events of the past few months have only confirmed my view that it's the right way to go."

Tommy stared back at him, his mind churning. "Legit as in?"

"Haulage. I've found a company that's ripe for a buy out, and it's a business I know from Australia. We can make good money, never have to worry about the Old Bill or the drug gangs again." Martin stopped, looked at them both, raising his eyebrow enquiringly.

Tommy took a deep breath. He could see Sharon beside him. She shifted in her seat, but said nothing. Typical Sharon. This was his moment. It was now or never - in for a penny, in for a pound. "I fucking hate it!"

Martin blinked at his vehement response, started to say something, but Tommy cut him off. "You had your say, now I have mine!"

Martin sat back folded his hands in his lap. "Go ahead."

"You talk about a legit business like it's the fucking bees' knees, the be all and end all. That's fine for you to say, you've been running the family business with Mickey. Me? I've been running a chain of dry cleaning shops! Fucking dry cleaning! Do you have any idea what that's like? Being a fucking Taylor and being shunted off to run a fucking dry cleaners! Fuck, if I ever smell that fucking horrible smell again I think I'll probably top myself!"

"Fine, we get a manager for the shops, put you in charge of - "

" - that's not the fucking point, Marty!" Tommy had never called his uncle by that name before, but it was time he stepped up, time he stopped being the little kid. "Do you have any idea what it's like being a Taylor and having everyone know you're nothing but a manager, a fucking errand boy!" Tommy could feel his temper rising and did nothing to hold it back. "I'm Mickey fucking Taylor's son! My dad is dead, and now it's my time, my turn! Dry cleaning? Haulage? That's not what the fucking Taylors do! You said we've been sailing close to the wind? I say bring it on! Let's sail right into that fucking wind!" He stopped, breathless, glanced at Sharon, implacable as ever, then back at Martin.

Martin shook his head. "You have no idea what you're getting into. This isn't a game, Tommy, this is fucking real! You think it's all like the movies? Women and cocaine and flash cars and shit? It's not! It's a rough, dirty game, where people get hurt, people die, where you're always wondering if today will be the day the police bust in, or a rival fucks you up, or someone you know gets killed! That's what you're asking for, you know that? Is that what you really want?"

"Yes! That's exactly what I want!"

Martin laughed, a cold, bitter sound. "You'd be way over your head."

"What? Like with the gypsies? I was way over my head there, wasn't I, yet I was the one who stopped a full on war between the families. I didn't notice you sorting that one out, Marty!"

Martin said nothing.

Sharon pulled out a cigarette, a gold lighter and tapped her cigarette pensively on the arm of the chair. "He's got a point, Marty."

"Fucking right I've got a point! I've also got a proposition. From the gypsies."

Martin shook his head. "No, no, we don't - "

"Let's hear him out." Sharon lit her cigarette, blew a cloud of smoke up towards the yellowed ceiling.

"Frankie Junior wants us to come in with them on a smuggling route. Duty free cigarettes from Europe." Tommy leaned forward. "I've done my research on this, there's a ton of fucking money to be made, easy money. They reckon almost half the fags sold in this country are smuggled in, it's a fucking gold mine!"

Martin ignored Tommy, turned to Sharon. "You know what I think, you know what he thinks. You hold the deciding vote."

Sharon looked between the two of them, savouring her cigarette. "I say we talk to Frankie, see what's involved."

Martin let out a sigh of exasperation. "What about - "

" – it's settled," said Sharon. "We all agreed, three of us, everything goes to a vote, we accept the decision. It was your fucking idea to do things democratically, Marty!"

"Yeah, I know. Not one of my better ones." He rubbed his head and reached for the glass of scotch that had sat untouched throughout their discussion. "All right, so Tommy talks to Frankie, gets all the info, then we make a final decision. What about the terrible twosome?"

Sharon grinned. "I spoke to them today. Georgie's happy as a pig in shit tearing the place apart and redecorating. Terri's keeping busy mothering him and trying to keep his hands off the young plasterer. I'm going to see them in a couple of days, got a present for Terri that should keep her happy."

"What you got her?" wondered Tommy.

"You'll see."

Martin frowned. "What?"

Sharon gave an enigmatic smile. "Let me enjoy my secret."

Martin drained his glass and stood up. "All right, that's enough for today. I'll talk to you both tomorrow." Without further ado he slipped into his jacket, grabbed his car keys and was gone.

Sharon watched him for a minute as Tommy stood up, looking towards Mickey's office. "You know he means the best for you?"

Tommy nodded.

"He's just trying to do what he thinks is right, what he thinks Mickey would have wanted."

"That's the problem. My dad held me back for years, now he's trying to do the same."

"Need a hand clearing his office out?"

Tommy was still gazing at his office. "It doesn't seem right. This place was his. That office is his."

Sharon stood up and stood beside him. "None of it's right, from Mickey's death onwards, but we have to move on. The last thing he'd want is a bleeding shrine in his name. Come on." She stepped forward, pushing open the door.

Tommy followed, but immediately paused. The office smelled of his dad - a combination of smoke and aftershave that had always hung around him.

Sharon saw his hesitation. "You don't have to change much, just tidy it up a bit - maybe even put up a few photos of the old man."

Tommy gave a wry shrug. "I don't have too many photos. Got this one the other day." He reached in to the folder he had brought in with him, handed the photo Big Bernie had given him. "It's a few years ago," he told Sharon, "but it's a good one of me dad, even if he is in prison clobber."

Tommy stepped into the office and looked around. The office was still as Mickey had left it the night of the fight with Frankie Junior, a musty towel on the floor, a whisky glass on the desk, cigarette stubs in the ashtray. "It could do with a proper cleaning, a lick of paint." He looked out through the big window to the gym beyond, the fighters working hard, sweating, grunting. Yeah, he could settle nicely in here if he allowed himself, but Sharon was right, he couldn't allow his old man's ghost to hang over him, he had to make his own mark, and this was as good a place as any to start. He turned back to say something to Sharon and was surprised to see her still staring intently at the photo that Tommy had given her. "You all right?"

Sharon looked up at him, a hawkish look in her eyes. "This photo, where did you say you got it?"

"From a bloke called Big Bernie, dad did time with him in - "

" - who's the fella in the suit?"

Tommy shrugged. "Don't know his name. Bernie said he was the governor of the prison."

Sharon slowly handed the photo back to Tommy, a smile creasing the corner of her mouth. "Interesting…"

Sharon

Fuck Paul!

Sharon lay in bed glaring at the ceiling, remembering all the nights she was alone without Paul, aching for him, dreaming of him coming to her, wanting him so much it was hard for her to admit even to herself how much she loved and desired him. She had lost the battle to hold onto her own self-control and deny the ferocity of her intense need for Paul, and now he had done this to her.

Paul who she had loved. Paul who she now hated with a white hot intensity that would have burned the skin from him if she could have got her hands on him right now. She should have known, should have been suspicious that it was all going too well, should have listened to her instinct - and to her friend Laura - when they were telling her the same thing: He will never leave his wife.

And last night it had come out.

It was no use, she couldn't sleep right now, she didn't want to sleep. She felt like she had a hundred barbarians running around her head, screaming and shouting and fighting and trying to escape. She just couldn't get her head around why he had done it again, why he let her down again, especially tonight, when he had built it up like he was going to tell her something special. What else had Sharon been expecting? Surely he was going to say that he had finally told his wife he was leaving her?

If he had known he was going to do this, why did he keep her hanging on? She had to know, had to understand, she had to get the answers. And why now, why had he let it go this far, why hadn't he just been honest with her from the beginning, when he knew all along he was never going to leave his fucking wife?

Anger, bitterness resentment; she felt the destructive lash of all these emotions. Paul had done this to her, but it was also her own fault it had happened, she was also responsible, she had invited it, encouraged it.

For years after they had parted she had thought about him, wondered how he would look if she saw him again, how his lips would feel on hers, how he would taste. Over and over again she had imagined the sensuous contact of his mouth on hers, the softness of his lips, their tongues entwining. Again and again she had dreamed of her hands softly stroking the contours of his handsome face, her fingers playing with his hair. A fantasy she had told herself – well now the fantasy had become a fucking nightmare, had fallen apart, the shattered pieces landing in her lap. Sharon felt like she was looking into a kaleidoscope, colourful, sharp, all the broken pieces mingling into one, all the different parts of her life knotted together in a broken pattern that would never be put back together.

She should have expected it. He'd had all these problems before, seemed to always have some drama or chaos going on. Did he thrive on that? Did he like living on the edge? But how could he have said all the things he'd said if he didn't mean them? He should have been on the stage, he was a fucking good actor. She started to focus on what tonight meant to them both, the cruelty of telling her tonight, but soon realized that it didn't matter what day or night it was, the simple truth was that he had done it again, let her down. Once again she had come second. She had never really been number one on his list. She thought she was, but she had been living in a fool's paradise. And in letting her down again, he had made her weak and vulnerable, made her needy. She hated him for that, hated herself for letting him do it to her.

Sleep was not going to come tonight. Sharon got up from her bed, padded barefoot into the kitchen, poured herself a stiff scotch, threw some ice in, watched as the cubes slowly melted. She couldn't let this go, she needed to know what he had been thinking - had he been leading her on the whole time? Nebulous feelings stirred inside her. She wanted to ask him, challenge him, but at the same time she never wanted to speak to him again.

She picked up the glass, looked at for a moment, then downed it in one, gasping as it burned the back of her throat. With the Dutch courage still fresh on her tongue, she picked up her phone and dialed his number.

She was ready to unload on him, ready for whatever excuses he gave, but the phone just kept ringing. Furious, she hung up and dialed again. No answer. Five times she tried with no answer, but Sharon was a determined, single-minded woman. On the sixth time she left a message, her voice filled with anger as everything spilled out.

"Why don't you grow up and just answer your fucking phone!" she screamed. "I really don't know who you think you are, but I'll tell you what you are, you're a cardboard cutout cunt! I hate you, I wish you were dead, wish I had never laid my eyes on you. There is only one word I have for you, and that is Karma."

She slammed the phone down, marched into her bedroom, swiped her hand across the top of her dressing table, knocking off the framed photos of Paul. As they crashed to the floor, she bent down, picking up what was left of them and hurled them against the wall, smashing them to bits.

She was so glad she had never introduced him to her family. What a show up that would have been. And now she was back to Sharon the dried up old spinster.

She paced around the bedroom, anger and sorrow mixing together in equal parts, then suddenly turned decisive. She rummaged in the top of her wardrobe, found an empty shoebox, then cast her eyes around the room, searching for everything he had ever given her. It didn't take long to track it all down, the perfume, the underwear, the books he had given her with special messages written inside, all the beautiful cards he had sent, the tickets from concerts and theatre productions they had been to, a beautiful parker pen, boxer shorts of his left here when he had stayed, his toothbrush, his electric shaver. All of them she gathered up, hurled in the box.

And still her anger wasn't spent. Next it was all the photos of them together, ripped into tiny pieces and crammed in the overflowing box. And finally the gold bangle engraved "xxx Always xxx". She threw it on the floor, put on her sturdiest shoes, then stomped on it over and over again until it was dented and mangled. Then that too went in the box.

She flopped back on the bed, looked around at the mess she had made. She didn't care. She wanted to scream, she hated him, hated him for what he had done to her, hated how he had made her feel.

She had wasted so much time trying to analyse herself, analyse Paul, now she'd had enough. She had given him all that she had, she had no more to give, didn't want to give anymore. She had opened herself up, had tried, and it had all come crashing down. Never again.

The truth was Paul had never really wanted her, it was all just a game to him, and he had amused himself at her expense, indulging in this reliving of the past.

Fuck, they had even glanced in jewellery shop windows together a couple of weeks ago, looked at engagement rings. She knew his divorce could take a couple of years, she knew it wouldn't be easy, but she was prepared to wait, she didn't put any demands on him. She understood what he had to get through.

She stared at the box, she didn't even want that stuff in the house anymore. She had to get rid of everything that reminded her of him. She didn't need to have any more contact with him, they didn't need to be in each other's lives at all. Fortunately, the likelihood of them just bumping into each again was almost zero, they lived totally different lives and had a different circle of friends.

She climbed to her feet, grabbed the overflowing box, carried it carefully into the kitchen and shoved everything into a black bin bag. The rubbish men came in the morning, so right there and then, in her night dress and dressing gown, she carried the bag outside and dumped it with all the other rubbish at the side of the road.

A black cat scooted across the road in front of her, startling her. She watched it as it hurried away into the shadows, then looked back down at the bag. For a moment she felt a wave of sadness wash over her, but she quickly brushed it aside. Fuck him. Fuck him to hell and back! She spat on the rubbish bag and marched back into the house.

Sharon lay curled up in bed in the darkness, still wide awake after several hours restlessly trying to sleep. She knew that the only time she would ever be with him now was in her dreams, she just wanted to go to sleep and dream, dream, dream that she was in his arms.

Her eyes started to flutter as the dream washed over her. "I love you, Sharon," he whispered. She smiled as she touched his handsome face. "I know."

Those were the words he had left her with when she last saw him.

Then suddenly she was wide awake, her thoughts clear and sharp. Paul didn't matter. He was nothing. Her place was with the Taylors, with her family. She had to take care of them, that was her mission now.

Everything else was gone, washed away.

She had loved him too much and was not loved in return.

She had never wanted someone so close to her in her life. It would never happen again.

She found out what passion brought, how it destroyed and maimed.

She was strong, needed nothing.

She buried her face in her pillow and cried herself to sleep.

Martin

Martin threw his keys on the table and looked around. "Graham?"

Silence.

Martin shook his head. "Don't pretend you're not here. I saw your car in the car park. I can smell your aftershave!"

He loosened his tie, undid the top button of his shirt and stepped into the dark living room. The view never ceased to amaze him. The flat was high over Canary Wharf with the lights of London spread out below, stretching away to the misty horizon; his own private light show every night, twinkling and dancing just for him. Graham was sitting on the huge leather couch, his back to Martin, with just the back of his head visible. "I tried calling you a couple of times," began Martin, "no answer. What's that all about?"

Graham spoke without turning around. "I'm sure she knows."

Martin said nothing and walked slowly to the corner of the room, his footsteps echoing on the highly polished wooden floor. He stopped at the bar, no need to turn on the lights, he could find everything he wanted in the dark - glass, ice, whisky. After the past few days he needed a stiff drink. He poured himself a double measure over the ice, the cubes cracking and dancing as the whisky seeped between them. "Can I get you one?"

Graham lifted up a large wine glass so that Martin could see. Martin shook his head. There was a wine bottle on the coffee table, almost empty. Graham had been hitting it hard while waiting for him. He took a sip of his whisky and watched Graham for a moment. If he was already half sloshed this was going to be another difficult evening. No point putting it off. "Why would you think she knows? You always go out on a Friday night, a few drinks with the boys, right?"

Still Graham said nothing. Martin came and stood by the window, his eyes adjusting to the light and looked at him. He still had the air of innocence that had so attracted Martin when they first met, his boyish smile, his fair, almost sandy hair now starting to thin. "You said she was going to stay at her sister's tonight, right? So what's the concern?"

Graham took a deep gulp of his wine. "She says she isn't coming home, but what if she does? It could all change just like that, just like it always does." He took another sip of his wine. "I should go." But he did nothing, just sat there staring past Martin, not even seeing the lights of the city, seeing nothing, lost in his own thoughts."

"You know it doesn't sit right with me not speaking to you," Martin told him. "When I put the phone down last night, I had decided I wasn't listening to your nonsense and lame excuses. You know what I've been going through, with my brother and everything, and yet I feel you have to fight with me over everything."

"I can't go on like this," gasped Graham. "The constant fear of discovery."

Martin sat next to him, gently stroking his shoulder. "We've been over this, again and again. We even spent a year of trying to stay away from each other, and we couldn't manage it."

Graham nodded slowly, reached up and took Martin's hand, holding it tight, like a drowning man.

Martin watched him for a moment, but he said nothing. "You keep telling me that it doesn't make you feel good - so why do you keep doing it then? You say you are so worried about Anita, but you seem to be able to get away whenever you want. If I was to say to you that I can't see you because of my ex, what would you say or think? We both know the answer to that."

Graham lifted his wine glass, drained it and reached for the bottle. Martin stopped him. "Don't hide inside there again. Be with me."

Graham pushed him away, grabbed the bottle, drained it into his glass and took a long sip, staring defiantly at Martin. "But what if she does find out? She could ruin me, ruin us."

"Why would she even do that? You really think she would embarrass herself that way?"

"She would do it just to spite me," said Graham bitterly.

"Most women in that situation just want to hush it up."

Graham gazed at Martin for a moment, then looked away. "I don't know what to think, Martin. You say you love me, but do I believe you? No I don't. I think you think something of me, but you are not in love with me, you have zero respect for me." He waved his arm around at the vast flat, filled with expensive artwork, with its stunning view. "You have all this, while I drive a ten year old Ford Fiesta! Sometimes I think you're just humouring me!"

Martin shook his head. "You know none of this matters, know what I think about you, feel about you."

Graham shook his head and sipped his wine.

"Come on Graham, don't make me do this again? You know I've never ever felt about anyone the way I do about you. Emotionally, physically, sexually, all of it. But I can't live another year, a month, a day, an hour like I just have – days of not talking, not knowing whether or not you're going to show up - that's not a future! And all you say to me is you're afraid your wife knows about us? That's not the response or the actions of somebody who is in love."

Graham sat and stared, saying nothing.

Martin stood up and paced in front of the big window. He was so tired right now, fed up with fighting with everyone. Fighting with the lawyers and Mickey's other families, fighting with Tommy and Sharon over the future of the business, fighting with Georgie and Terri about their new circumstances, and now, when he just wanted to relax, wanted someone to hold, to love, he was fighting once more with Graham. He sighed, sipped at his drink and looked towards Graham for something, anything. "I sometimes feel that all you want is for me to keep chasing you," he began, "just to keep me there. But you know how much I love and care for you. There is nothing more I can do or give to show you anymore. You tell me what to do, what you want from me?"

Graham drained his glass and finally looked up at Martin with tears in his eyes. "I just wish she were gone, out of my life…"

Martin hurried over to sit beside him, hold him. "I want that too! You meet people for a reason, a season, or forever - I so want you to be the last one. Martin and Graham. That's it. No more."

Graham looked up, teary eyed. "Do you really feel that?"

"How can you doubt that? I don't have one single thought in a day that doesn't include you in some way. All I've thought about today is coming home, to you. I'm tired, weak, needy today, all I want is a cuddle, to put my arms around you and hold you there forever."

They both fell silent, Martin gently rocking Graham as he sobbed softly in the darkness.

Tommy

Tommy parked his car outside Frankie's office. It was hard not to recall the last time he had been here; the night of the big fight. That time the atmosphere had been very different, guns bristling, Mickey and Frankie on the verge of a family war that would have devastated both of them. And Tommy had fixed it, brought the two families back together. Fuck, he was such a fucking hero now that he had even been forgiven for seeing Frankie's daughter, Jeanette. Not that Frankie actually approved - Tommy was a married man - but he had at least refrained from cutting Tommy's balls off, given him a few months to sort his personal life out.

Tommy climbed out of his car, stepped into the grimy outer office. The office at the gym was messy enough, but a scrapyard, fuck, there was dirt and oil and mess everywhere. Tommy avoided touching anything as he nodded to the boys on the way in. All of them were relatives, distant cousins or whatever, many of them over from Ireland. They gave Frankie a steady workforce he could trust - trust to do the job, and trust to keep their mouths shut.

Frankie was sitting in his office, the phone glued to his ear. He waved Tommy to a chair and carried on talking.   Tommy looked around, chose the least dirty looking chair he could find and carefully lowered himself into it.

He was excited, nervous, everything at once. This was it, what he had wanted, what he had waited for all these years. He was the boss, representing the Taylors, not just a kid, not just Mickey's son, shunted out of harm's way to look after a poxy dry cleaners shop!

He knew he had to get this right. Martin hadn't wanted him to come, but Sharon was backing him. Both of them would be looking to see how he did, one of them wanting him to fail, the other hoping he would succeed. No pressure then!

But despite his nervousness, he felt good. This felt right, what he was supposed to do. He was Mickey fucking Taylor's son, for Fuck's sake! And as much as Mickey had tried to protect him, Tommy had always known that sooner or later he would come into his own. You can't keep a Taylor down forever, the cream always rises.

"Tommy, how are you?" Frankie leaned forward, engulfing Tommy's hand in his huge paw. He crushed half the bones in Tommy's fingers before finally releasing him. "Can I get you a drink?"

Tommy nodded his head. "Sure. Why not?"

"Good lad." Frankie turned towards the doorway. "Seamus! Get us a couple of coffees you dozy bastard!"

There was a grumble from the next room, but Tommy heard someone get to their feet, heard the tap run as he filled the kettle.

Frankie turned back to him. "So how's your family?"

"Good. Everyone's getting used to, you know…"

Frankie sighed. "He was a good man, a big man." He gave Tommy a knowing glance. "Tough boots to fill, eh?"

"Impossible boots to fill," replied Tommy quickly. "All I can do is be my own man."

"Smart lad," growled Frankie. "And don't even think about asking me about my family - you see more of Jeanette than I do!"

Tommy grinned.

Frankie's face turned serious, his heavy brows knitted together. "So what about our little business venture? Are you in?"

Tommy paused as Seamus, a big, dark haired geezer with a strong resemblance to Frankie, ambled in, set one coffee on the table for Frankie and handed the other to Tommy. Tommy took the grimy mug and peered through the steam at Frankie as he took a sip. "We're in!"

Frankie grinned. "Good! It's about time the families worked together again. I'll set up a meeting with the boys on the coast, let you know when we are sorted."

Tommy nodded, sipping at his coffee. "There's something else I wanted to ask you about, Frankie."

"Anything. We're family."

"It's about Mickey. Have you heard anything?"

Frankie's face turned serious. "A fucking tragedy that - no, a fucking disgrace!" He sighed. "Makes me wish I'd knocked the fucker out, then he wouldn't have been out celebrating!"

Tommy noticed Frankie's hands as he held his coffee mug, his knuckles were still bruised from the fight.

Frankie sipped his coffee, set the cup down. "I've put some feelers out, like you asked, but I have to admit we are drawing a blank so far." He set his coffee cup down and leaned forwards. "It's downright spooky to be honest. Usually, someone like Mickey - a name, a king - well, if someone like that goes down, it's hard to keep it quiet. People talk, boast, show off. Everyone wants to feel like they are a part of it, they know something, you know what I mean?"

Tommy nodded.

"But this?" Frankie sat back, gazed out of the window, thinking, seeing nothing.

They sat in silence for a moment, the growl and rumble of machinery from the yard the only sound. Finally Frankie picked his coffee cup back up and drained it. "But sooner or later, someone will say something to the wrong person, and we'll know about it. And then, then, you can take revenge for your dad, find the fuckers that did it and rip them to fucking shreds!"

Tommy felt his stomach tighten at those words. Revenge Mickey. That was something he had to do, he needed to do. But when the time came, would he be able to do it? Would he have the guts to punish someone? To kill them in cold blood? He was Mickey's son, the one who should revenge his father's blood, but could he do it?

Sharon

Sharon woke up abruptly, feeling like a bag of shit. Traces of her nightmare still haunted her mind, dark, shadowy thoughts and fears going through her head. She had been dreaming about her childhood, about her dad, a sickening feeling as she remembered looking into his evil eyes, his face full of contempt, dislike and disapproval of her. What her dad had done to her made her sick with loathing and disgust. She hated him for the hateful things he had done.

But worst of all was her own feelings of guilt, her destructive belief that she was responsible for what had happened, that she had invited it, encouraged it. Deep inside herself she knew she was all those evil disgusting words he called her as he fucked her. Sharon touched her face and wasn't surprised to find that it was wet with tears. She closed her eyes for a moment, trying to forget the look on her dad's face. It wasn't just dislike, it was hate. Then his face disappeared into the darkness and it wasn't her dad looking at her anymore with that look of resentment and contempt, it was Paul. And suddenly everything came rushing back to her, the night before, what had happened. She knew with deep certainty that she would never find happiness and true love - it could never exist for her, she had been fooled into thinking it would. She was so angry, so hurt.

She thought of how often Paul had whispered, "I love you, Sharon." He had used those words so many times, a meaningless repetition of an emotion he didn't really feel for her. And yet she also somehow felt that she had seen the love in his eyes, felt the love in his touch, felt it in his kisses, those same kisses that made her stomach do a somersault just at the thought of them. But in the end he had betrayed her, made a complete fool of her.

She climbed out of the bed, her anger and heartbreak merging into an angry, cold feeling. Who the fuck did he think was? He wasn't a Taylor, he wasn't one of them, and he wasn't going to ruin her life.

She strode into the office determined to give nothing away, but was greeted by Tommy and Martin, grinning at her. "So who's the love of your life?" asked Tommy.

Sharon paused, her stomach flip flopping. How could they know?

"Come on, tell us more," added Martin, pointing to the dozen red roses sitting on his desk.

Sharon caught her breath, forcing a fake smile to her face. She glanced briefly at the roses, then turned and sat down, pulling out her cigarettes and lighting up to buy herself time. With a huge effort of will she kept her hand steady as she clicked her lighter and held it to her cigarette. "I haven't got a clue who they're from," she said evenly. "I must have a secret admirer." But behind the false bravado she felt gutted. He was at it again, playing his game, one that he had played often before with her. She was tired of it, sickened by it, filled with disgust. What was he thinking? She didn't know and didn't care. It was over, finished.

Martin and Tommy were chatting about something, but Sharon couldn't focus on anything, their words just washed over her. She felt herself trembling as she sat smoking, her outer poise a mask for the feelings that boiled just beneath the surface. She had learnt from a young age that the best way to survive was to hide your true feelings. Why hadn't she listened to her own counsel when Paul had shown up again? She started to panic. She was feeling vulnerable, afraid that she was going to reveal visible signs of her emotions. Whatever she did she must not give way to the hurt and pain she felt, she must not break down in tears. Take control of yourself, Sharon, she thought.

Martin glanced over at her. "Oh, and a bloke called Dave rang earlier, can you call him back? He said it was urgent."

Sharon felt her heart skip a beat, wanting to vomit she felt so nauseous, but she managed to control herself, forcing out an answer. "My business is finished with him, he's a waste of time. If he calls again, tell him I'm out of the country for a few weeks, no need for a return call. If I need his services I'll call him."

She realised she was biting the side of her mouth to stop her bottom lip trembling, but Martin didn't seem to notice.

"Has he been bothering you?" asked Tommy, a concerned look on his face.

"No," Sharon lied, "he's just one of those persistent salesmen. You say one thing nice to them and they stalk you for weeks."

"Fair enough. We'll give him the brush off if he calls."

Sharon nodded her thanks, glancing over at the flowers. She didn't want to see them, didn't want to touch them, but she couldn't help herself. She climbed slowly to her feet and walked over to the flowers. Martin and Tommy weren't paying her any attention. She bent down, picked them up, her hands shaking. The card read "XXX Always XXX". She ripped the card in half, threw it in the bin, turned and handed the roses to Tommy. "Give these to your wife, or one of your girlfriends," she told him.

Tommy grinned. "Thanks, Shal. I'll give them to the old lady, keep me in her good books for a few days."

As Sharon turned away, her eye was caught by a couple of photos on Martin's desk. She picked them up. "Where did these come from?"

Martin grinned. "I was listening to a few old tunes the other night, going through some photos from mum's. Who's Sorry Now, Crazy, you know the ones? Anyway, I saw these photos, thought you'd like them, maybe they'd put a smile on ya face?"

Sharon looked at the photos. Martin was right, she couldn't help but smile. "Tommy, look at this one. You in your dad's arms when you was christened. Look at ya, like an angel," she laughed.

"And look what he's turned into!" laughed Martin.

Sharon looked at Tommy. "He loved you so much ya know, he was really proud of you how you've turned out."

Tommy smiled. "Thanks."

"He kept you out of the business because he wanted to protect you," she continued. "But you're the spitting image of your dad." She smiled. "I dunno if that's a good or a bad thing, Tommy."

Sharon looked at Tommy. What would it be like to have a child? That was her biggest regret in life, not having a baby of her own. Even without the abortion she would always have ached for a child. It was an essential part of her nature to protect and nurture and being denied that in such cruel circumstances, so early in her life, meant that she had always carried a heavy burden of bitterness and resentment.

She flicked through the photos, shaking her head. "Bloody hell! There's some dodgy hairstyles and nasty wallpaper here!" she laughed. "Oh my god, look at the state of me in that one, what I'm wearing, my hair!"

Suddenly a photo caught her eye. She looked at it for a moment, and showed it to Tommy and Martin. "Here, have a look at this one, what I've got to tell ya will make you laugh." The photo was of a Sunday lunch at Terri and Jimmy's place.

"As you know," began Sharon, "I hated Jimmy, the weaselly little fucker, only tolerated being around him for Terri's sake. I told her many times, if he ever says or does anything in front of me you know I will go for him - and Tel knew I meant it."

Tommy nodded.

"I know you didn't like him Shal, nobody did, he was one horrible bloke. Terri was married before wasn't she?"

Sharon looked at Tommy. "Yes" she said slowly, "poor fucker was only twenty one, a tragic accident. She never got over him, it broke her heart. She's never been the same since."

Tommy could see the sadness in Sharon's eyes, he heard it in her voice.

"Anyway, let me tell you about this day, you'll crack up. There were a few of us there for dinner, about nine or ten maybe. We had a lovely dinner because the prick wasn't there, he came back late from the pub as usual, and Jimmy being Jimmy he just had to spoil everything for Terri.

When anyone went to hers for dinner she always did a good job decorating the table, nice serviettes, she would get her posh glasses out, really make an effort. You might not remember it, Tommy, but she was an excellent hostess. Anyway we waited for a bit, but we knew Jimmy wasn't coming back, so we decided to have dinner without him.

So after dinner, it was getting late, everyone had gone home except me. The kids were in bed, and me and Terri were just sitting there chilling, having a nice glass of wine. We hadn't even washed up we were so bloated from dinner.

Then the phone rang, it was Jimmy. I'm on my way home he says to Tel, I'll be back in ten minutes, so make sure my fucking dinner's on the table! I could tell it was him from the way Terri's face instantly changed when she knew Jimmy was on his way back. She was a nervous wreck, looked like she was going to have a heart attack or something.

"Come on, Terri," I said, "let's sort his dinner out." I dragged her into the kitchen, but when we looked around, there wasn't nothing left but scraps. "He's going to fucking kill me!" moaned Terri. "No worries," I told her, "I've got it sorted." I grabbed the dirty plates, scraped all the leftovers onto one plate, then scavenged the bin for whatever else we could find. We was laughing the whole time, imagining what Jimmy would say if he saw where his food had come from. We arranged it nicely on the plate, then we both spat in it!

Tommy laughed. "You're kidding?"

Sharon gave a wicked smile. "You don't know the half of it." She was really warming to her story. "I'll make the gravy," I told Terri, "just get the kettle on, throw an Oxo cube in." She did as she was told while I nipped off to the loo, came back a minute later with a nice cup of warm piss.

Terri just stared at me. "Sharon, you can't!" she gasped. "Just watch me!" And before she could stop me, I grabbed the gravy, poured my piss in it, handed it back to Terri. "Go on then."

Both Tommy and Martin were watching her now.

"It gave me so much pleasure watching Terri pouring it over his dinner." Sharon was laughing hard now. "But not as much pleasure as we got as we sat and watched him eat it! It was so funny we had to go outside in the garden, we were laughing so much we were crying.

He ate it all, the daft cunt, thought we were laughing because we were drunk."

"Blimey," said Tommy, "remind me to check what you're serving next time you invite me over for dinner!"

Martin looked at Sharon and thought how different she was to Terri. Sharon was a strong, independent woman. Throughout all of the shit they had been through, Sharon never ever refused to give up on Terri, or any of them. She was a survivor.

Terri and Sharon had become closer over the years, but Martin wished Terri had Sharon's attitude on life. Terri definitely needed to grow a bit of backbone. But then Terri and Sharon had always been so different; on their future, their outlook, their expectations. Terri saw herself married with a couple of children living happily in Dagenham forever after, that was the limit of her ambitions.

Terri had a good sister there, thought Martin. They had had their moments, their times not talking, and he'd seen a few of their fights - he wouldn't like to get in the ring with either of them! Like most sisters, there were times they hated each other, but they were always there for each other no matter what, they had all got through the shit together. After all, family was family.

Sharon picked up another photo. "Tommy, look at this one." She handed him a photo of herself sitting on the bonnet of her first car, a Ford Capri. "Your Dad got it for me for my eighteenth birthday," she told him. "I passed my test the week before. You remember that motor don't ya, Martin?"

He nodded. "Oh yes. I was just little, but you strapped me into the front seat and took me drag racing up and down the Heathway, scared the crap out of me."

"It was the best pressie I'd ever had, all my mates were so jealous," said Sharon, smiling. She frowned suddenly. "Then a month later it just seized up on me. Your Dad was fuming. Turned out it was a ringer. So Mickey went over to see the bloke, I ended up getting a convertible Mercedes out of it. Now that was a car! You'd better believe the car dealer didn't take the piss again."

Sharon fell silent, didn't share the rest of the story with the two of them, although she had replayed it in her head over and over again down through the years. Why did it stick in her head? Because that was the day she witnessed how Mickey dealt with things when the piss was taken out of him or his family...

The manager at the garage was a proper liberty taker; thought Mickey Taylor would just take it. No way. Seriously, why would he think that anybody could take a liberty with Mickey Taylor, with Dangerous?

"Get in the car, we're going over there." Mickey had turned up to rescue Sharon when her car died. One glance at the look on his face and she did as she was told, grabbed her handbag and off they went in his Stag, Slade blasting out on the radio. As she threw her handbag in back she clocked a gun underneath Mickey's coat on the back seat. She glanced at him, but knew enough not to mention it.

Following Mickey's instructions, Sharon went in first with the MOT and all the paperwork while Mickey just wandered around the car showroom, looking like an interested customer ready to purchase a nice new motor. As far as this dodgy car dealer knew, Sharon was alone.

He was a short, fat geezer who wore loads of gold. He had a ring on every finger, pierced ears, and a bundle of gold chains hanging around his fat neck; wanted people to know that he had a few quid and was worth a few bob. He was a local hood, into debt collecting, property development and car sales, a flash, lairy bloke. He drove a big Rolls, had a house like a fortress, always had two minders with him wherever he went. Sharon could see them sitting in the back of the office watching them on the forecourt.

As Mickey had predicted, the bloke gave her the brush off. It was a used car, bought as is, if she'd knackered it, that was her problem, he couldn't do anything about it.

That was when Mickey came in. "What's going on here?" he asked.

The manager looked at him dismissively. "None of your fucking business, mate." The minders stood up as Mickey approached. "Fuck off, it's got nothing to do with you," Mickey told them. "He stitched my sister up on a motor. This is between me and him."

The dealer glanced between Mickey and the minders, trying to defuse the situation. "Come into my office, son, let's talk about this."

Mickey turned to Sharon. "You go back and sit in the motor, Shal, I'll sort this."

Sharon hesitated. She didn't want to leave him and paused in the doorway, worried about him. She knew Mickey could handle himself but there were two big blokes, three if you counted the car dealer.

"I said go back to the car." Mickey's voice was cold, flat. She'd heard that tone before and knew better than to argue. She did as she was told, just a quick glance back as Mickey strode into the office.

Sharon got back into the car, didn't know what to do. All she could think of was Mickey in the office with those three blokes. Then she remembered the gun on the back seat. He hadn't taken it with him, had he? He wasn't going to shoot them? She turned around, frantically searching under Mickey's coat - it was still there.

She picked up the gun, and another thought crossed her mind. He needed her, he was alone, and she had a gun... Without thinking it through, Sharon clutched the gun to her stomach and raced back to the office.

She threw the door open, holding the gun out like she'd seen on TV.

"Fuck, Shal, what the hell are you doing? Put that thing away before you hurt someone!" He was rummaging through the top drawer of a filing cabinet.

Sharon looked around the room. One of the minders was sitting on the floor his hand clutched to his bloody nose. The other was lying in the corner, his face also bloody, out cold. Then there was the manager, sitting behind his desk, an expression of pure fear on his bloody, battered face. Sharon blinked, trying not to look at the blood. She had learned to never be surprised by what she found once Mickey got involved in something,. "I didn't know who you was!" blubbered the manager. "Didn't know she was your sister! Honest, Mickey, if I'd known..."

Mickey ignored him, continuing to peer in the drawer. He glanced outside at the forecourt, then back at the manager and held up a set of keys. "How about these?"

The manager's eyes widened as he squinted through the blood that ran down from a cut on his forehead. "That car cost me - "

Mickey cut him off. " - Do I look like I care how much it fucking cost you? Is it sound or is it a ringer?"

The manager gulped. "It's a beauty. Full service history, the real deal."

"Perfect." He tossed the keys to Sharon. "There you go, sis. Happy birthday."

Sharon looked at the keys. "A Mercedes? You're kidding me?"

"No kidding," said Mickey. He turned to the manager. "Tell her, it's hers, legit."

The manager gulped. "My pleasure," he said, forcing the words out.

Sharon gave Mickey a big hug and ran out to check out her new car. "Take it for a spin," Mickey shouted after her. "I'll sort out the paperwork, see you at home."

Mickey watched until Sharon had started the car, driven away with a wave. Then he softly closed the door of the office, turning back to the manager. "Let's get finished up here, shall we?"

"Penny for your thoughts, Sharon?"

She blinked away the memories and met Martin's gaze.

"There's something we need to talk about," Martin continued.

Sharon nodded. Time to put everything behind her. From now on it was family, nothing else. "What's up?"

"We need to talk about Terri," said Martin. "I'm worried about her, she's not in a good place. She's self-harming again."

A look of distress crossed Sharon's face. "No! For fuck's sake! I can't believe she's cutting herself again!"

Martin shook his head, "No not good at all Shal."

"Ahh," continued Sharon. "I have something that might help her get herself back together a little bit, put a smile on her face. Give her something to love, a reason to get up in the morning."

Martin and Tommy looked at each other. "What are you brewing up?" wondered Tommy.

Martin continued, "Is this that secret of yours we have been waiting to find out about? I reckon it might be..." he said smiling.

"Well if either of you fancy a drive to Wales with me tomorrow, I'm picking up a Great Dane pup for Terri."

"Wicked! She's always wanted a Great Dane!" said Martin. "That's a blinding idea. I'll come along for the ride."

Sharon grinned and gave a deep sigh. "I could do with a distraction," she said softly to herself.

Tommy

Big Bernie's face lit up as he saw Tommy walking towards him. "Here's the man!" he croaked, his voice thin and raspy.

Tommy set the fruit basket on the bedside table, reached out and shook Bernie's thin hand. The first time he had come to see Bernie, Tommy had not wanted to be there, could barely stand to touch the old geezer. But now, well, it seemed right. It was what he had to do. Bernie was part of the wider family, and that meant something. Bernie was a big man, but as the cancer had eaten away at him he had turned to skin and bone. He held Tommy's hand for a moment. "It means a lot you coming to see me," he said quietly. "I know you must be busy, what with all that's going on."

Tommy laughed it off. "Nah, no worries. If I can't come visit one of my dad's old mates, what's the world coming to?"

Bernie nodded, but still looked concerned. "What is the world coming to, that's what I wonder?" He nodded around the ward, at the other beds. "The other fellas in here, don't never get no visits, know what I mean? But they're all somebody's dad, somebody's granddad. Why don't their families come visit them, eh?"

Tommy dropped into the low chair, shook his head. "Don't know. But it's not right."

For a moment they were both silent. It was Big Bernie who spoke first. "I remember you, you know?"

Tommy squinted. "From when?"

"When you lot used to come up and visit your old man. Regular as clockwork you lot was."

Tommy nodded. "Yeah, I remember those days. My mum hated going up there, was right ashamed she was, but I never felt that way. I was going to see my dad, didn't matter where it was, what he'd done, he was my dad."

Bernie nodded. "Your grandma was the one that made me laugh."

"Lizzie?"

"Yeah. Lovely lady she was, there every week, year in, year out, and whatever the weather. She always looked smart that woman. Always wore a hat and coat with a matching bag and shoes. Her face always impeccably made up."

Tommy smiled at the recollection. "She was such a smart woman, she always looked good wherever she went. She had a thing for bags, shoes, hats and coats. Her bedroom was chock-a-block of shoes and bags and coats."

"Your dad adored her," Bernie told him. "Really hit him hard when she died just before he got out. Blamed himself he did, said the stress of him being inside, the long trip to see him each week had worn her down."

For a moment the sadness washed over them both, remembering Mickey, Tommy thinking of Lizzie's funeral and his dad there with the cops. Fuck, they had been through some hard times.

Then suddenly Bernie laughed, and the spell was broken.

Tommy looked at him. "What?"

"I was just remembering your dad," said Bernie. "Most of the time he was ok about being inside, knew he'd been nicked, had to do his time. But every so often it got to him, and he started talking about breaking out. Come up with some real hairbrained schemes, he did."

"Like what?"

Bernie thought for a moment, then suddenly started laughing. "My favourite was the one with the prison visitor."

"Go on…"

"There was this woman used to come into the prison every week for a while. Right old battle-axe she was, we used to reckon she only came because it was the only way she could get a bloke to talk to her. I reckon she was about sixty, real old fashioned matronly type. You know the sort, short hair, flat shoes, tweed skirt and jacket. You could imagine her out walking the dogs, or singing in the local church choir, that kind. She was a real bible basher, used to try and bring God into that godforsaken place. Anyway, one day Mickey comes up with this idea to somehow kidnap her, dress up like her, and just walk right out the bleeding place dressed as a woman!"

Tommy laughed. "How the hell was he going to manage that?"

Bernie shook his head. "I don't remember the details, like I said, it was harebrained and more, but I do remember him suddenly starting to pay this woman lots of attention, request to meet with her every week and talk about his problems or whatever guff it was she did to try and save his soul. Oh, and the make-up!"

"Make up?"

"Yeah. He needed makeup and a wig in order to pull it off, so he tapped up the poofs - there's always some inside who have make-up and stuff like that - and got him some to start practising." Bernie dissolved into paroxysms of laughter that soon turned into a miserable racking cough. His face turned red as he coughed harder and harder, but eventually brought it under control.

Tommy looked on, concerned and held a glass of water out to him.

When Bernie had finally got his breath back he took the water, sipping it. His eyes were watery and his voice barely a whisper when he looked back up at Tommy, but he still had a smile at the corner of his mouth. "Some things are just wrong," he whispered, "and your dad in make-up was one of them! It's a sight I'll never forget."

"What happened in the end?"

Bernie shook his head. "Truth is stranger than fiction. She stopped coming one day, just never showed up no more. We found out a few weeks later that she'd run off with the local vicar!"

Tommy smiled. He liked hearing stories of his dad - he had been gone so much when Tommy was growing up, it helped to fill in the big blanks in his memory.

Bernie reached out, pulled a grape from the fruit basket, and chewed thoughtfully for a moment. "You heard anything? You know, about your dad?"

Tommy shook his head, his good mood quickly dissipating. "Nothing. It's kind of spooky. No one saying nothing."

"Did you talk to the gypsies?"

Tommy nodded. "Yeah. They've put feelers out, but nothing yet."

Bernie settled back on his pillow, looked exhausted from the talking and coughing. "Just give it time, Tommy, give it time. If anyone can find out what happened, who done it, it's the gypsies."

Tommy blinked, looked away. Give it time. Right. Easy for him to say. He wasn't the one who felt that with each passing day he was letting his dad down more and more...

Terri

How had her life got this bad? Terri just wanted to wake up in the morning and feel good. She wanted to feel... actually she didn't know what to feel, how she should feel after all that had happened. Happy, yeah, that was what she wanted; to feel happy, like she did when she first met John. It such a short time they were together - three years, two months, sixteen days and seven hours - before he was cruelly taken from her. The moment the love of her life died, and Terri's life ended. Her husband, just twenty one years old, was snatched from her by a drunk driver, and that's when Terri died inside. That's when she turned to drink. Instead of John being the meaning of her life, drink became her life.

Terri never had learned how to deal with death. She had lost Sheba, had lost her husband, had lost her mum, not coped well with any of them. Now there was nothing in the world that could hurt her any more unless one of her children died. At times it felt like everything she loved was taken away from her. If it hadn't have been for her mum she would never have got through it, she would have had her children taken away from her, but her mum had been there for her, as always. God she missed her mum so much. She wished she could have her back to for five minutes, just so she could hear her voice, see her beautiful, calm face, have her arms wrapped round her. Lizzie would make it all right.

Mornings were always a bad time for Terri. She would lie in bed with her eyes closed not wanting to open them, fighting the fact she had to move her arse out of bed to face another miserable day. Hours she could spend like this, not wanting to get up till late afternoon, then at the other end of the day she would wind up sitting up most of the night, just thinking, thinking, thinking. She didn't want to face the world, didn't want to talk to anyone, just wanted to be left alone in her own misery. She wanted John back, wanted her husband. The day he died her heart was broken, and she knew that life would never be the same again.

When she did eventually make it out of bed, Terri needed five coffees and five fags before she could function. She scared herself looking in the mirror, she looked like Medusa. She splashed her face with cold water, then stared at herself again. Where was the Terri she used to know? She was not the woman she once was, that was for sure.

As she stared at her tired, haggard reflection, the reality of how she had let herself go hit her straight in the face. Terri hated the way she looked, the extra weight she had put on disgusted her, and her teeth were brown from years of smoking, too much coffee, too much whiskey. What a dissipated demeanour she presented. Welcome to my crushing, stifling, suffocating mad world, she thought, my own lunatic asylum in my head. John would be horrified if she saw the state of her, he would be so upset and disappointed with her, she felt like she had let him down. She had let her children down, didn't deserve to be happy, didn't deserve to have any kind of life. Why should she? She was a bad mum, a bad person.

Terri wanted to hide away and have a nervous breakdown. She didn't want to go out, she was a complete and utter wreck, her mind everywhere, she couldn't focus on anything. She hid herself away for days at a time, just couldn't face the world. There were so many questions running through her mind, but she just didn't have the answers.

At times she had considered suicide, but she knew John would say it was the coward's way out, and she couldn't do that to her kids. She wished that she were thirty years older, so she would be near the end of her life.

She sat on the bed, thinking about John. He had treated her like a lady, respected her, listened to her, talked to her, helped her get through her issues with herself. When she was with him she had stopped all the self-harming. They had made so many plans together, things to do, places to visit, but after his death her life stopped, an overwhelming feeling of grief enveloped her. He would be so disappointed in her.

Even now, all these years after losing him, every part of her still mourned for him, ached for him, refused to accept that he was gone from her forever. She hadn't stopped needing him, she had lost part of herself the day he died, and she was incomplete without him. Her heart was an open wound that would never heal. She didn't think another man like him existed. He was kind, he was gentle, something that had been a whole new experience in her life. He wasn't threatening at all, she felt safe with him. He talked to her, not at her, listened to her, really wanted to know what she felt, what she thought, what she wanted.

When he told her about himself, about his family, she found herself envying him, almost wishing to exchange her past for his. Someone whose childhood could be looked back at with pleasure. A dad that loved him. That was new to her.

She was compulsively drawn to him. The more she got to know him, the more she liked him. He was someone who she looked up to. She treasured his kindness, his compassion drew her to him. She always felt safe with him, never uncomfortable the way other men made her feel. When she looked into his eyes she just melted, felt every single bit of his love for her.

Terri was always different from her friends and other girls, she was a bit of a loner, didn't want anyone to know how dirty and bad she was. She could never flirt or tease, have a bit of cheeky banter with the boys, could never make love. Those words made her skin crawl. Not one friend knew what she had done with her dad. When they laughed and talked about what they had got up to with their boyfriends, she couldn't help but wonder what it would be like, fun loving, not forced and brutal.

Terri wondered how many woman actually liked it, enjoyed it? For her it was filthy and disgusting, men using women and their bodies. It was just sex to them, no emotion involved. She knew what she had read about it, what her mates had said, how it should be, but the thought of allowing any man near her to do what her dad had done to her made her sick with hatred and disgust. Her own feelings of guilt were her punishment for being bad and wicked.

Terri withdrew further and further into herself, concentrated on her school work and exams. That's what led her to John - they met in her local library. Just like in a book or a film, she dropped a book on the floor, and John picked it up, smiling as he handed it back to her. They began chatting straight away, and something just seemed to click, there was a powerful connection instantly. But all that was snatched away in one moment, leaving her bereft, alone.

Terri sighed. She could still remember every last detail of the day he died – the green sweater he had been wearing when he left for work, the ham and cheese sandwich she'd made him for lunch, with Branston Pickle, his favourite. The kiss and smile he'd given her as he left, like they were a pair of newlyweds.

And especially she remembered the police coming to the door later that morning to tell her he was dead. She'd answered the door to the coppers often enough when she was growing up, that was nothing new, but the second she saw their faces she knew it was something different, something wrong, something terrible. It was the first time she'd had a copper look at her with sympathy, first time there had been a WPC at her door.

Her hand had gone straight to her mouth, she'd not really heard a word the coppers had said, but somehow it had sunk in.

The next thing she remembered was sitting on that lovely flowery couch they'd just bought – they'd thought it was so posh – the Old Bill sitting next to her, the WPC handing her a cup of tea. But if that was bad, what happened next was worse, that moment when they left her, alone. Alone with her thoughts, the vision of her beautiful John in her head, smashed and killed in a car crash, his beautiful face bloodied and mangled.

After John had died, Terri didn't want to ever face the world again. The fact that she did eventually manage to muster up the courage to venture out of the house was entirely down to Sharon. She simply couldn't have done it without her.

She couldn't wish for a better sister. Like all sisters, they had had their moments, their fights, but they were always there for each other no matter what. There were times they hated each other but they had got through it - family was family, after all.

Terri and Sharon were so different - they had always been so different. Take their future outlooks. Whereas Terri had always seen herself married with a couple of children living happily in Dagenham, Sharon knew there was a big wide world out there. She wanted to travel and see a bit before she settled down. And she had, she showed no sign of settling down yet. Because Sharon had never had children she could go wherever she wanted, do whatever she wanted, with whoever she wanted, no responsibility but to herself, and she had taken full advantage of it.

She had bought herself a lovely place, was always on holiday, seemed happy with her life, the things she had. Mind you, Sharon wouldn't let people take this piss out of her, wouldn't tolerate anything that gave her grief. She worked hard to get rid of all the shit from her life, all the negativity and nonsense, always seemed to surround herself with people that made her feel good.

She had money, had a good life and good friends, didn't suffer fools gladly.

Whenever Terri thought about her sister she pictured someone strong and independent, cocky, clever and confident.

But despite all of the shit they had been through, all the fuckups Terri had made with her life, Sharon had never given up on her. Terri knew that more than anyone else in the world, Sharon understood her. Understood her, and told her the home truths she needed to get herself moving again after John's death. "You've got to take control of your emotions, Terri," she had said. "Nobody else can do it for you." Sharon had wrapped a protective arm around her. "If I could wave a magic wand and take all your hurt and pain away and make it all better, make you happy, I would. I fucking hate seeing you in this state." She had held her tight. "You know I will always be here for you, Terri, always."

So how come Terri felt so alone? It was how she'd felt then, when John died, how she'd felt every day since.

It was what she deserved, that's what she told herself. She was a bad person, had done terrible things, and God's punishment was that she was doomed always to lose the ones she loved.

Terri lay and gazed at the ceiling. She knew she should get out of the bed, but what was the point? Another dreary, empty, depressing day lay ahead of her. She rolled over, buried her face back in the pillow, hating herself, hating her laziness, hating the –

"Terri? You'd better get your arse down here right now!"

Georgie's voice came to her from downstairs, loud enough to penetrate her apathy.

"Fuck off," she grumbled. "Whatever it is I don't care!"

Again he yelled up at her. "Believe me, you're going to want to see this!"

Something in the way he said it caught her attention. She sat up, ran her fingers through her tangled hair. "All right, all right, I'm coming!" She hauled herself out of the bed, dressed as usual in a baggy old t-shirt and jogging bottoms. She grabbed her robe and wrapped it around her, glancing in the mirror and immediately wished she hadn't. Fuck, what did she look like? Oh well, no time to do anything about it now, Georgie had seen her like this enough times before. She crammed her feet into her old slippers, reached in her dressing gown pocket for a packet of fags. Fuck, none there. No worries, she had plenty in the kitchen.

She staggered out into the upstairs hallway. "You'd better have a fucking good reason for getting me out of bed before midday," she grumbled as she headed towards the stairs.

"Oh, believe me, we've got a good reason." It was Sharon's voice.

"Shal? What are you doing here?" Terri hurried down the stairs. "Is everything OK?"

"No it's not fucking OK?" Georgie this time, clearly with a right royal hump on.

"What?" Terri reached the bottom of the stairs and froze as a ball of excited brown fur came leaping towards her.

"We thought you could do with a bit of company out here," smiled Sharon.

"Oh my god, he's adorable!" Terri bent down, scooping up the wriggling pup as he hurled himself at her. He squirmed around in her arms, licking her face as she squeezed him tight.

"That is disgusting!" sneered Georgie, and headed into the kitchen.

Sharon was still smiling. "What are you going to call him?"

Terri's face was wreathed in smiles as she held the puppy, who seemed quite happy to be cuddled. "I don't know…" She looked thoughtful for a moment. "What was that geezer called who lived on the Heathway when we was kids, had that gorgeous Great Dane?"

Sharon furrowed her brow in thought. "Yeah, I remember him, funny bloke, always wore that parka with the furry hood, winter, summer, whatever the weather…Jasper, Mr. Jasper?"

Terri grinned. "That was it, Mr. Jasper." She held the puppy out at arm's length, examined him, took in his bright eyes, his big floppy ears, his black nose. "Yeah, Jasper, that will do nicely." She set him down, watched him as he sniffed around the hallway. "Jasper, come here boy!"

Whether it was the tone in her voice, or something in the way she said it, but the pup immediately came trotting back over to Terri, sniffed her outstretched hand. "See, he knows his name already."

Georgie shuffled past, staying away from the dog, a cup of tea in his hand. "Lord help us," he moaned, "as if I didn't have enough mess to deal with, you have to bring that flea bitten mongrel into the house!" He glared at Sharon, who gave him a sarcastic grin.

"Give you something to do," she replied, "you know you love cleaning."

"Not after something disgusting like that!" He stomped loudly up the stairs.

Sharon turned back to Terri. "You'd better keep an eye on Jasper, get some newspaper down, get him trained as quickly as possible or you'll get all kinds of grief from your brother."

Terri nodded, but she was barely listening. The moment Jasper had come bounding towards her, Terri had felt young and alive again. The sparkle was back in her eyes, the love she felt for Jasper was there instantly. "Yeah, yeah, yeah, course!" She was like a breathless school girl as she hurried into the kitchen, Jasper at her heels. "Come on boy!"

Sharon watched her, could see the instant transformation. Getting Jasper was exactly what Terri needed to bring her back to life, get her out of the slump she had been in. Then she glanced up the stairs towards Georgie. He was not going to be so easy. She could tell already that there was going to be conflict over the dog, that Georgie was not going to be happy while it was getting house trained.

Sharon sighed. Isn't that always the way? You solve one problem and you create another. The sound of Terri's excited voice and Jasper's happy barking came to her from the back garden. Fuck Georgie. He would just have to deal with it. Terri was happy for the first time in years, and that was worth any amount of moaning from her brother.

Sharon

Sharon poured herself a glass of sparkling water, set it on the wide, wooden table and stood for a moment gazing at the shoe box before sitting down, slowly lifting the lid. The words 'Pandora's Box' sprang into her mind, but she pushed them aside. She had waited long enough, for the right time, 'til she was strong, ready, able to face this chapter of her past. She had paid her dues - enough for several lifetimes - and now it was her time.

She reached into the box and pulled out the first photograph. It was grainy, black and white, but despite the poor quality, the low light, it was clear enough for anyone to see what was going on.

A middle aged man was naked, his hands bound and chained above his head, his back and buttocks covered in angry welts. On a table near him was a collection of BDSM paraphernalia.

Sharon peered at the photo. "Come on, who are you?" But there wasn't enough of the man's face showing to recognise him. Sharon peered at the photo for a moment longer, then set it aside, pulling the next one from the box. "That's better..." It was the same man, but this time his face could be seen, eyes shut, head turned to one side in agony or ecstasy - who could tell which?

Sharon set the photo on the table, then reached for a scrapbook. She opened it up and began turning the pages. It was full of photos of men, all cut out from newspapers or magazines, each with a name and job title underneath.

She turned several pages, then paused, a smile on her face. "I knew I'd seen you somewhere before," she muttered.

There was the same man, though this time he was wearing rather more clothes - an expensive suit in fact, as he climbed from the back of a large limousine, smiling for the camera. The caption underneath read: William DeBruin, CEO DeBruin Holdings.

Sharon couldn't resist a smile. "Billy Boy, that's what you liked me to call you, wasn't it?" She looked up, remembering. "Billy Boy's been naughty, wasn't that what you liked me to say as I whipped your sorry, fat arse?" She pinned the naked photo of William DeBruin into the scrapbook next to his official photo and turned to the next photo in the box.

Sharon gave a little chuckle as she looked at the photo, another middle aged man, this time with a dildo buried in his rear end, his face turned conveniently to the camera. "We all know who you are, don't we?"

It took her just a few seconds to find the man this time. Rupert Morgan, MP. Again Sharon clipped the naked photo next to the 'official' one. "Like shooting fish in a barrel," she laughed to herself.

It wasn't long 'til Sharon had worked her way through the box. About half the photos she couldn't identify, but there were now a considerable number that had been matched up with their public photos. As she worked she had written each name on a list - her notepad was almost full as she scanned the page.

MP.

Judge.

CEO.

Prison Governor.

Minister.

Television personality.

Each in turn had fallen foul of the hidden camera that Sharon's mate Peter had installed for her. It had no flash, for obvious reasons, and was carefully hidden behind a long mirror at the end of the hall, but it still did its job, taking a photo every minute while Sharon was working. And while many of the photos showed the backs of heads, or were blocked by Sharon as she moved around her clients, there were still enough for her to fund her lavish lifestyle for the rest of her life without turning another trick or ever raising a whip in anger again.

She had already got rid of all her gear, the latex basques, the whips, dildos, plugs and paddles, the ropes, chains and handcuffs. She had even had the decorators in to completely redo the place. Gone were the hooks and attachment points, gone the long mirror, gone the camera. Her flat no longer looked like a nineteenth century French boudoir, now it was a stylish, elegant sanctuary, somewhere that Sharon actually liked coming home to. For the first time in many years her flat was hers, it was her home, nothing more.

She had considered moving, severing all ties, but she had been there too long, didn't want to get to know somewhere new. No, this was her home, and she was finally going to enjoy it.

She carried the scrap book, the notepad and her glass over to the couch, settled herself down, her legs tucked up underneath her. She started leafing through the pages, gazing at all the famous faces, all the compromising photos.

Suddenly she stopped. A smug face gazed out at her from the page. "I never liked you," she sneered at the page. "Sweaty, nasty little man!"

And just like that she had made her choice. Judge Lionel Winthrop would be the first of Sharon's former clients to discover that their private peccadilloes were not as private as they had hoped.

Tommy

Tommy navigated his big BMW through the narrow streets of the Harwich docks. A nervous energy buzzed through him, a tingle that seemed to start in his stomach and spread through his body to his arms and legs. The last time he'd felt like this was when he had raced to Big Frankie's yard to stop the war between the families. This felt just as big, perhaps bigger even. After years being shut out, kept in the shadows by his dad, he was finally stepping up. This was it. This was Tommy's moment to prove that he could make it on his own, bring some serious money into the family.

His reputation was resting on this, he'd burned his bridges, couldn't go back to fucking dry cleaning shops. Frankie Junior seemed happy to be working with him, and his Aunt Sharon had given him a little pep talk before he left, but Martin wasn't happy. Not only did he think it was the wrong direction for the family to go, he also didn't think that Tommy was the person to be making the deal. But Sharon had told Martin to get off Tommy's back - the look on his face was a sight to see when she'd laid into him - and so here he was, heading to a big meeting as the head of the family, the Taylor's official representative.

He checked his satnav. This was the place. A big, rundown warehouse with nothing to distinguish it from hundreds of others on the industrial estate.

Tommy checked his watch - ten minutes early. He didn't want to go rushing in like some new kid, so he pulled into an empty car park across the road, lit a cigarette, opened the window and sat back.

Frankie was a tough nut, but Tommy trusted him. If Frankie thought it was a good deal, Tommy would go along. But only so far. If there was one thing Tommy did know, it was that in any business deal with Frankie and the gypsies, there were looking out for themselves first and foremost. Nothing against Frankie, it's what he should be doing, but Tommy wasn't going to rush into anything without making sure that the Taylors were making their fair share.

Frankie's strength was the contact across the channel - some Romanians or Albanians who could get the ciggies from Europe - and in finding outlets for them in the UK. But where the Taylors came in was moving the stuff. They could provide reliable drivers to make the pick-ups and deliveries, muscle to protect the goods, warehouses to store them. Without Tommy, without the Taylors, they would have no distribution. And to be fair to Martin, despite his reservations about the deal, about Tommy's involvement, if there was one thing he knew about it was distribution. He had spent a couple of days talking Tommy through all the ins and outs of shipping until his head spun, wouldn't let him go 'til Tommy could answer all his questions, show he knew how to estimate costs, figure out sizes of vehicles, tonnage...

Fuck, he'd never had to work that hard even in school – but then he'd never had a reason to. Tommy blew a cloud of smoke out the window. Even though Martin was trying to block him, you couldn't fault the guy - he only wanted the best for the family.

Tommy's eyes picked up a car heading towards him. Frankie. Frankie had a sense of style, loved old Rolls Royce's. Not very subtle, but that was his way.

This one was a light colour, grey or silver, a 1970s classic, looking incongruous as it rolled through the empty streets. Hiding in plain view, Frankie called it. No one would expect a crook to show up for a business deal in a car like that, so they would ignore him! Stupid, Tommy called it, but who was he to tell Frankie what to do? He'd been running his family's business in his own distinctive way for over twenty years and had never served time, so he must be doing something right.

The Rolls pulled into the car park across the road, up to the big roller doors of the warehouse. Someone must have been watching for him, because the doors immediately rolled up, and the car disappeared inside.

Tommy took one more puff on his cigarette then flipped it out the window, the burning butt tracing an elegant glowing arc as it flipped end over end into the darkness. Tommy closed the driver's window, slipped the car into drive and eased forward, noticing with a brief smile that the nerves, the tingling had gone. He was ready.

As Tommy climbed out of his car the warehouse door rolled shut behind him. The warehouse was crammed full with high metal shelves, a jumble of boxes and pallets stacked high to the dark ceiling, some thirty feet above.

"Tommy!" Big Frankie strode forward, extending his huge bony hand for Tommy to shake. "Come on in." He led Tommy into a small office on one side of the building. "My cousin Danny," he waved towards a small, dark haired man with a big smile, a long scar that ran across one cheek.

He offered Tommy his hand and held out a whisky bottle. "Drink?"

Tommy nodded. "Cheers."

"And my other cousin, Dmitri."

Dmitri was as big as Danny was small, a giant of a man with a crushing handshake, thick eyebrows that met in the middle and an intense stare. He held Tommy's hand for a moment, his eyes boring into him. "So you Tommy Taylor, Mickey's son?" He had a deep voice, a thick accent.

Tommy nodded, meeting Dmitri's stare.

Dmitri looked at Frankie. "Your dad, he beat the shit out of this guy?"

Again Tommy nodded.

Dmitri suddenly let go of Tommy's hand and let out a big roar of laughter. "Any guy whose father beats up Frankie is a friend of mine!"

Tommy took his drink from Danny and perched on the edge of the desk.

Danny held up his glass. "Here's to making fuck loads of money!"

Tommy lifted his glass. "Fuck loads!"

They all emptied their glasses and held them out to Danny for refills. He filled the glasses one by one, his own last and set the bottle on the table. "Frankie explained the situation to you?"

Tommy nodded. Let them do the talking until he was ready. That's what Martin had told him. That's what your old man always did. Let them show their hand first, make them wait, so that when you do speak, they want to hear what you say, they need you.

Danny looked at Tommy, who just sipped slowly from his glass. "We can get hold of a lot of cigarettes, ten thousand, twenty thousand a week, more if we have buyers."

Still Tommy said nothing, fighting back the urge to speak.

Danny glanced at Frankie, Dmitri. "We can get a little out here, but the big quantities, we are shut out."

Finally Tommy spoke. "So I heard." That was enough. Say no more...

Danny licked his lips. "This area, there is another group, they are, how shall we say, very territorial."

Tommy nodded again, another sip of the drink.

"The Carlton Crew they are called. They have stopped some of our shipments, stolen our goods. Frankie says you know them?"

Now was the time. Tommy slowly drained his glass, set it on the table. "Cocksuckers!"

Danny looked confused. Dmitri furrowed his thick brow. "Cock - " began Danny.

"The Carltons. Cocksuckers." He paused, grinned at Frankie. "Didn't I tell you I went to school with Ronnie Carlton?"

Frankie shook his head.

"Right little weasel he was. I used to beat him up, steal his lunch money." Tommy grinned at the memory. "Threatened to tell his dad. I told him, bring it on. Your dad and mine can sort it out. That shut the little cunt up." Tommy looked from one to the other, making sure he had them all. "So here's what's going to happen. We are going to start running shipments. We'll start at ten thousand a week, get the ball rolling. At some point, the Carltons will fuck with us. Chances are my boys will sort it out - they'll be tooled up and ready. If that does happen - and it will - we'll retaliate, fuck with one of their shipments. And when we fuck with them, they'll stay fucked." Tommy glanced towards Frankie. He gave him a small nod of encouragement. "That's the way it will happen. We fuck with them, they stay fucked. Know what I mean?"

Danny was scowling. "Then what? Won't it just escalate?"

Tommy shook his head. "Nah. Cos that's when I'll call Ronnie up, remind him about how I used to nick his lunch money, and ask him if he wants me to keep on doing it."

Danny laughed despite himself and grinned at Frankie.

"What did I tell you?" said Frankie. "These Taylors are the real, fucking deal!"

Tommy stood up straight, adjusted his cuffs, buttoned his jacket. He'd seen his dad do it a thousand times, never realised 'til then how naturally it came to him. "Our share is forty percent, take it or leave it."

There was a moment of stunned silence.

Danny frowned. "Frankie said twenty five?"

"Course he did. That would leave more for you lot. But if you want the Taylors on board, handling distribution, security, shipping - twenty, thirty, a hundred thousand fags a week, then it's forty percent."

Dmitri looked at Danny, who was thinking, his face serious. It was clear who was the boss.

Frankie looked uncomfortable, glancing from one to the other.

Danny rubbed his hands together, staring at the floor.

Tommy stood very still, ready to react to whatever happened next. While he might look relaxed he was alert, on his toes. If Dmitri moved towards him, even half a step, Tommy would have the whisky bottle in his hand, ready to defend himself.

Finally Danny looked up and shook his head. "You know, I did some checking. About you, your dad, your family." He glanced at Frankie. "It's just like Frankie said - you Taylors are the real fucking deal!" He held out his hand, grinning. "Forty percent it is!"

Frankie stood by Tommy's car as the roller door eased up, clanking and grinding. He bent down and leaned in the window. "You took a real fucking chance there, you know? These boys don't fuck around."

Tommy looked at Frankie's craggy face, close to his, the smell of whisky strong on his breath. "And now you know – I don't fuck around either."

Frankie grinned. "Fuck me. Your old man would be proud of you!" He reached in and squeezed Tommy's shoulder. "It's going to be good doing business together, Tommy!"

As the door fully opened, Frankie stood up. "You sure you won't come get a drink with us? There's a great strip club these guys own, really nasty women if you get what I mean?"

Tommy grinned but shook his head. "Another time. There's something else I need to do tonight."

He pulled out of the warehouse, already dialing on his phone.

"I didn't expect to hear from you again."

Tommy felt himself growing stiff at the mere sound of Melissa's slightly breathless voice. "I'm in Harwich. I want to see you."

She gave a light laugh. "That's the way it is, is it?"

Tommy felt his throat tighten at her provocative tone. "Yes."

"And when you say you want to see me again, you mean you want to fuck me?"

"Yes."

For a moment he thought she wasn't going to respond.

"There's a hotel on the outskirts of Ipswich. The motor lodge."

"I'll find it."

"Text me the room number. I'll see you in an hour."

Tommy hung up, the blood racing through him, his hands gripping the wheel tight. Danny might own a strip club with some seriously nasty women, but Tommy had something much better - a hot woman who he shouldn't go anywhere near, his own half-sister for god's sake. And he was going to fuck her.

Tommy lay on the bed, gazing at the ceiling. The hotel room was small and functional, bland 1990s decor, a small bed, faded yellow curtains, but none of that mattered.

He had told himself he wouldn't call her, shouldn't see her again. What had happened was madness, an aberration, a moment of weakness at a difficult time. His half-sister, his own flesh and blood - the most sacred of forbidden fruit. Even as he was getting changed to drive up to Harwich he had tried to believe the lie, as he shaved and showered, picked out his best suit, his pale grey silk tie, everything down to his black Armani boxers. But he had known, deep in his heart he had known that he would call her, and that if she had given him any encouragement he would do anything to see her again.

The knock on the door was firm, confident. Tommy sprang up, quickly checked himself in the mirror, and opened the door, a cocky grin on his face.

Melissa breezed past him into the room, barely giving him a second glance, her perfume wafting over him as he stood watching her. "Nice place."

Tommy quickly shut the door and turned to face her. She wore a tight dress, above the knee, which clung to her slim figure, her blonde hair cascading across her shoulders. Her eyes met Tommy's, and he grinned. "So, how have you been?"

For a moment Melissa said nothing. Then she sighed. "Really? You called me up this late at night to exchange small talk?"

"No, I just - "

"Do you want to talk or do you want to fuck?"

Tommy needed no second invitation. With two strides he was across the room, his strong arms around her as his mouth met hers. Just like before it was instant passion, the kiss long and deep as their bodies pressed together. Tommy was already hard from anticipation, but he could feel himself growing as he pressed himself against her flat stomach, one hand in her hair, holding her neck, the other on her firm behind.

His mind was full of the memory of their last encounter - he had replayed it in his mind a hundred times - as he reached up to her shoulders, wanting to push her to her knees, feel her mouth on his cock once more.

But Melissa resisted. "Uh uh."

Tommy froze, puzzled. "I thought - "

"Bad habit, thinking," she teased. "We have a deal, remember? You owe me?" Melissa reached up to Tommy's shoulders, pushing him downwards.

He needed no second invitation and dropped to his knees in front of her.

His hands held her slim hips as he began kissing at her knees, his lips brushing her soft skin. She wore no stockings this time, her legs bare, so he could taste her soft skin as he slid his mouth upwards.

She moaned softly, reached down and slid her tight skirt up for him, rucking it up around her hips.

Tommy kissed up her soft thighs, soon reaching her tiny black g-string. He kissed her through the soft cotton, felt her squirm with pleasure as he pressed his mouth against her. He kissed her like that for a moment, but he wanted more, wanted to see her, touch her, taste her. He quickly peeled her g-string down, exposing her smooth, shaved sex.

As he gazed at it for a moment, Melissa looked down at him. "I do love a man who repays his debts in full."

Tommy looked up, smiling. "By the time I'm done, you'll be deep in my debt."

She reached down and wrapped her fingers in his hair. "I do hope so!" Her hand pulled him forward and he buried his mouth against her.

Tommy felt her soft lips against his, probed and teased with his tongue, tasted her wetness, all the while her hands in his hair holding him in place.

His tongue darted between her lips and she gasped. He began thrusting, forcing his tongue deep inside her as she pulled him against her, again and again, forcefully, rhythmically, pounding his face into her.

She came with a shiver, a small gasp of delight, staggered backwards to sit on the edge of the bed, her legs apart. She smiled at him. "Consider your debt repaid."

Tommy stood up, never taking his eyes off her. He wanted her more than he had ever wanted a woman.

With trembling hands he unzipped his trousers, dropped them and his boxers to the floor, and stepped out of them.

She reached out for his stiff cock, pulled him towards her, and wrapped her mouth around him.

For a moment he allowed himself to enjoy the sensation of her mouth on him, but he wanted more, wanted it now. He pulled out. "Turn around."

She looked up at him with her pale eyes and did as he commanded.

"On your knees."

Without a word Melissa knelt on the bed, Tommy behind her.

For a second he admired her beautiful body, then he quickly grabbed her hips and thrust inside her.

She gasped as he forced himself inside, but she was wet and ready. He began thrusting, knew it wouldn't take long, he was too full of desire. His pace quickened, Melissa meeting his rhythm and pushing back against him.

Tommy wanted to make it last, wanted to savour the moment, but his lust, his passion was too great. Faster and faster he thrust, his hands holding her hips, and then with a cry of ecstasy he came, gasping, falling on top of her as she collapsed onto the bed.

For a moment Tommy felt as though he was in a dream, outside of himself, looking down at the bed, lying naked, Melissa wrapped in his arms.

She slid out from underneath him and nuzzled up against him. "I'll give that seven out of ten," she murmured.

Tommy propped himself up on one elbow, gazing at her. "That's it?"

Melissa's eyes sparkled back at him. "And that's making allowances for the fact that that was our first fuck."

Tommy laughed. "Maybe I don't rate you that highly."

She played idly with the hair on his chest, then ran her hand down across his flat stomach, took his cock in her hand and began softly stroking it. He instantly began to stiffen. "Really?"

Tommy laughed and kissed her neck.

She continued to play with him. "This is the last time we do it like this - in a cheap hotel I mean."

He lay back, allowing her hand to revive him. "And what did you have in mind?"

"Once a month or so, I come to London. You take me out to a nice restaurant, buy me lovely presents, then afterwards we go back to a beautiful, boutique hotel, and I do this..." She slid her head down across his chest, kissed his stomach, took his hard cock into her mouth and sucked for a moment. She paused. "Deal?"

Tommy grinned, pushed her head back down so that she engulfed him again. "Whatever you say..."

Terri

She could hear Jimmy screaming at her - even in her dreams that voice haunted her. "Your children hate you, you've never looked after them," he ranted. "Never loved them." He sneered at her. "Drink and weed, that's all you care about. They hate you, you know? They told me they wished you were dead. You're more hassle to them alive, you cause them endless problems. You're like the child, and Georgina's like your mother looking after you.

"The grandchildren don't know you because your kids don't want to bring them round," he continued, "You're just an embarrassment to them." He stood over her. "Your children are embarrassed by you. Can't you see it?"

Terri wanted to escape, wanted to get away, but his voice bored into her, no mercy, no respite. What could she do? What could she say? She lay on the couch, nursing her bottle, too drunk to get up, too befuddled to fight back or argue.

"Useless you are, Terri," he continued. "You're making everyone miserable. They all detest you, your behaviour." He flicked a hand towards her stained dressing gown. "Look at the state of you, you're a fucking embarrassment to us all." His eyes narrowed, his face turned nasty. "Here's an idea - why don't you just kill yourself and put everyone out of their misery? No one loves you or cares about you, you're a selfish bitch. All you do is cause everyone hassle, phoning people up at ridiculous hours of the morning, pissed, shouting, screaming, crying, looking for sympathy. Either that or looking for a drink." He shook his head. "What a fucking loser!"

He went to the dresser, picked up a bottle of whiskey, poured a large glass, held it out to her. "Here you go, have that." Terri turned her head away. Jimmy leaned in, shoved the glass towards her mouth. "Go on, drink up you useless slag!" She tried to resist, but he pushed the glass against her face, forced her mouth open, poured the whiskey down her throat, spilling half of it down her chin.

He threw the glass on the floor, shook his head. "The one thing you do, drink, and you can't even do that right!"

He turned towards the door, casting his eyes around the room. "Look at the state of the house. It's a shit hole. And you, you stink, you dirty shit bag. You haven't bathed for days, have you? Lucky for him that your first husband died. He was lucky enough to escape you and the shit that comes with you and your fucking family!"

Terri glared up at him. "Don't you ever mention John! Never mention his name!"

"Or what?"

She climbed to her feet, unsteady, pointing the vodka bottle at him. "I will fucking kill you!"

He looked at her with amused disgust. "In your fucking dreams!" He reached out, gently prodded her in the chest, watching as she flopped back onto the couch. "I'm going out," he told her. "Clean up this pig sty before I get back or you'll feel my belt across your fat arse when I get home!"

Terri sighed. There were times she had tried to escape, tried to get out and break free, even for just a few hours, but he always seemed to know, always found a way to shit on her plans.

"You don't think you're going out looking like that do you?"

Terri stood in the doorway in a mini skirt and low cut blouse. Her mate Lucy was having a big party, and she had managed to convince to Terri to come.

"You old slapper. You're not some teenager. What do you think you're wearing? Showing all your tits off like that, you're an old bird, not a stunning twenty year old. And as for that fucking skirt…"

He glanced at the kitchen table. "It's Tuesday today," he said coldly. "You fucking know the drill. Monday, the meat from Sunday with chips. Tuesday, sausage, mash and beans. Wednesday, spag bol, Thursday, lamb chops, boiled potatoes and runner beans. Fish on a Friday, and Saturday Chinese takeaway."

"I know, Jimmy," she pleaded, "but I told you I was going out to Lucy's party, so I got you a pizza."

He said nothing, just stared at the table.

"You like pizza…"

Without warning he grabbed the table, flipped it over, spilling everything on the floor - the pizza, his beer, the cutlery, everything. "It's fucking Tuesday, and that means sausage, mash and beans, not fucking pizza!"

"Jimmy!"

He rounded on her, fury in his eyes. "Clean it up! Then get out of those fucking clothes and fix my dinner!"

"But I'm going - "

" - you're fucking going nowhere whore!"

Terri started to say something, but he took a half step towards her. "Do I need to slap you to make you see sense?"

Terri shook her head, scurried past him and started cleaning up the mess.

Jimmy looked down at her, her short skirt, her tits hanging out the front of her blouse. "And if you're a good girl, I might give you a good fucking later…"

The memory bit at her. Why did she put up with it for so long? What was wrong with her? Just remembering it made her want to crawl back to bed to just sleep and sleep and sleep, allow the depression to creep over her, envelope her. She didn't wanted to see anyone, talk to anyone, she had nothing to say, just wanted to be left alone in her misery to die.

Even after all these years she couldn't cope without John. Even though she was sober now, she would still often wake up without a clue what day it was - it didn't matter, every day was the same. Once her life had meaning, now it was just a long yawning series of nothingness stretching away into a dark, bleak, lonely future...

"Terri!" Georgie's shrill squawk cut through the air. "That fucking dog has gone and done it again!"

Terri pulled herself out of her bed, wrapped a robe around her, hurried down the stairs, through the immaculate living room into the kitchen, where Georgie stood over the cowering puppy, Jasper. Terri looked around in confusion. "But he did it on the paper, like he's supposed to!" She hurried over, scooped Jasper up in her arms, giving him a hug. He licked her face gratefully.

Georgie looked on in glowering disapproval. "That is so disgusting! He was licking his bollocks earlier!"

Terri met his fierce gaze, continued to allow Jasper to lick her face. "I don't care, do I sweetheart? Mummy loves you!"

Georgie turned away in disgust.

Terri grinned. "You're just jealous because no one ever licks your privates, aren't you?"

Georgie tried to ignore her, busying himself with the kettle.

But Terri wasn't done baiting him. "See Jasper, Georgie's upset because he's all dressed up with nowhere to go."

It was true. Georgie was in full on Samantha mode, wearing a sleek red dress, an auburn wig that cascaded down across his shoulders, and enough make-up to hide even the most masculine of features.

He sighed as he gazed at the kettle. "I can't even remember the last time I gave anyone a blow job!"

Terri set Jasper down and began clearing up the newspaper where Jasper had peed, Jasper fussing around her and getting in the way of everything she did. "Course you can," replied Terri. "It was that fat fuck you killed!"

Georgie gave her a sharp glance, looking away before she noticed. "I meant apart from that. I'd prefer not to remember that night."

Terri was on her hands and knees. She shoved the soggy newspaper in a carrier bag, reached up and grabbed a disinfectant spray, giving the floor a quick squirt and a wipe. By the time she had laid some fresh newspaper down and washed her hands, Georgie had tea ready for both of them. Terri took her cup and sipped gently. "Yeah, well we've all got nights we'd rather forget, haven't we?"

Georgie still seemed ill at ease as Jasper sniffed round his feet. "It's not natural, you know, having a dog in the house? How can I keep the place clean with him pissing and crapping everywhere?"

Terri looked around. The house had been cleaned and tidied within an inch of its life. At first she had loved having Georgie doing all the cleaning and tidying - after a lifetime looking after slobs of husbands and lovers, it seemed wonderful, no mess to deal with, the house always clean, always smelling fresh. But the novelty soon wore off. Every time she took her cardigan off and set it on the couch she could see Georgie fidgeting, could practically count the seconds until he said, "you're not going to leave that there are you?" Tea cups got short shrift too - half the time she hadn't even finished her cuppa before he whisked it away, washed the cup and put it away. And woe betide her if she dared to put a cup down without a coaster underneath it.

And if things had been getting bad before, the arrival of Jasper had really put his nose out of joint. All of Georgie's OCD tendencies came out in full - he literally followed Jasper around, watching for any signs of misbehaviour, and freaked out should the poor puppy dare to actually piss or shit anywhere!

Fortunately Jasper was a well behaved little fellow, and was toilet training really fast, but it would never be fast enough for Georgie, who regarded the dog's very presence in the house as an affront. He had suggested they buy him a kennel and chain him up outside, "where dogs belong", but had lost that argument - Terri might look frail, but when push came to shove she didn't back down.

And so an uneasy truce had settled over the house, Georgie watching like a hawk, Terri protecting Jasper from his ire, and Jasper the happy go lucky one in the middle, completely oblivious.

Georgie sat at the table with his tea, crossed his legs elegantly. Terri knew what was coming. "I can't see what harm one little trip into town would do?"

They had been over this ground a hundred times, but Georgie kept coming back to it. "We could go together?" he pleaded. "Tell me you wouldn't like a good shag? You could be my wing man, we could pick up a pair of handsome fellas, bring them back here? What do you say?"

"I wouldn't like a shag."

Georgie looked at her, puzzled for a moment.

"You said, tell me I wouldn't like a shag. So I did."

"You're lying."

Terri sighed. "Actually I'm not. Since the last time, I've pretty much lost my appetite..."

Georgie glared at her, then softened. "What if just I went? You wouldn't have to - "

" - to tell Sharon and Martin?"

Georgie nodded.

"Actually I would."

Georgie went into full on pout. "Bitch!"

"Georgie, they put us out here for our own safety. Neither of us have a good track record you know, and if you fuck up again you're going back to Broadmoor. You know that, don't you?"

The look Georgie gave her was hateful. He climbed to his feet, threw his cup in the sink, the tea splashing up the shining white tiles, stormed from the room. "I am never going back there!"

As Georgie stomped from the room, Jasper came scurrying round Terri's feet, disturbed by the loud noise, the raised voices. Terri reached down and petted him. Thank God she had Jasper. Sharon knew what she was going when she bought him for Terri. Terri scratched his head, played with his floppy ears. "Shall we go walkies? Walkies?" That was a word Jasper knew already. He raced to the door, barking excitedly, skipped around Terri as she put her shoes on, clipped his lead on him.   "I'm going out for a walk!" she shouted up the stairs.

There was no reply.

With a sigh Terri opened the door, following Jasper outside.

When they had first moved out to the coast Terri had hated it. It was so desolate, she didn't even want to leave the house, wanted to stay in bed all day, or curl up on the sofa under a big blanket and watch TV until she finally fell asleep. But since she'd got Jasper, she'd had to go out, and little by little the quiet beauty was getting to her.

It was still sparse, wind-blown, more brown than green with the muddy estuaries and the wind-blown reeds, but the cries of the gulls seemed a little less plaintive, and when the sun shone, throwing a million sparkles up off the water as she walked along the sea wall, it was actually quite beautiful.

Having Jasper helped too. His antics kept her amused as he raced back and forth, chasing and barking and scampering and playing, the whole world a box of magic things to discover and explore. Terri sighed. How long since she had felt like that about anything?

Although the sun was shining there was a chilly wind blowing in off the sea. Terri wrapped her cardigan tight around her, looking around for Jasper. She couldn't see him. She looked further afield, but suddenly froze as she saw a figure in the distance. Was someone following her?   She peered back, the sun bright in her eyes.

Someone was there, but they were too far away for her to see them clearly. And why should she even imagine that they would be following her?

Then she remembered. She had seen someone before, more than once, a figure in the distance, never getting closer, but always there.

Just at that moment Jasper came galloping up through the reed beds, covered in mud. Terri sighed, laughing. It was hard to be cross with him. "Look at the state of you!" she tutted. "Georgie's going to have a shit fit when he sees you!" Jasper wagged his tail and galloped after a butterfly, and Terri glanced back again. No one there. She blinked, shook her head. She was getting old, imagining things. She hurried after Jasper before he got into more trouble.

Tommy

Tommy rolled his shoulders, stretched his neck. Being in the gym, getting changed into his old grey sweats, always got him in a good mood, reminded him of fighting, his own career as a boxer. At the time it had seemed like it would never end, but like everything else it had vanished before he'd had time to really appreciate it.

As he slipped his t-shirt on he noticed something on his ribs - he peered in the mirror. Teeth marks. He knew it had got a bit wild with Melissa the other night, but he hadn't realized it was that rough! Even just thinking about her he felt himself start to harden. She was wildfire, screwed like a fucking feral woman. He had never experienced anything like it. She went from submissive to dominant in the blink of an eye, every time he thought he was in charge she would turn the tables on him, do something that would turn him to putty in her hands. He was going to be careful though. It wouldn't do if his missus - or his girlfriend Jeanette for that matter - saw another woman's teeth marks on him.

He slipped his t-shirt on, changed his thoughts to something safer. The cigarettes. That was a good topic. Sharon was well impressed with him, even Martin had stopped moaning for a day, though he was reserving judgment until they started. What was that phrase he liked to roll out? "There's many a slip twixt cup and lip," or some such bollocks. Well fuck that, and fuck you, Martin, thought Tommy, there'll be no fucking slips on my watch.

He stepped out onto the floor, felt the eyes on him, heard the friendly greetings as he made his way across to where Kenny was training.

For a minute Tommy just stood and watched him work. The speed bag was his thing, he had the fastest fucking hands Tommy had ever seen, pure natural talent, and it was a joy just to watch him work.

The trick, Tommy had found, was adding some power to those lightning hands without slowing him down. Right now he was a bit like a swarm of mosquitoes, always in your face, always buzzing around, but not doing any real damage. Add just a little power to those pesky punches, though, and he'd be a real handful for anyone in his weight division.

Kenny paused, seeing Tommy watching him. He gave the bag a final flurry of punches then skipped over to Tommy, the sweat rolling down his face. "Morning guvnor."

Tommy threw him a towel. Morning guvnor. He never tired of hearing that, never tired of finally being recognised - by some people at least - as the new boss. He glanced back at Martin, in his office, on the phone. He may do a lot of the work, thought Tommy, but people don't see him as the boss. Too quiet, too business like, not enough hard edge showing. He had it all right - Tommy knew from some of the things that his dad had told him that Martin could be a right cold bastard when he needed to, always calm, never panicked. But as the face of the Taylors? The one people looked up to? That he was never going to be.

And then there was his aunt Sharon. Tommy knew how tough she was, what she was capable of, but it was different. She was a woman, she'd never be the one to do the real dirty work when it had to be done. No, if the Taylors had a new boss, a new leader that people were looking to, it was him.

Kenny sipped from his water bottle, peering at Tommy. Tommy had learned to read the boy. He was shy, never really spoke unless he was spoken to. "What's on your mind, Kenny?"

Kenny paused, took another sip and cleared his throat. "I was just wondering. You know, about your dad, about Mickey?"

Tommy met Kenny's eyes, but Kenny quickly looked away.

"I mean, who did it, like?"

Tommy shook his head. "Don't know, Kenny, and that's the truth. Not for want of trying, we've got Frankie and the gypsies, all our people out there with their ears to the ground, but no one's said a word yet."

Kenny nodded, looking thoughtful. "It's fucking wrong," he said suddenly. Tommy had never heard him speak with such vehemence. Now Kenny had started, he didn't seem able to stop. "If I fucking knew, knew who'd done it, I'd beat them to death with my bare hands!" he continued, almost breathless. "Mickey was fucking everything to me, and it's just not right him not being revenged, know what I mean?"

Tommy nodded slowly, his eyes drifting across to where his uncle sat on the phone. "Yeah, I know exactly what you mean." He turned back to Kenny. "Now, let's see you put some of that aggression into the heavy bag. What's your mantra?"

"Same speed, more power!" replied Kenny seriously, as though he'd managed to remember some complicated formula.

"That's fucking right!" Tommy exhorted, "same speed, more power. Now let's see it!"

Tommy was still drying his hair with a towel as he joined Sharon and Martin in Martin's office. Sharon and Martin were staring at each other, saying nothing. Tommy looked back and forth between the two of them. "Did I miss something?"

For a moment they were both silent, then Martin turned to Tommy. "No. I've just had Georgie on the phone giving me grief about the dog, nothing I can't handle."

Sharon still looked sour faced. "He blames me, thinks I never should have got the ruddy dog in the first place, but I swear, Terri would have gone fucking loopy if she didn't have something to take care of."

"What about Georgie? You'd think looking after him would be enough for any one."

Sharon shook her head. "That's different."

Tommy dropped into a chair and sipped from a water bottle. "This sounds like something I'm going to stay out of."

Martin gave a dry laugh. "Good decision."

Tommy leaned forward. "Listen, before we get down to business, there's something I wanted to ask. What's happening about Mickey?"

The muscles around Martin's face tightened, his eyes narrowed. "Nothing's happening about Mickey, and nothing will happen until we have some firm information as to who was responsible."

Tommy scowled, shaking his head. "That ain't right."

Martin leaned forward, fixed him with a glare. "I don't care what you think is right, until I say - "

" - And who made you fucking king?" Tommy glared at him. "You think this is your decision? He was my fucking dad, and the longer this goes on with us sitting around doing nothing, the more we look like a bunch of yellow cunts who don't give a toss - or worse, don't have the balls - to deal with whoever killed Mickey!"

Martin started to say something, then leaned back in his chair, breathing hard.

Sharon glanced between them. "He's right, Marty," she began. "It's starting to look bad, making us look weak. Someone tops Mickey and we do nothing? That's not good."

Martin steadied his breathing and looked at them both. When he spoke, his voice was low, icy. "You think this is simple? Like in a fucking movie? We just get a tip off from someone, go in and take the fuckers out, end of story?"

Tommy glared back at him. "Why the fuck not! If we think we know who did it, we've got the manpower, we fucking take them out! Fuck, half of east London would be on our side!"

"It wouldn't be enough," said Martin softly.

Tommy glanced at Sharon, scowling. "What the fuck is that supposed to mean?"

Martin looked uncertain for a moment, then sighed. "Because if I had to put money on who was responsible, I'd put it on the Vietnamese."

"Fine. Let's go fucking take them down!"

Martin gave him a dismissive look. "You don't get it, do you? You don't take down the Vietnamese. They are too big. Fight them you're fighting a whole fucking country!"

"So we just do nothing?"

"You're damn right we just do nothing! That's a fight we can't win. Ever hear of the Vietnam war? Does that ring a bell? They beat the fucking Americans, Tommy! What do you think they would do to us?"

"So that's it? We just give up? Wave the white fucking flag!" Tommy stood up, his face red.

"Sit down, Tommy."

Tommy looked around at Sharon. "What? You're taking his side now?"

"No! I'm not taking his side. We have to revenge Mickey, and we have to be seen to revenge Mickey, but we can't go off halfcocked. And like Marty says, we can't start a war we can't win. Mickey wouldn't have wanted that."

Tommy stood for a moment longer then slowly sat back down.

Sharon leaned forward. "We all know how strong the Vietnamese are in the drug trade right now, we can't confront them. So we back off in the London drug trade - make up the slack with your cigarettes, whatever else we can rake in - lie low a bit, and press all our contacts harder to find out who did it. Then we go in hard - whoever it is - and cut them off at the fucking knees. Agreed?"

Neither Tommy nor Martin looked happy, neither said anything.

Sharon glared from one to the other. "I said, agreed?"

And eventually, first Martin, then Tommy, nodded their heads in reluctant agreement.

Martin

Martin closed his eyes and lay back on the couch. He was getting too old for this. Even when Mickey was alive he had started to wonder if he could do it anymore. Now it was ten times harder. Nothing against Tommy and Sharon, they both meant well, but they were both starting almost from scratch, and this was a tough business.

Martin wondered if he should be more assertive - what would they do if he put his foot down, said he was the boss, and they either did what he said or pissed off? Would they buckle down? Walk away? Or fight back? He laughed softly to himself. They were Taylors, what the fuck did he think they would do?

No, all he could do was keep doing what he was doing, try and keep Tommy on a short leash while he learned the ropes, and hope he didn't get himself into any trouble he couldn't get out of. It's not like he and Mickey had exactly gone to college. It was in at the deep end for Mickey when Bobby died, using his fists and his nose and not much else to carve out a chunk of business that was far bigger than anything Bobby had ever imagined was possible. And Tommy was a lot like Mickey, but he had the added benefit of being older when his old man passed away.

And as for Sharon, she had a canny head on her shoulders, and while she clearly supported Tommy a lot, she wouldn't want to see him get himself in over his head. His mind wandered for a moment, thinking about Sharon. She was a strange one, different from all the other brothers and sisters, she kept herself more to herself, always had, worked hard to preserve her privacy.

Not that Martin - or Mickey before him - couldn't have found out more about her if they'd wanted to, but she clearly worked hard to protect her privacy. Martin had his own ideas of course - she wasn't married and made good money without having a job, and there weren't too many ways a woman could do that - but that was her own business.

But now she seemed different. Even before Mickey's death something had changed, and since, well she was a different person, more part of the family than she had ever been.

And as for the other two, Georgie and Terri, well there was an odd couple if ever he'd seen one, but at least Sharon's idea of shunting them out of town seemed to be working out, even if Georgie kept bending Martin's ear with his moaning and complaining. It was like -

The doorbell interrupted Martin's flow of thoughts. He checked his watch. It was after eleven, it could only be Graham.

Even as Martin peeled himself off the couch the bell rang again, and was immediately followed by the sound of a fist hammering on the door.

"Hold your horses!" grumbled Martin as he walked slowly to the door. If Graham was showing up this late, unannounced, it could only mean one thing - another row with his wife.

Martin reached the door and peered through the peephole. It was Graham, and he looked rough.

"Martin! Let me in! I know you're home!"

Martin opened the door and Graham spilled in. He was a mess, his tie askew, shirt half untucked, hair all over the place, and he stank of booze. "What took you so long?"

Graham gave him a cursory peck on the cheek, tottered into the living room where he stood swaying, gazing at the lights of Canary Wharf and the city spreading out in the distance.

Martin followed him more slowly and stood watching him, waiting for him to begin, to unload his latest tale of woe. It always began the same way - "I can't do this anymore..."

For a moment Graham seemed hypnotized by the lights, but finally he shook his head and turned back to Martin. "I can't do this anymore!"

Martin motioned to the couch. "Why don't you sit down before you fall down?"

Graham glared at him. "Don't you fucking patronize me!"

Martin padded over to him in his socked feet and gently took his arm. "I'm not patronizing you, you look tired."

At Martin's touch Graham turned, collapsing into his arms, sobbing. "You can't imagine what she's like! She never stops nagging, I'm sure she knows!"

Martin steered him to the couch and sat down beside him. "You just need to–"

"Get rid of her for me, Martin!" He stared at Martin, wild eyed. "I know you could do that, I mean, have someone do that, and then we would be free, you and me!" He was giddy, breathless, his words tumbling out. "We could run off together, anywhere, Spain, the Seychelles, anywhere in the world, and be happy together!" He stared at Martin, wild-eyed, breathless.

Martin sighed and shook his head. "That's not me, that's not what I do." Graham started to speak, but Martin cut him off. "It's not that I don't love you, I do. I miss you, want to be with you - but not like that."

Graham glared at him and pulled away. "You don't care about me! You wouldn't care if I topped myself tonight!"

"That's not true!" protested Martin. "Don't start playing the victim again, you know I've never felt like this before, about anyone. When I'm working I find myself thinking about you, wondering what you are doing, where you are, wondering if you are thinking about me."

Graham said nothing, glanced quickly at Martin then turned his head away again to stare towards the window.

"But we have to work this out sensibly. If you are going to leave your wife, leave her. But don't come here at night banging on my door and demanding that I kill her! That's not the way I want us to be!"

Graham still stared ahead, not meeting Martin's eyes. "What if it was the only way? What if I said do that for me or I'll walk away?"

Martin shook his head. "Now I need a drink!" He stood up, walked slowly to the bar in the corner of the room and poured himself a large brandy. He stood by the bar gazing at Graham, who finally looked up at him. "I feel mixed up and empty and confused," admitted Martin. "I'll be honest, a part of me doesn't like the effect you have on me. I'm used to being in control, but you sweep that away from me, I feel like a stick being carried down a river, out of control."

Graham stared at him. "You should try my life for a day, living with the bitch!"

Martin sipped his drink. "Then you come here, like tonight, making demands, and I have this fear, every single day it haunts me, that if I don't do what you want, you will remove yourself from me, vanish from my life."

There was a long silence, both of them staring across the half darkened room at the other. Finally Graham smiled. "Why don't you pour me one of those and come back over here?"

Martin hesitated.

"It's OK, I'm a bit drunk, but I can handle one more." He gave a sly grin. "And anyway, one more drink and I'll let you do anything you want to me..." He gave a coquettish smile.

Martin laughed despite himself. "You know I can't resist you..." He pulled out another glass, pouring a small measure into it.

"Rationing me?"

Martin grinned, adding a splash more.

Graham patted the couch beside him. "I'm sorry I came on so strong earlier," he began, as Martin sat down beside him, "I just want us to be together."

Martin lowered himself into the seat and handed Graham his drink. "We will. We just have to be patient..."

Tommy

Darren, Ricky and Spud. These were exactly the blokes you wanted by your side on a job like this. Tommy sat quiet, listened to the banter as they chatted about football, women, jobs they had done together in the past. And now, for the first time, Tommy was out on a job with them.

Part of him was nervous, but the other half was excited - this was it, this was what he had wanted to do for years, what his dad had never let him do. Get out there and get his hands dirty. Martin knew nothing about it, of course, but what was the point of talking to him about it? No reason to ask someone a question when you already know the answer. But the boys were restless, they missed the game, missed the extra money, and so they had come to Tommy direct. Come to Tommy because he was the man now. He was the new king, and well, if you want a decision, you go straight to the top, right?

It was hot and crowded in the car, but Tommy didn't care. He'd had enough of being safe, being comfortable. That was Martin's way, not his. Fuck comfort, he wanted to be uncomfortable, wanted to feel that tingle in the pit of his stomach that he had right now.

He'd only ever really experienced it before when he was boxing, before a bout, and he had loved it, had loved knowing it was there, then defeating it, overcoming it, going out in the ring, jacked up and ready, and beating the shit out of some poor sucker.

And that was how he felt right now as he sat crammed in the back of the car beside Darren. Darren was one tough cunt, had always done all the dirtiest jobs for Mickey, never blinked, never backed down, just got on and did the job. Exactly who Tommy wanted beside him.

Spud was sitting in the driver's seat. He was well named - he had a bullet head completely devoid of hair, and small eyes. He glanced in the mirror. "Heads up, boys!"

Tommy twisted round in his seat, could see a big lorry coming slowly towards them down the darkened street. The lorry rolled past them, coming to a halt at the traffic lights. As it did so, a battered transit van appeared out of the darkness, stopping right in front of the truck. At the same moment, Spud pulled forward, alongside the lorry. Tommy pulled a stocking mask over his head, scrambled out the car with the others, the buzz in his stomach fierce, a huge grin on his face underneath the mask.

Darren clambered up the side of the lorry and jammed his gun against the drivers' window. "Open up, darling!" he shouted to the driver. "We got a present for you!"

The driver stared wide eyed at the gun for a moment, then nodded, pointing at the door handle.

Darren dropped down to the ground and the door swung open. The driver looked down at him, fear etched across his face. "Don't shoot, please!"

"Course we won't!" Darren growled through his mask. "As long as you're sensible."

The driver nodded. "I've really got nothing you want. Dog food, that's all it is."

Tommy stepped forward. "Nice try, sunshine, but that's not what we heard. Keys!"

The driver's eyes took in the four of them, and all the fight went out of him. He sighed. "It's plasma TVs…"

"Yeah, we know that. Keys!" repeated Tommy.

The driver reached in the ignition, pulled out the keys and tossed them down to Tommy. He caught them, handed them to Spud. Spud had been a lorry driver, knew how to drive a big truck like this. "Now, you, out!"

The driver slowly climbed down, still looking nervously at Darren and the gun.

Tommy reached out and grabbed his face in his big hand to get his attention. "Here's how it works. First, you give me your phone."

As the driver dug in his pocket and pulled out his phone, Spud clambered into the cab of the lorry, slamming the door. The transit pulled away, and Spud fired up the engine.

Tommy took his phone and gave it to Ricky, who pocketed it. "Now, strip!"

The driver looked surprised and glanced back as his truck began to pull away. "What?"

"Strip!" As Tommy repeated it, Darren waggled the gun at the driver as a reminder. He didn't need any more encouragement, quickly pulled off his t-shirt, shoes, socks and jeans, which Ricky gathered up.

Tommy looked at his pale, flabby body. Not a pretty sight. "And your keks!"

The driver stared at him bug eyed, then peeled his underwear off. Ricky grimaced, picked them up between his fingertips, jogged over and threw all the clothes in the boot of their car.

As the lorry pulled away into the darkness, Tommy reached out, patted the driver on the cheek. "There's a good lad. You have a nice day now, all right?"

Darren roared with laughter, raised his voice to be heard over the noise of the pub. "You have a nice day? I thought I was going to piss myself at the look on his face!"

Spud nodded. "And taking his clothes. Right smart that was!"

Tommy sipped his drink. It couldn't have gone any better. They'd pulled off the job without a hitch, and the boys were looking up to him for his part in it. All he needed now was -

"I've seen your picture in the paper, haven't I?" The girl was in her late twenties, maybe early thirties, bleached blonde hair, silicone tits. A typical Dagenham slapper, but good looking for all that.

Tommy grinned. "Yeah, you might have." He had to lean in close to speak to her, liked the way she smelled.

She gave him the once over, obviously liked what she saw. "Go on then, who are you? Are you in films or something?"

Tommy shook his head. "No love, not films, real life."

She looked confused. "Real life?"

Tommy gently took hold of her arm as he leaned in again to talk. "I'm Tommy Taylor."

The girl looked at him for a second, then realization dawned. "Fuck me, you are too!"

He could smell the alcohol on her breath as she spoke, see the sparkle in her eyes. "Can I get you a drink?"

"Don't mind if I do. Vodka and cranberry please."

As Tommy ordered her drink he slipped his arm around her, and she made no effort to pull away. He turned back to her, smiling. "So what's your name, love?"

Mindy. At least that's what Tommy thought she had said, but it didn't really matter. Two drinks had been all she needed, then they were outside and into the back of Tommy's BMW, Tommy humping her like there was no tomorrow while holding on tight to her silicone tits, the buzz from the hijacking finally dissipating as he came inside her, collapsing forward to nuzzle her firm breasts.

"Fuck me," gasped Mindy happily. "I just fucked Tommy Taylor!"

Sharon

Somewhere public, that was her first priority. And then it had to have a classy look, business people, lots of suits, so that neither she nor her client would look out of place. And then she needed space outside for Ralph to park, so that if things got sketchy he was right there.

It took a little looking around, but Sharon had found a place that suited her down to the ground. It was in the heart of the city, and at lunchtime was comfortably full of business men, traders in expensive suits, professionals every one.

Sharon had arrived early and found herself a small table from where she could watch the door. She had dressed conservatively, a professional woman's two piece skirt and jacket, white blouse, easy on the make-up, just enough jewellery to look well off.

She sipped at a small glass of sparkling water and looked around. It was a mostly younger crowd, but there were some older men in there, the type who just a short time ago would have been prospective clients, a bit of money in their pockets, a fat, boring wife at home, sex a distant memory. They were the easy marks for her, desperate, needy, weak, pathetic. She could see several of them giving her the eye. Even though she was dressed demurely, there was no hiding her figure, no burying that pure sexual aura that Sharon had always had, that men had always picked up on.

What was it someone had once said to her? "I knew you were up for it, the moment I first saw you." That was over forty years ago, just after she had finished blowing the bloke in the back of his Ford Cortina. No one had ever said anything like that to her, so she had quizzed him on it.

He zipped his jeans, looked at her. "Some women," he had explained to her, "you can just tell."

She still looked mystified.

"It's like, you look round a pub, and you can tell, nine times out of ten, if a girl's up for it. Some of 'em, you know they wouldn't give you a blow job if you gave 'em a million fucking quid. Others, well, you know that if you play your cards right, they'll do just about anything you want."

Sharon glared at him. "And I'm one of them?"

He shrugged, gestured to his car. "Here we are..."

Even though she had stormed off, effing and blinding at the bloke, she had never forgotten what he'd said. Never forgotten it, and used it to her advantage when she had decided that having sex was by far the easiest way for her to make a living.

She looked up as a man moved towards her from the bar, a drink in his hand. He was one of her typical clients, slightly overweight, probably early fifties, an expensive suit that did nothing to improve his debauched looks. "I was wondering..." he began, but Sharon cut him off.

"The answer's no."

He stopped in front of her, tried to grin. "But you don't even know what I was going to ask?"

"Yes I do. You were going to ask me if I wanted a drink. And then, if you got a couple of drinks inside me, you were going to whisper to me about this lovely little hotel round the corner, and then you were going to try and get inside me." She gave him a challenging look. "And that's why the answer is no."

He stood still for a moment, thinking, frowning, and finally managed one word. "Bitch!"

Sharon laughed. "More than you could ever imagine. Now fuck off before I dump my drink on your head and embarrass you even more!"

With a last scowl he scuttled off to the bar.

"You got rid of him easily enough."

As soon as she saw him she knew he was her contact. Well dressed, nothing showy, just a good suit, a crisp white shirt, a sober tie. She had seen him approaching and was ready for him. She sipped her water, nodded for him to sit down at her table. "I'm used to dealing with the likes of him."

The man sat down. "Evidently." Sharon put him in his mid-40s, probably a lawyer, used to acting with discretion. It looked like she didn't need Ralph at all.

As he sat down he extended his hand to her. "Saunders."

Sharon felt his soft skin, observed his carefully manicured nails. Definitely a lawyer. "Thank you for meeting me."

Saunders sat down, placed a slim, black leather briefcase in his lap. "My client was surprised to get your letter."

"I'm sure he was." She couldn't keep the smile from her face. "Did he show you the photos."

Saunders shook his head. "No. He simply told me that under no circumstances should they be allowed to become public."

"That's why we are here."

"Just so." Saunders looked around and coughed. "The issue that concerns my client is the question of this incident being repeated."

Sharon nodded. "I understand. There's nothing I can do except give you all the photos I have and my word."

Saunders studied Sharon carefully. "He said you would say something like that." Saunders chose his words carefully. "He saw you more than once, seems to have developed something more than just casual feelings for you…"

Sharon smiled to herself. She had definitely chosen the right mark to start her new business. "He knows me well enough. If I say this is it, then that's what I mean."

Saunders thought for a moment longer. "Very well then. The photographs?"

Sharon reached into her large purse, pulled out an envelope and slid it across the table to him.

Saunders looked at the envelope with suspicion, as though it might bite him.

"Go on. Have a look. You want to make sure you get your money's worth."

Still Saunders hesitated. Finally he peeled open the envelope and slid the photos up just enough to be able to see what they are. Sharon watched his face carefully as he quickly scanned the contents. One by one he glanced at them, then up at Sharon, a shocked look on his face. "Oh my!"

Sharon laughed. "It takes all sorts, eh?" She nodded towards the brief case. "I think that's mine?"

Saunders licked his lips, closed the envelope, then reached down and slid the briefcase under the table towards her. "It's all there."

Sharon picked up the briefcase, felt the weight, then lifted it into her lap. Making sure that is was turned to the wall so no one could see, she undid the clasps, lifted the lid a couple of inches and peered inside. Rows of neatly stacked fifty pound notes met her gaze. She nodded, closed the case. "Then I reckon we are all done here." She stood up, looked down at Saunders, still sitting peering at the envelope as though it were about to explode. "Nice doing business with you."

The handshake he gave her this time was a lot less assertive, thought Sharon as she strode out of the pub. You would think he'd never seen a man with a dildo up his arse before!

Ralph was waiting for her, jumped out the car and opened the back door for her, just like a real chauffeur. "Everything OK?"

Sharon grinned as she slid into the back seat. "Absolutely peachy, Ralph, absolutely peachy."

As Ralph climbed in and pulled out into traffic, Sharon set the briefcase on the seat next to her, pulled a small leather address book out of her purse and began flicking through it. "Who next?" she muttered to herself. Suddenly she stopped skimming through the pages, grinned. "Judge Stephens I think!"

Tommy

"What the fuck were you thinking?"

Tommy gave a small smile as he dropped into the chair opposite Martin's desk. "Hello, Marty, I'm doing great. Thanks for asking. And how are you?"

Sharon   grinned,   despite   Martin's   furious expression.   There was no doubt about it, Tommy was becoming more and more like his old man every day. And no bad thing either, she had a feeling that the business would start floundering pretty soon without his drive, his ambition, his bloody minded cocky self-assurance.

"It's not a joke!"   Martin scowled, rubbing his forehead. He looked older than the last time Sharon had looked at him closely. He was her kid brother, the baby of the family, with natural, boyish good looks. So when did he start looking old for heaven's sake?   He looked to Sharon for support, but she said nothing. Martin leaned forward, calmed himself down. "You can't just go off by yourself taking risks like that. You don't have the skills, the knowledge - "

"And where am I supposed to get them?" Tommy spat back at him. "Certainly fucking not from you! If you had your way I'd be stuck in that fucking dry cleaners for the rest of my life!"

"And what's wrong with that?"

Tommy stared at him. "You're taking the fucking piss now " He felt his skin crawl at the thought of it, the smell, the little old ladies with their fifty year old coats smelling of mothballs and cat piss.

"Give him a break, Marty," chipped in Sharon. "He's a Taylor, that's all you need to remember."

"Still, going off alone like that..."

"I wasn't alone," Tommy informed him. "I had a good crew - one of my dad's crews. Darren, Spud, Ricky."

Sharon gave a nod. "Good boys. How much did you clear?"

"After the boys are paid out we'll net eighty grand."

Sharon gave a low whistle. "Not bad for a night's work." She looked at Martin. "What else have we done lately that's brought in eighty grand in a night?"

Martin sighed. "That's not the point."

"That's exactly the fucking point!" scowled Tommy.

"No! The point is that you took a big risk without talking it through first!"

"Why would I tell you first? I already knew what you'd say!"

"That's not the way we do things!"

"Isn't it? Did Mickey come and ask for your permission before he went out on a job?"

"You're not Mickey!"

Tommy jabbed his finger at Martin. "And neither are you - but someone has to step up and fill his shoes, and right now it looks like I'm the only one who's got the bollocks to do it!"

Martin pushed his chair back and jumped to his feet. For a moment Tommy thought he was going to come round his desk and punch him in the face. He stood staring at Tommy, clenching and unclenching his fists, then suddenly took a deep breath and exhaled hard. "I don't have the energy to argue this shit right now!" he snarled, and grabbing his jacket off the back of his chair, he stormed out the office.

Tommy started to go after him, to say something to him, but Sharon called him back. "Let him go," she told Tommy. "He's got a lot on his mind right now."

Tommy watched Martin till he was out the door of the gym, then slumped back into his chair. "Who rattled his fucking cage?"

Sharon laughed. "After that conversation you really have to ask that?"

Tommy shrugged.

"Come on Tommy, you don't have to play the innocent with me. Your dad's death has left a huge hole in this family, and you're the one who's filling it." She grinned. "And you're loving it!"

Tommy couldn't hide a little grin.

"Your dad held you back for too long, we could all see that, but he just wanted to protect you. But now he's gone, you've got to figure it out for yourself."

Tommy nodded. "Thanks, Aunt Sharon. For supporting me and everything."

She shrugged. "What choice do I have? There's clearly no holding you back." She leaned forward. "But be careful. I see that look in your eye, and it's the same one I used to see in your dad's eyes. You are loving this, and that's OK, but don't let that cloud your judgment, you know what I mean? There's times when that fire and passion will serve you well, but there will also be moments when a cool head is called for. And that's the trick. Knowing when to let the fire burn, and when to cool everything down and be the one who's thinking clearest. That was your dad's gift, and that's what you have to learn."

Tommy nodded. "I will, promise."

Sharon stood up and yawned. "But eighty grand, that's not a bad start."

Tommy grinned as she put an arm round his shoulders. "Yeah, not bad, eh?"

Terri

Jimmy stood over the bed, looking down at Terri with a face full of loathing. Terri stared at him in disbelief. "Sharon is lying to you," he sneered. "They are all lying to you. You tried to kill me, you dirty whore, but you couldn't even do that properly, could you?" He held a long knife in his hand, the blade catching the light. "Now it's my turn. I'm going to kill Sharon, Martin, Tommy, Georgie, you're whole rotten family one at a time in front of you. I'm going to make you watch, make you suffer so much you'll want to die."

Terri looked up helpless. "No, no, you can't. You're dead. I killed you!"

"I can, and I'm going to. One at a time, nice and slow."

"No!" screamed Terri. "Get away from me!"

Sharon could hear Terri screaming as she approached the house. She sighed to herself. "What is going on?"

As Sharon reached the door, Terri came running out, wide eyed, her hair plastered to her face, wearing just a long, white night dress. "Jimmy's here," she screeched. "He's here! He's alive, he's not dead! He's going to get me, kill me, and you, and Georgie - "

Sharon grabbed her, wrapped her arms around her. "Stop! Stop! There's no one here, only me and you."

She wiped Terri's lank hair from her terrified, sweat-covered face. "He's dead, Terri, he can't hurt you."

Terri looked around, bewildered, trembling. Suddenly all the energy went out of her; she could barely stand. Sharon put her arms around her, led her back into the house and over to the settee, sat her down. Terri leaned forward, her head drooping between her knees.

Sharon sat beside her, an arm around her shoulders, feeling her sweat soaked nightdress with her fingers. "He's gone Terri," Sharon told her. "He can't hurt you no more. No one is going hurt you again. I will always look after you. I will never let you down."

Terri said nothing.

"Come on," said Sharon, "let's get you upstairs, get some clean, dry clothes on you."

"No! No!" shrieked Terri. "I'm not going back up there! Jimmy's up there! He'll kill me!" She was petrified.

"He's dead, Tel. You killed him, remember? That bastard is dead and buried and will never bother anyone again. You made sure of that."

Slowly, slowly, Terri lifted her head, meeting Sharon's eyes. "Then why does he keep coming to see me?" Without another word she buried her face in Sharon's chest, sobbing.

Sharon sighed. Just five minutes ago she had been sitting in her car gazing at Terri and Georgie's house and thinking that everything was falling into place, marvelling at how well things were going for her. Four old clients contacted, and three of them had paid up. The other had told her to fuck off, but she figured sending a choice selection of his photos to his office would soon get him in line.

With the money she was making she had even upgraded her car. A baby blue Bentley convertible, that's what she had treated herself to. She sighed as she settled into the deep, ivory-leather seat, waiting for the song to finish on the radio before she went in to sort out Terri's latest crisis. It was an old Motown song, real music as she liked to call it, and it seemed a crime to turn it off before it ended. And anyway, the longer she could spend cradled in her car's soft seat, the longer it was till Terri unloaded her latest bunch of bullshit on her. But she certainly wasn't expecting a full blown hallucinogenic nightmare.

She shouldn't have been surprised though - trying to deal with Terri and Georgie was worse than dealing with kids. Not that Sharon had much experience dealing with kids, life had conspired to make sure that never happened, but from the limited time she had spent around nieces and nephews, that was probably not a bad idea. She had no real idea how to deal with them, and her notoriously short temper would have made life difficult, to say the least, if she'd had kids of her own.

She never got any peace when she came to visit. The last time she'd come up, she had been sitting outside for a minute, letting herself relax before going in, eyes closed while the music washed over her, when the sound of someone tapping on her window had pulled her out of her relaxed reverie.

It was Terri, of course. "Come on Shal! You can't hide in there all day!" she had shrilled.

More's the pity, thought Sharon. The song faded out and Sharon reluctantly turned off the ignition, shoved the door open, forcing Terri to step back.

Terri had her skinny arms wrapped tight around her, securing her stained cardigan in place like a shield. Her eyes took in Sharon - dressed to the nines as usual, from her freshly coiffed hair to her high heels - then the car. "Someone's doing all right."

Sharon couldn't keep the grin off her face. "Long term investments paying off."

Terri tore her eyes from the car and met Sharon's fixed gaze for a brief second before flicking back towards the house. "Well you'd better come in. I put the kettle on."

Sharon glanced up at the sky. A morning shower had just blown over, and the clouds were scattering like torn strips of paper chased by the wind, leaving behind a sky as bright as cornflowers. Sharon stepped carefully around the puddles and followed Terri into the house.

Sharon settled herself into a kitchen chair, watched as Terri moved around making tea, putting some Rich Tea biscuits on a plate. It was hard for Sharon to see how Terri had let herself go. She'd been a lovely girl, slim, nice tits, pretty face, but now… It was all still there, but she just didn't seem to give a shit. Her hair was unbrushed, she never wore any make-up, and her clothes were shapeless, baggy. Give me a day with her, thought Sharon, and I could turn her back into an attractive woman who would still turn a few heads.

"Penny for your thoughts?" Terri set the teacups on the table, looking anxiously at Sharon.

Sharon looked away quickly, forced a smile to her face. "You look all right, the sea air must suit you?"

Terri gave a tired sigh. "I like it here, but…" She paused suddenly, looked towards the back door. There was a whining, the sound of a paw scratching against the door. Terri smiled, and hurried to the door. As soon as she pulled it open, Jasper bounded in, tail wagging, sniffing excitedly round Sharon before turning his attention to Terri. Terri left the door open, and the breeze carried the briny scent of the mud flats to them on the warm air.

"In your bed," instructed Terri, and Jasper reluctantly curled up on his bed. Terri looked up at Sharon with sad eyes. "I don't know what I'd do without him, Shal," she began, leaning over and scratching Jasper's ears. He wagged his tail, licked her hand. "He's the only thing that keeps me sane, but Georgie says he's going to kill him!"

"I'm sure he doesn't mean it," said Sharon, sipping her tea. "You know what Georgie's like, he makes a drama out of everything."

"No! He means it!" She leaned forward, her eyes staring, filled with fear and concern.

Sharon patted her hand. "Come on Tel, you know - "

" - he said he would poison him one night when I was asleep, put weed killer in his food, then chop him up and throw him in the sea!" Terri was starting to get hysterical. "He means it, he really does, I just know it!"

Sharon leaned forward. "Terri, just think about it, think about Georgie. Does he have any weed killer?"

Terri frowned. "No, but - "

"And chop him up? Georgie? He won't even top and tail a fish when he's cooking! He still gets you to do it, right?"

Terri's certainty started to fade. "Yeah. But - "

"And how many times has he walked to the sea?"

Terri bit her lip. "Never."

"There you go." Sharon sat back, took another sip of her tea, leaving a deep red lipstick mark on the cup. "He's always been like that, all mouth and no trousers, you know Georgie."

Terri still didn't look convinced.

"I'll have a word with him, OK?"

Terri looked up, her tired eyes pleading, grateful. "Would you?"

"Of course."

Terri hesitated a moment. She looked down at the floor, wringing her hands together.

Something is about to come out, thought Sharon.

Finally Terri looked up. "I know you think I'm a bit of a psycho these days," she began. Sharon started to protest, but Terri pressed on. "No, I get it. I know I'm not always thinking straight, and I probably do blow things up, make a meal of them, but it's hard, Shal." She looked up, her eyes pleading. "I still see him, you know? Still see his body in the bed, bloated, those swollen lips, half his head - "

"Stop it!"

Terri looked up, startled.

"Don't torture yourself. He was a bastard, a right cunt, and he had everything coming to him. You did the world a bleeding favour when you topped him, so don't keep obsessing over it."

Terri gave Sharon a quick glance, then stood up, and drifted over to stare out the window. The sky to the East was clear, a haze rising up over the flat estuary as the sun started to warm the damp ground. Terri stared into it, as though by staring hard she could see something that was hidden. "They're out there, Shal," she whispered.

Sharon looked at her, puzzled. "Out there? Who?"

"I don't expect you to believe me," said Terri quickly, "but I see them. I see them when I'm out with Jasper. In the distance, so far away that you might think it's a ragged bush, a tree stump, but I know, I know they're watching me." She still stared off into the distance.

Sharon scowled, then pushed herself to her feet, came and stood beside her sister, gazing out into the bright emptiness. "Who's out there?"

Terri glanced at Sharon, then returned her gaze to the hazy distance. "I've never seen them close - they're too clever for that - but they follow me, watch me."

Sharon looked at the side of her sister's face. Fuck, she was really losing it. She took a deep breath. "You've seen them for sure?"

Terri nodded vigorously.

"Describe them to me."

Terri's eyes never left the sky, bleaching out as the sun heated up the day. "They're always there, always watching." She blinked. "But like I told you, they're much too clever to let me see them."

Sharon sighed. "It's not much of a description, is it? I can just imagine you doing one of them little sketches for the police. It would look like a bleeding tree! Who's following you, they'd say, Twiggy?" Sharon couldn't keep the bitterness and frustration out of her voice.

Terri turned suddenly. "I know what you think. You think I'm losing it, imagining things. I'm not!" For a moment her eyes were clear, bright, feverish almost, then just as quickly she looked away, started fumbling with the tea towel, wiping imaginary crumbs from the immaculate kitchen counter.

Sharon reached out, briefly touched Terri's shoulder. She could feel the tension coursing through her body. She was like a deer that had just heard a noise, poised, ready for flight at any moment.

Sharon turned away. "I'll have a word with Martin and Tommy, have one of the boys come and take a look around, real discrete. OK?"

Terri nodded, her eyes deep pools of fear and relief. "And Georgie, will you talk to Georgie?"

Sharon nodded. Why not? She'd talked to one lunatic in the asylum, why not complete the set?

"Georgie?" Sharon stood outside the bedroom door, rapping lightly on it with her knuckles. "Can I come in?"

"Fuck off!" The voice that answered wasn't Georgie, but rather his alter-ego Samantha. Sharon's heart sank. Georgie was hard enough to talk to when he was himself, but Samantha added another level of difficulty, another level of weird to proceedings, throwing a protective cloak around Georgie that made it almost impossible to get through. "How are you, Samantha?"

There was a moment's pause, then. "I told you to fuck off!"

"I just want to talk."

"I don't!"

Sharon drew a deep breath. "The house looks nice."

The pause was longer this time. She'd got Samantha thinking.

"Thank you."

"I can tell it matters to you."

"We can't live in a messy house," Samantha informed her.

Sharon leaned on the doorframe and closed her eyes. "I know. I'm the same. Everything has to be just right." Sharon reached up and rubbed her forehead with a manicured finger. She wasn't in the mood for this. Think! Concentrate! "But you're not the only one who lives here," she said finally.

"More's the pity," came the quick reply. "That messy bitch and her stinking, slobbering animal should just fuck off out of our house!"

"It's her house too."

There was a long silence this time.

"Terri's your sister," continued Sharon. "She loves you."

"We don't need anyone else!"

"Maybe not. But she needs you."

Silence.

Sharon wondered if she'd gone too far. It was so hard when she couldn't even see Georgie - or Samantha - so hard to know what he was thinking.

Sharon was so deep in thought that she didn't hear the footsteps, was startled when the door suddenly popped open and Samantha stood there, in an exotic cocktail gown, high heels and more make-up than even Sharon wore in a week. Samantha stared at her for a moment. "Terri really needs me?" It was Georgie's voice that came out, so different from the supercilious tones that Samantha adopted.

Sharon nodded. "She really needs you, Georgie."

He met her eyes for a moment, then stomped back into the room, a big man in a woman's dress and heels, no longer Samantha, now just a middle aged man in drag. He pulled off his wig and set it on the dresser, sat down and began wiping off his make-up.

Sharon was fascinated, she had never seen the transformation from Georgie to Samantha or back again, it felt as though she was witnessing something deeply personal, almost intimate.

Georgie wiped roughly at his face, smearing the make-up as he scooped it off, one baby wipe after another covered in it then dumped in the rubbish bin. "And I suppose you're going to tell me she needs that horrible hound too?" He glanced over at her for a second, then returned to his clean up job, working hurriedly as though he had to finish the job quickly lest Samantha re-merge.

Sharon gave a soft smile. "Yes, she needs that horrible hound. He helps keep her sane."

Georgie snorted out a short laugh. "Really? Have you seen her? She looks like a fucking bag lady, moping around in those horrible clothes. And now she's taken to peering out the window and muttering under her breath, thinks the boogie man is out there watching her or something." He shook his head, opened his eyes wide to wipe away a thick layer of mascara. "Too much weed and vodka if you ask me. Half her brain is soaked with booze, the other half is lost in a ganga fog."

"And you want to take away the one thing she cares about, the one thing that gives her life any meaning? Good luck with that!"

Georgie stopped, gazed in the mirror for a second, then stared out of the window. He took a deep breath. "You've got a point." He resumed scrubbing his face. "But couldn't you have chosen something less messy, less intrusive? A gold fish or something?"

Sharon laughed. "Tough to take for a walk." She walked over to stand behind him, met his eyes in the mirror. "Try to be a bit nicer? Don't threaten to kill the dog?"

He gave a weary shake of his head. "If I must."

Sharon rested her hands on his shoulders and was delighted when rather than pulling away, he reached up with one hand to hold hers. "You must."

Georgie frowned, but his eyes were smiling. "All right. I'll play nice."

Tommy

Tommy cracked his knuckles, his cigarette hanging from his lips, and peered into the darkness. Another night, another job. He could get used to this. Instead of being cooped up in the stinking fucking dry cleaners, he was out with Darren, Ricky and Spud once more, following up a lead that Darren had got. A warehouse that was sometimes used by a dodgy Polish importer called Piotr, who Tommy had met a few times. They all knew he did some dodgy business, a bit of low level larceny, handling stolen goods, that kind of stuff, but he never interfered with them, so they left him alone.

But now, apparently he had taken a step up, got too big for his boots, bringing in a big load of duty free fags through his buddies back home. So not only was he getting ideas above his station, but he was also stepping into an area that Tommy wanted to carve out for himself. That couldn't be tolerated. The solution was simple - hit his warehouse while the goods were there and clean him out. In one stroke they would put him out of business and make a good few bob themselves.

Tommy grinned, his mind playing with that phrase from the A Team - "I love it when a plan comes together." That he could relate to. He took a drag on his cigarette, flicked the butt out the window, gazing out into the darkness.

He felt like a different person these days. Finally, he was stepping out from his dad's huge shadow, establishing himself as the big man, the boss. Sharon was on his side, even Martin had stopped arguing with him at every turn, stopped treating him like a kid, started listening to him at times, at times even giving him some credit for knowing what the fuck he was doing.

The confidence was seeping through into every area of his life. At the gym Kenny looked at him with different eyes, hung on every word he said, trained like a fucking demon whenever he was around, whenever he thought Tommy's eyes were on him.

And then there was Melissa. He'd never met a girl like her. She was so fucking hot, so dirty, did things - and made him do things - he'd only ever seen in porn movies before. Just thinking about her got him hard. He closed his eyes and started to recall the last time he'd seen her. He had never imagined a girl could have an appetite for sex that was bigger than his, never imagined a woman could be that imaginative, that filthy.

"Heads up!"

Tommy sat up, startled, and found Darren, Ricky and Spud staring at him. "What's the score?"

Darren squatted down by the door, his muscular arm, criss-crossed by dark tattoos, resting on the wing mirror. "We've cut the fence, Ricky's had a snoop around, can't see anyone on guard. The electric box is on the wall outside, so even if there is an alarm we can turn it off before we go in."

Tommy grinned. "Like taking candy from a baby."

"Stupid fucking Polack!" grunted Spud, the faint light gleaming off his shaved head.

Darren stood up and Tommy climbed out of his car, gazed across the road at the dark warehouse. He nodded to the truck, parked beside him. "Ricky, you wait here. As soon as we're sure it's all clear, we'll call you. Spud, got the bolt cutters?"

Spud held the bolt cutters up, grinning. "These fuckers would cut through Fort fucking Knox!" He slipped them back into a black canvas duffel, hauling the duffel up onto his shoulder.

Tommy turned back to Darren. "Let's do it!"

They turned and crossed the road, slid along the dark fence to a spot under a tall tree, then eased through the gap that Spud had cut earlier.

Tommy scanned the darkness as they hurried across the dry gravel car park, flitting from shadow to shadow. It certainly looked quiet, no lights on inside. But would you really leave a hundred and fifty grand's worth of ciggies unguarded? Surely there had to be something they had missed?

Tommy felt a tingle in his stomach and struggled to keep a grin from his face. Just a bit of nerves, enough to keep him on his toes, not enough to make him freeze or slow down at a critical time.

They reached the shadow of the building and slid up against it. Spud flipped open the electric box and played in it for a moment while Tommy looked around. Apart from a couple of old cars on the far side of the car park, there was no evidence that anyone was around.

Spud muttered something, and then all went dark, the faint exterior lights shutting off to leave them in total darkness. Tommy patted his jacket pockets - flashlight in one, gun in the other. What more did he need? Still grinning, he followed Darren and Spud round to the rear of the building.

They paused by a small rear door. Darren reached into Spud's duffel, pulling out a long crowbar. He glanced around - nothing, no one moving, not even a rat or a bird - then jammed the end of the crowbar into the door, level with the lock and cranked on it.

They could hear the sound echo through the building, but the door didn't budge.

"If there's any fucker in there, they'll know we're here now!" whispered Spud, glancing around uneasily.

Darren adjusted his grip on the crowbar, then cranked again.

Once more the noise echoed through the dark, and this time the door moved a little.

As he positioned himself for a third try, Tommy moved close beside him, wrapping his big hands around the bar alongside Darren's. "Three, two, one," he whispered, then together they wrenched on the bar. With a loud crack the edge of the doorframe splintered, and the door swung open.

They peered into the darkness as the echo chased off into the silence. Spud stuck his head in the door.

"Knock, fucking knock!"

Silence.

Spud shouldered his duffel, flicked on his flashlight and led the way into the dark warehouse. Tommy followed, and Darren brought up the rear, carefully closing the broken door behind them.

They were in a narrow corridor that led along the side of the warehouse towards the front. They passed a small office, a dirty kitchen, a smelly toilet, their flashlight picking out scraps and images as they passed - a cluttered desk; an old Playboy calendar on the wall; a dirty sink with several chipped coffee mugs on the drainer; a rickety table with three orange plastic chairs; a toilet with no seat, the toilet paper sitting over the handle of a filthy toilet brush.

At the end of the corridor they stepped out into the warehouse, and there they were - a large stack of boxes, sitting pretty in the middle of the floor. Tommy smiled. "Looks like they were expecting us!"

Spud stepped forward, running his flashlight over the large stack of white boxes. There was a crest they didn't recognise on the boxes, something written on them that they couldn't decipher.

"Check 'em," said Darren.

Spud stopped at the stack of boxes, clamped his flashlight under his arm, reached in his pocket and pulled out a switch blade. He flicked it open and reached for the nearest box.

Before his blade could cut into the box, a light flashed into their eyes from the far side of the stack of boxes, blinding them. "Stop there!"

Tommy raised a hand to shield his eyes, peering towards the light. He could see nothing but the bright glare.

"I knew some fuckers would try to steal my goods!" snapped the voice. "You greedy bastards better turn around and walk out now before I shoot your arses!"

Tommy squinted, trying to see better, but the light was bright, shining straight at them. "Easy now," he said, slipping his hand into his jacket pocket.

"No! No easy! Fuck off! Leave!" The voice had a strong accent, Eastern European. "Now! Before I shoot you bastards!" Held alongside the light, the shiny barrel towards them, was a shotgun, shaking slightly, but always pointing in their direction.

Tommy lowered his other hand, palm down, a calming gesture. "OK, OK, we're leaving now."

Spud flipped his blade closed and slid it back in his pocket. Darren started to back up too, and as he did so, his shadow, which had partly been blocking Tommy from the full glare of the light, moved to one side, totally exposing Tommy.

"Fuck me! You fucking Tommy Taylor!"

Tommy's face fell. He knew the voice. It was Piotr himself, taking the night watch, guarding his merchandise. He stared back into the bright light. "So what if it is?"

"You fucking Tommy Taylor!" squawked Piotr. "Tommy fucking Taylor trying to rob me? You know me you cunt, and you try to rob me!"

"I didn't know it was you Piotr," lied Tommy. "We just heard there was a load of fags, ripe for picking."

"Don't you lie to me, you cunt!" screamed Piotr. "If you know the cigarettes are here, you know it's me! I did some business with your dad - he was good man, not thieving scumbag like you, who try to rob Piotr!"

Tommy frowned. "Fuck you! You don't know me! Don't know what I do or don't do!"

"Everyone going to know what a scumbag you are!" screamed Piotr, the shotgun shaking as he shouted. "I tell everyone what a thieving cocksucker you are!"

Tommy felt calm, icy almost. He knew exactly what to do and how to do it. He stepped forward, his hand still in his jacket pocket. "You're not going to do that, Piotr," he said slowly.

The shotgun shook towards him. "Stand still. What the fuck you mean?"

Tommy took another step forward. "You're not going to say anything to anyone." Another step forward.

"Stand still or I fucking shoot! What shit you talking? I gonna tell - "

He never finished his sentence, his last words drowned out by the blast of Tommy's gun as he shot from the hip, from his jacket pocket, his hand clamped tight to his side as he fired four quick shots.

The sound was almost deafening in the confined warehouse, the blasts echoing off the concrete floor, the corrugated iron roof.

As the shots spat out in the darkness, Piotr's light disappeared, the shotgun too, both clattering to the floor. They were soon followed by the heavy sound of Piotr's body slumping onto the bare concrete.

Darren and Spud hurried forwards, their flashlights quickly finding his slumped figure, half propped against the back wall, two red stains already spreading out across his dirty shirt. He looked up at them, a look of disbelief on his face, almost childlike in its confusion. "He fucking shot me!"

Tommy walked over more slowly, stepped between Darren and Spud and look down at Piotr. The bullets had hit him in the stomach, throwing him backwards, one leg underneath him at an awkward angle. His face looked pale, eyes squinting as he peered up into the bright lights towards Tommy. "What you fucking shoot me for?"

Tommy squatted down in front of him, staring at him eye to eye. "What's my name?" said Tommy coldly.

Piotr scowled. "What you mean?" he gasped. A trickle of blood ran down from the corner of his mouth.

Tommy reached out, gripped his jaw, forcing him to meet his eyes. "What's my fucking name?"

Piotr coughed and pulled his face free from Tommy's grip. "Tommy Taylor," he grimaced, the pain etched across his face.

Tommy nodded. "That's right. Tommy Taylor." He stood up, wiped his hand on his trousers, his gun still in the other hand. "And you threatened me!" His cold eyes bored into Piotr. "You threaten a Taylor, this is what happens." He half turned away, then turned swiftly back, the gun pointed right between Piotr's eyes. "You fucking die!"

Piotr didn't even have time to raise his hand before Tommy shot, one blast, splattering his brains against the wall of the warehouse.

He turned away without even glancing at Darren and Spud. "Darren, call Ricky, let's get this shit loaded. Spud, clean up this mess."

For a moment neither of them moved, their eyes meeting in shock and surprise. Then, "Yes, guvnor!" answered Darren quickly.

"Yes, boss," added Spud.

Tommy walked slowly back down the narrow corridor, turned into the dirty bathroom, then suddenly leaned over the filthy sink and vomited, once, twice, his guts heaving, seeing Piotr staring up at him.

But just as suddenly he shut the image out, banished it. He would deal with it later, but right now there was work to be done. He turned on the tap, let the water run for a moment, then leaned over, splashed the water over his hot face, swirled some round his mouth to get rid of the taste of vomit, then spat it out. He straightened up, wiped his face on the sleeve of his jacket, found that he still had his gun in the other hand. He peered at it for a moment in the darkness, then kissed it, slipped the safety on, slid it down the back of his trousers.

"You all right?" said Darren when he heard Tommy step back into the warehouse.

"Why the fuck wouldn't I be?" said Tommy smoothly.

Darren grinned in the dark. "Right, guv. Why the fuck wouldn't you be?"

Tommy looked around, knew what he had to do, what he needed to do, now more than ever before. "You lot finish up here without me?"

Darren nodded. "We've got it from here."

"I'll see you tomorrow, then." Without another word he turned on his heel and strode off down the corridor.

Darren watched until he heard the back door scrape closed, and turned to find Spud staring at him. "What you think of that, then?" said Spud, his small eyes gleaming in the dark.

Darren laughed softly. "I reckon the old man would be fucking proud, that's what." He glanced over at Piotr's body, still slumped against the wall. "Now, are you going to stand around all night yakking, or are you going to clean up that fucking Polack mess?"

Tommy tore his phone from his pocket as he stepped outside, frantically punching the buttons. He held the phone to his ear, holding his breath.

After several rings a sleepy voice answered. "Tommy? What the fuck time is it?"

"I want you!"

Melissa's breathy voice whispered down the line. "Of course you do."

"I want you right now!"

There was a moment's silence. "It's late. I'm tired."

"I don't care. It has to be now." He clamped the phone tighter to his head, willing her to say yes.

"I don't know..." She paused, yawned. "What will you do to me?"

"I'll fuck you like you've never been fucked before!" he told her.

"I don't know, Tommy, I've been fucked pretty much every way there is, you know…"

"Not like this!" he growled.

"Go on then…"

Tommy leaned against the cool metal wall of the warehouse, gazed out into the darkness, picturing Melissa's lithe body. "From behind, that's where I'll start."

"You know how much I like that…"

"My hands on your hips, forcing you down on the bed, forcing myself inside you."

"Deep inside me?"

"Deeper than you've ever felt," he croaked…

Tommy

Tommy was still bleary eyed from the night before as he slid into a chair at the greasy spoon. The smell of fried food nauseated him, hanging thick and heavy in the air like a cloud. All he wanted to do was sleep, but the call from Frankie was impossible to ignore, and so he had dragged himself away from Melissa, climbed into his car, hammered back down the A12 for an early morning meeting, his big BMW eating up the miles as he raced through the droves of bored commuters driving their salesmen's cars to another day of dreary appointments.

And, of course, Frankie was late. Tommy nursed his coffee, closing his eyes. Instead of being here he could still be with Melissa. He'd left so early he hadn't even had time for a morning shag. In fact, he had barely fallen asleep from the previous night's activities when Frankie called. Fuck me, the girl could wear him out. He'd convinced her to meet him at a nice hotel near Ipswich, one they had used a couple of times before, and they were barely through the door before they were ripping each other's clothes off.

Melissa was like a woman possessed, tearing at him with her teeth and her nails, wrapping her limbs around him like sinuous tentacles, or the branches of some horror movie tree that coil around you and don't let you go. They'd gone at it for a couple of hours, ebbing and flowing, faster and slower, an outpouring of raw lust that never seemed satisfied, until they had finally fallen asleep together in the early hours of the morning, her limbs still coiled around him like an anaconda that had ensnared its prey.

Tommy would have to be careful when he got home, his back, chest, legs, were scored with dozens of bite marks and scratches; no way he could let the wife see those, she'd have a fucking shit fit. She knew he played away from home a bit - she had to, she wasn't stupid - but this would be too much, the evidence shoved right in her face. He gave a little smile, recalled what a South African bloke he once met had said about a girl: "She fucks like a rattle snake!" Tommy wasn't sure exactly what he'd meant at the time, but now, now he understood. No two ways about it, Melissa fucked like a fucking rattle snake!

Tommy felt a heavy hand on his shoulder and opened his eyes. "Morning, Tommy. Did I wake you up?"

Tommy grinned as Frankie lowered his big frame into the seat opposite.

"No fucking kidding! Six o-fucking-clock and you wondered if you woke me up?"

Frankie looked into Tommy's face and grinned back. "No rest for the wicked, eh?"

The waitress bustled past, bleached hair and orange make-up, mascara laid on with a shovel, thirty-five trying to pass for twenty. "What can I get you?"

Frankie peered up at the menu board above the counter. "Full English for me, love," he growled, "and a cup of tea."

She nodded, turned to Tommy. "And are you ready to order now, love?"

Tommy held up his empty coffee cup. "Just keep this stuff coming and I'll be fine."

She nodded, scurried off.

Tommy leaned forward, propped his elbows on the table and cradled his jaw in his hand. "So?"

Frankie's face turned serious, and he leaned in closer, dropping his voice from its normal booming baritone. "We got a lead. On your dad."

Tommy froze, his eyes locked on Frankie. For a moment, it seemed as though everything else had stopped, the café had fallen silent, the only sound was his blood pulsing in his ears, the words repeating over and over: "We got a lead. On your dad."

"There you go love."

Tommy took a second to break from his reverie, looked up at the waitress as though surprised to see her there. She held a coffee jug towards him. "Keep it coming you said, right?"

Tommy blinked away his surprise, licked his dry lips, held his coffee cup out to her. "Yeah, right, keep it coming."

She filled his coffee then hurried away.

Tommy took a slow sip of the scalding coffee, then turned back to Frankie. The shock had passed, now he was all business, cold, calculating. "What you got?"

The waitress had left a cup of tea for Frankie. He took a sip, leaning in even closer. "Word from a reliable source is that it was the Vietnamese that hit your old man."

"How reliable?"

"Someone I really trust. He's - " Frankie paused as the waitress set his breakfast on the table, smiling politely until she was gone. "He's solid, really solid. Says a couple of their boys have been boasting about it, how they helped knock off Dangerous."

Tommy's jaw locked tight, his eyes narrowed as he processed this. The Vietnamese. It made sense. They had been locked in an escalating war with them, a war that Mickey thought he had won when he destroyed their HQ. But clearly they were a bigger threat than even his old man had reckoned. And now, it seemed, they had had the last word. Or so they thought.

"Tommy? Tommy? Are you all right?"

Tommy snapped his cold eyes up to meet Frankie and nodded slowly. "Yeah, I'm all right."

Frankie reached his massive hand across the table and gripped Tommy's arm. "I know what you're thinking, Tommy, and I totally understand it. Blood is blood, and when your blood has been spilled, someone has to pay. That's right, that's the way it is. But be very fucking careful with these boys. They are nasty, they are cunning, and they are growing like a fucking weed. If you do something, and there is any fucking hint, any clue at all linking it back to you, they will wipe your whole fucking family from the face of the earth. Do you hear me?"

Tommy lifted his coffee cup, drained it, set it back on the table. "I hear you Frankie." He stood up, vengeance and caffeine coursing through his veins. He knew what he had to do, he just had to figure out how to do it. "I owe you one. Thanks." He turned and strode out of the café, Frankie's eyes following him all the way.

Finally Frankie turned to his food. He loaded his fork, took a big bite, chewed slowly and washed it down with a sip of hot tea. "If he's not Mickey Taylor reincarnated," he muttered to himself, "then I'm a fucking kosher butcher!"

"It's out of the question!" snapped Martin.

Tommy had tried to broach the subject calmly, at their regular morning meeting, but no matter how subtle he had been about it, Martin had jumped on him the moment the words were out of his mouth.

"We have to be smart about this," Martin added, perhaps sensing he had reacted too strongly. "Our business is just starting to recover, we can't afford a war right now, especially with the Vietnamese. They are just too big, too strong."

Tommy stood before Martin's desk, too wired to sit down, the scratches and bites on his back stinging, reminding him of Melissa, her energy, her passion, her lust for life. She made him feel alive and alert. "So we do nothing?"

Martin shrugged. "I don't know, Tommy. Would you risk wiping out the whole family for the sake of revenge?"

Tommy stopped, leaned his hands on the back of a chair and glared at Martin. "I would fucking do something, that's for fucking certain!" He turned to Sharon, who had so far said nothing. "For fuck sake Sharon, back me up here. Now we know who killed Mickey, we have got to do something, right?"

Sharon sighed. She had been dreading this day. "I don't know. You're both right. Martin's right that the Vietnamese are too big to mess with, but you're right too - it doesn't sit right to know who killed Mickey and just do nothing."

"Exactly!" exclaimed Tommy. "People have to know! If you fuck with the Taylors, there's a price to pay!"

"Like Piotr?" said Martin quietly.

Tommy froze. "How do you know about that?" he hissed.

Martin's calm gaze met him. "You think you're the only one who hears things?" He shook his head, eyes half closed. "There's not much you do that I don't know about."

Tommy stared at him for a moment, then turned away. What was that supposed to mean. The stinging from his back suddenly intensified. Did

Martin know about Melissa? Is that what Martin meant? Or was Tommy just being paranoid?

"Piotr?" questioned Sharon. "Who the fuck is Piotr?"

Martin gave a small smile. "Tommy had his first kill last night. Think you're the big man now, don't you? You're all fired up after killing some small time Polish crook, think you can take on the whole fucking Vietnamese army, right?"

Tommy span around, anger coursing through his veins. "You cunt, at least I'm not some fucking cowardly old poof, running home to my boyfriend every night, too scared to even revenge my own brother!" As soon as he'd said it, Tommy regretted his words, but it was too late, they were out there.

The silence lay heavy on the room, the background noise of the gym suddenly loud in their ears, the grunts of the fighters, the clank of metal weights, the incessant beat of the music that pounded out all day long. Normally it faded away, they didn't even notice it, but now it was loud, insistent, filling the void between their words as they all paused, waiting to see who would break the silence, what the fall out would be.

Tommy took a deep breath and glanced at Martin. Martin's face was unreadable, as usual. What was he thinking? Did he even care what Tommy had just said? Everything just seemed to wash over him - but was that just a front, an illusion? Surely he wanted Mickey revenged? And if so, Tommy's comments must have really hurt.

"For fuck sake, you two!" It was Sharon who spoke first, glancing back and forth between the two of them. "You killed someone last night?" she asked Tommy.

Tommy nodded. "Little fucker made us, threatened to run his mouth off." He scowled. "You don't threaten a fucking Taylor…" The words, that had seemed so important the night before when he'd had a shotgun pointed at him, sounded hollow, empty now.

Sharon didn't take her eyes off him. "Are you all right?" There was concern in her voice, in her expression.

She reached out and gently touched Tommy's arm as he stood beside her.

Tommy gave her a short nod. "Yeah, I'm fine."

Sharon tugged on his sleeve. "Then you need to apologize, right now."

Tommy started to say something, but Sharon cut him off. "Marty may be a lot of things - a cold blooded bastard for one - but he's no fucking coward."

Tommy pursed his lips, fought back the lump that was trying to rise in his throat. He had never been good at apologizing, was never good at backing down. He'd spent a lifetime biting his lip around his dad, but now, now that he was no longer in his massive shadow, he was finding it harder and harder to say the right thing just because he was supposed to. But then he remembered something, a story his dad had told him, about Martin coming to his rescue when he had been kidnapped. Martin breezed in and took out two geezers while Mickey was tied up, helpless. Sharon was right. Martin was no coward… "Sorry." He had to force the word out, but once that first, bitter word was out there, the rest came easy. "I was out of order," he continued. "I shouldn't have said that."

For a moment Martin said nothing, just turned his cold eyes slowly onto Tommy, as though measuring him up, assessing him, deciding how to respond. Finally he gave a slight nod. "Apology accepted." They shook hands.

Tommy heard Sharon exhale sharply beside him.

"But let's leave our private lives out of it next time,

eh?" He met Tommy's eyes. "We all have secrets we would prefer to keep that way, right?"

He knows, thought Tommy, as he nodded his agreement. He fucking knows about Melissa.

"That's better," added Sharon. She glanced back and forth between the two of them. "But that still leaves the issue of the Vietnamese unresolved."

Martin leaned forward, his face impassive, as though the argument had never happened. "We keep an eye on them. We take our time, look for an opening, an opportunity. If the chance arises, we strike back. But we don't advertise it, we don't shout about it. If there is the slightest risk of anything being traced back to the family, I'll veto it."

Tommy shifted uncomfortably. "I don't know Marty, that still doesn't sit right. People are watching us, waiting, wondering when we are going to do something. We're losing a lot of face on this."

Martin shrugged. "So be it. I'd rather lose face than lose another member of the family." He looked from Sharon to Tommy. "Nothing until we all agree, and nothing that puts any of us at risk. Agreed?"

Sharon nodded and glanced up at Tommy.

He could feel both sets of eyes upon him and knew this wasn't a fight that he could win right here, right now. Martin wanted to wait, to take his time. Fine, Tommy would play along, keep his nose clean. But he would never stop looking for the chance to strike back, whether Martin approved or not. "Fine," he said finally. "We wait."

Martin nodded, leaned back in his chair and suddenly broke into a big smile. "So you were a busy boy last night, Tommy!" He reached in his desk, pulled out a bottle of scotch, two glasses. He poured a small measure into both glasses and held one out to Tommy.

Tommy took the glass, held it up to the light, the cut glass refracting the pale light into sparkling diamonds across his face.

"Welcome to the family business!" declared Martin.

It sounded almost mocking, but Tommy had no choice but to join in. "Cheers." He drained the glass in one, the fiery liquid burning his throat. Whatever Martin might think, even if he had his doubts and reservations, Tommy knew the truth of it. He was a real member of the family business now. He had crossed a line. And he wouldn't stop until Mickey was revenged, and he was firmly established as the guvnor, the new, undisputed boss.

Sharon

Sharon was almost starting to enjoy her visits to the country. It was such a contrast to the city, heading out of town, each minute taking her further away, the buildings and clutter falling away, the fields appearing on the side of the road, the sky opening up.

She had never really noticed the sky much before, it was just there, sometimes blue and sunny, mostly grey and cloudy. But heading out to the coast on a regular basis she had started to look at it differently. It was different. It was bigger, brighter, more open. Whereas in town you only got small glimpses, a patch appearing between the buildings if you happened to look up, out near the coast it was impossible to ignore. It was everything, everywhere, eighty or ninety percent of what you saw, a vast canopy that filled your field of vision as far as you could see.

Today the sky was pale, slightly washed out, like an old t-shirt that has had most of the colour washed out of it, but she knew it would soon change. They were into the dog days of summer now, late August, and the weather had fallen into a consistent pattern for a couple of weeks - cool mornings under a clear sky, then a steady buildup of heat through the day, the sky gradually turning a deeper blue. Then around mid afternoon the clouds would start to build, wispy at first, then thicker and thicker, the air getting heavier, the light, if light could do such a thing, also seeming heavier and more intense, until around tea time when a sudden storm would rip across the land.

And then the air would lighten, the sky would clear, and as night fell the whole cycle would start over.

Sharon turned her attention back to the girl sitting next to her. Lydia, that was her name. Cute little Polish girl, the agency had recommended. She couldn't have been more than twenty, with a slim figure and a bleached blonde pixie haircut. Fuck knows what she would make of living out in the middle of nowhere. Oh well, that was her problem, as long as she did her job and stuck around, Sharon didn't care what she did to entertain herself.

"So you understand your duties?"

Lydia gave a little nod. "Clean up after the dog, stay out the way the rest of the time."

Sharon grinned. Had she really been that curt in her instructions? "Right. That's the most important thing. Georgie will do lots of tidying and cleaning anyway, but if you are there to help, he will stop wigging out so much."

Lydia looked puzzled. "Wigging out?"

"Going crazy, getting angry."

Lydia nodded, processing this. Her English was pretty good, a bit of an accent, but she spoke well, understood pretty much everything. "And this Georgie, your brother, he is the transvestite?"

"Yes, but don't call him that," said Sharon quickly. "It looks like that, but that's not really it. It's more like he's two different people." She paused. "It's actually quite easy to deal with. When he's dressed as a man, you call him Georgie - "

" - and when he's a woman, Samantha, yes?"

Sharon nodded. "Yes." Good, the girl was sharp.

"And your sister, Terri. I keep an eye on her, tell you if she is too drunk or high?"

Another nod from Sharon. "Just in case."

Lydia gazed out the window, saying nothing.

Fuck me, thought Sharon, this is going to be interesting.

Samantha eyed Lydia moodily. "You could have found someone with better dress sense."

Sharon sighed. "Amazingly that wasn't the most important criteria I used when choosing someone."

Samantha gave Lydia another sulky once over then sashayed into the kitchen. "I suppose if she stops me from killing that stupid dog that would be something."

As if on cue, Jasper came bouncing in from the garden, sniffing Lydia vigorously, his tail wagging furiously.

Sharon started to ask Lydia if she was ok with dogs, but there was no need - she was rubbing his head and cooing to him. Clearly a dog lover.

"You can start by cleaning up this mess!" snapped Samantha from the kitchen.

Sharon followed his pointing finger - some grass that had tracked in on Jasper's paws as he had dashed in to see the visitor.

"Of course." With a little smile at Sharon, Lydia trotted into the kitchen. She took a quick look around, passed Samantha in her ruby cocktail dress and headed for the kitchen sink. A quick look in the cupboard and she found what she was looking for; a bottle of spray cleaner and a cloth.

Within seconds the grass was gone, the cloth rinsed and hanging across the edge of the sink.

Samantha watched Lydia's every movement carefully, his deep brown eyes in a slight frown, but her work was above reproach. "If you can make a good cup of tea too, we might just get to be friends," said Samantha in the husky tones that Georgie changed to when his alter ego was in control.

"Of course." Lydia grabbed the kettle, filled it and started rummaging through the cupboards to locate everything.

Samantha strolled out of the kitchen towards the stairs. "You can bring it to my room." He ignored Sharon and headed upstairs, narrowly avoiding Terri on the way.

"Where is she then?"

Sharon had to suppress a smile. Terri, often so sloppy in her dress and appearance, had made an effort, cleaned herself up, put on a fresh cotton dress. "In the kitchen." She followed Terri into the kitchen. "Terri, this is Lydia, Lydia, Terri."

The two shook hands, sizing each other up. Thank God we came on one of her up days, thought Sharon.

Terri on a down day was a scary sight, with her greasy lank hair, dark, hollow eyes, sloppy food stained clothes. But on an up day she was…

"Lydia. What a lovely name!"

Manic. Breathless almost.

Lydia gave a little smile and continued making tea. "Would you like tea or coffee?" The question was addressed to both Sharon and Terri.

"Coffee for me," replied Sharon.

"I'd love a cuppa!" gushed Terri. "Do you need any help?"

Lydia shook her head, smiled. It was true. She already had three mugs on the counter, had found the coffee, the tea, the sugar, the spoons.

Sharon took Terri by the arm. "Let's go outside for a bit of fresh air," she suggested, leading Terri gently into the back garden. Jasper followed them, hoping someone would play with him, but as Terri and Sharon settled on a small bench in the shade of a mature apple tree he settled down by their feet and chewed on a stick.

"How are you?"

Terri looked back at Sharon, blinking in the bright light, like a nocturnal creature suddenly exposed to daylight for the first time. "I'm good." She paused, as though considering it. "Yeah. Good."

Sharon nodded, looked up and smiled as Lydia brought their drinks to them.

"Is there something I need to do now?" she asked Sharon.

"Take Samantha his tea - his room is at the end of the hallway - then maybe start a bit of cleaning, finding out where everything is?"

Lydia gave a little smile, a half curtsey, and trotted back into the house. Terri's eyes followed her. "She's so young," she whispered. She turned back to Sharon. "Looks so innocent. Remember when we were like that Shal?"

Sharon sipped her coffee. "We were never that innocent. Never had the chance to be. Our old man beat and raped every drop of innocence out of us before we were sixteen years old."

Her cold words fell on them, silencing them both, taking them back to a place they had spent a lifetime trying to avoid. Sharon immediately regretted what she had said. She usually kept a lid on it, kept her bitterness buried, didn't think of or refer to the past. She couldn't change it, so why even think about it? But glancing at Terri she could see the effect it had had on her - this was the last thing Terri needed right now.

"She'll be good for you," added Sharon quickly. "Agency said she was the best they had, hard worker, good attitude."

Terri dragged herself back up from the abyss, meeting Sharon's eyes briefly. "That's good. She looks like a lovely girl. Just as well Georgie doesn't like girls, eh?"

Sharon forced a smile to her face. "First time I've thought that was a good thing!"

And suddenly the ice broke and they both laughed, a genuine laugh that pushed back the dark clouds, giving them both the space to recover, push the memories back into the dark corner where they always lurked, replacing them with something better, brighter.

"I still remember your face the first time you found out that Georgie played for the other team," laughed Sharon. "Looked like you didn't know whether to laugh, cry or knock his lights out!"

Terri nodded. "Well, it was a shock, wasn't it? A good looking bloke like Georgie, the birds always hanging round him?"

They sat in silence for a moment, sipped their drinks, the only noise coming from Jasper, working hard at the stick he had found.

Sharon sat back, gazed at the sky. Who would believe it? Sharon, the lady about town, sitting gazing at the sky and quite content?

"They're still out there," said Terri suddenly.

It took Sharon a moment to realize what Terri was talking about. "They?"

"The watchers. That's what I call them. The watchers. I don't see them every day, but I always know when they're around, even when I don't see them." She turned her eyes to Sharon, deep pools of misery and hurt, suspicion and paranoia. "I know you don't believe me, but it's not just in my mind."

Sharon didn't know what to say. She already had one crazy sibling, and Terri had never had a strong grip on reality. Was she completely losing it now? After years of abuse she had killed her husband, and now here she was stuck out in the middle of nowhere with Georgie, who was certifiably bat shit crazy. Then suddenly Lydia breezed into the kitchen, and an idea shot into Sharon's mind. She reached across, resting her hand on Terri's thin leg. "Tell you what, why don't you get Lydia to keep an eye out for them? Two heads better than one and all that?"

Terri glanced up at her. "Right. I get it. I'm crazy, so have the normal girl keep an eye out - and when she doesn't see anything, then you'll know for sure that I'm off my head, lost the plot!" Terri pulled away from Sharon and stood up. "Don't fucking bother. I know what I've seen, and I don't need your little spy coming here to prove that I'm imagining things, that I'm deluded!" Before Sharon could reply, Terri stormed back in the kitchen, slammed her teacup on the counter and raced upstairs.

Sharon was grateful for the sanctuary of her car. She'd said goodbye to Samantha and tried to talk to Terri through her bedroom door - like trying to talk to a sulky, fucking teenager - and gave Lydia her final instructions. And then she couldn't get out of the house quick enough.

She slumped in the soft leather seat, turned on the radio and the air conditioning. The sun had already burned through the morning haze, and now the sky was bright, sharp, a glare from horizon to horizon that had her reaching for her sunglasses. She took a deep breath, slipped the car into drive and pulled slowly away.

Her mind was preoccupied, her attention elsewhere, so there was no chance of her noticing the shadowy figure lurking behind a wind blasted tree, his eyes fixed on the house.

Tommy

Tommy paused in the hallway of the hospital. He hated this place. Everything about it. The smell of sickness and disinfectant reminded him of when he was a kid and one of them had thrown up, his mum used to wash the loo with Dettol. Then there was the look. They tried to brighten hospitals up a bit these days, but it still had the post war industrial look, no matter how hard they tried. Institutional, that was the word. He always felt like when you came into a place like this you might never get out, you could be sucked into its big jaws, processed, shoved in a bed somewhere and left to rot. Too much time visiting prisons had warped his mind.

He was dying for a fag, was trying to quit for the twentieth time, and as usual, a couple of days in the itch was starting to really bother him. It was all he could think of, when could he have his next fag - and never was the answer he came up with. He could feel the nicotine patch on his arm, wrapped his hand tight around it in an effort to get a bigger hit, then shook off the feeling, marched into Bernie's room and took a deep breath. "All right, big fella?"

The name was a travesty these days - Bernie was visibly shrinking from one visit to the next, the cancer eating him away from the inside and leaving just a shell, a large framed man hung with sagging skin, like an old, grey sheet hung across a wooden clothes horse.

Bernie was sleeping, his breath coming fast and shallow as his devastated lungs tried desperately to suck enough air in to keep him alive. The cannula hooked to his nose gave him a steady stream of pure oxygen to assist the process, but it was not enough, and day by day he was losing the battle.

Tommy paused by the bed. Should he wake him? He knew Bernie loved his visits - he'd never actually said it, but Tommy was pretty sure he was his only visitor - but it seemed somehow wrong to wake him when he was sleeping. It was probably the only time he got any peace, and relief from pain, from the hacking cough that tormented him when he was awake.

Tommy reached up and once more rubbed the nicotine patch through the sleeve of his jacket. If looking at Bernie lying there dying wasn't enough to convince someone to quit, nothing ever would.

He turned and glanced around the ward. Visiting this place was enough to put you off almost any form of vice, a bunch of withered up old geezers all just lying there waiting for the grim reaper to pay them their visit. What a way to finish life.

"Wondered when I'd see you again." The voice was a rasping croak, like dry leaves crushed in your hand, rattling round the quiet room.

Tommy forced a smile to his face as he turned around to meet Bernie's gaze. "All right, mate?"

Bernie's look spoke volumes, but he still forced out the words, the lie. "Feeling peachy, Tommy, feeling peachy."

Tommy settled into the chair next to Bernie and set the bag of oranges on the bed. It had become a ritual, Tommy always brought him oranges, they reminded him of holidays in Spain, reminded him too of the orange his mum had always put in their Christmas stockings when they were kids.

Bernie took an orange from Tommy, held it to his nose to take in the aroma, then handed it back for Tommy to peel and feed to him, slice by slice.

Bernie savoured two pieces before finally speaking again. "I always thought people were taking the piss, just saying it, that when you get old, it's like being a kid again," he gasped, his blue lips barely moving. "But it's true. My mum used to feed me orange slices…" He laughed, a harsh, rasping sound that sucked the air out of him for a moment then reduced him to a fit of coughing. Finally he got his breath back under control, and to Tommy's surprise, looked back up at him with a sparkle in his pale, watery eyes. "You don't look much like my mum though."

Tommy smiled back. "That's a relief. An ugly fucker like you, who knows what your mum might have looked like."

Bernie's face went momentarily peaceful. "Ah, she was beautiful, she was Tommy. Auburn hair, and the softest skin you've ever laid hands on." He sighed, settling back into his pillows. "Unfortunately for me, I take after me dad."

"There can be worse things."

Bernie glanced over at him.   "Nothing better if you've got a dad like yours."

Tommy nodded.   He knew the question was coming, knew he should lie, dissemble, say nothing. But this was Bernie, and he'd promised…

"Have you heard anything? Any news on your dad?"

Tommy was looking down at his hands, knew he had to keep quiet, knew what Martin would say and do, knew it was the smart thing, to keep it to themselves, sit on it… Tommy looked up, meeting Bernie's tired eyes. "Yeah. We know who did it."

Bernie's eyes bored into him. "Who? Who would have the nerve to touch Mickey Taylor?"

Tommy glanced around at the room of sleeping old men, then leaned in closer and whispered to Bernie. "It was the Vietnamese."

Bernie looked puzzled. "Them? I thought they just ran restaurants and stuff?"

Tommy shook his head. "Nah, really big in drugs these days."

Bernie settled back on his pillow. "Who would have guessed it…" He gazed up at the ceiling for a moment, then turned his eyes back to Tommy. "So when do you hit back at them?"

Tommy looked troubled and said nothing. Bernie glared at him. "You're having a fucking laugh with me, ain't ya?"

"We can't. My uncle Martin said we have to be careful - they're big, not just some local rival gang you can intimidate or take down.   They're like one of those creatures, what you call them, you cut off one head, three more grow back…"

Bernie's eyes never left him. "This ain't fucking right. Knowing who did your old man and doing nothing. No, it's all wrong."

"Fucking tell me about it," growled Tommy. He could feel his blood pressure rising at the thought of it, needed a cigarette to calm his nerves. He reached in his pocket reflexively, felt for his packet of fags. His fingers wrapped around it before he remembered that he'd quit, that he didn't need the calming shot of nicotine that only a cigarette could bring… He pulled his hand out of his pocket, looked up and met Bernie's eyes.

"I would kill for a fag," whispered Bernie.

Tommy scowled at him. "A man in your state? The last thing you need is - "

" - two weeks. That's what they said."

Tommy frowned. "Two weeks? What's that supposed to mean?"

"That's about how long they reckon I've got left. After that it's sayonara, turn out the lights, party's over."

"Fuck," muttered Tommy. "I'm sorry mate."

Bernie was still looking at Tommy's jacket, towards the packet where his cigarettes nestled. "What difference can one more fag make?"

It took some doing to get Bernie out of the bed, but once he was upright he seemed to find his strength, shuffling along with his IV trailing behind him. Tommy pushed the IV stand on its little wheels and offered to support Bernie, but he was having none of it. "I can still walk by meself," he wheezed.

Tommy had a hard time not laughing when they got outside. Right there at the hospital entrance half a dozen sick and dying patients were clustered - not to mention several nurses - all sucking on cigarettes.

Tommy pulled out the packet, Bernie's eyes following his every movement, and flipped it open. Bernie's shaking hand took a cigarette, held it up to his nose to sniff, then set it between his lips. Tommy flicked his gold lighter, watched as the flame quickly lit the cigarette, Bernie sucking in the smoke with a serene expression of bliss, eyes closed, experiencing nothing but the slow inhalation of the smoke.

Tommy lit his own cigarette, leaned back against the wall, all of the smokers huddled under a small awning as a summer storm lashed down, the falling rain bouncing off the black tarmac of the car park, creating bright rainbows of oil in the quickly growing puddles.

Finally Bernie opened his eyes. "So what's your plan?" There was a bright feverish flush to his cheeks.

"Plan?"

"Your dad."

Tommy drew the smoke into his cheeks and looked around. No one else was listening to them, each person was lost in their own little world, a small nicotine room that held their attention for a few brief moments. "What can we do? Martin's right. If we do anything, if they get one sniff that it's connected to Mickey, they'll wipe out the entire family."

Bernie sucked on his cigarette, gazed out into the rain, saying nothing.

"It just fucking burns me though," continued Tommy. "Knowing those fuckers are out there, thinking they've got away with it, thinking they got one over on us, on me, on the Taylors, on my dad!"

Bernie took another drag on his cigarette, looking at Tommy through a haze of smoke. "You'll figure something out." He started to take another drag, but a fit of coughing shook him, forced him to lean over, almost choking, gasping for air for a moment, Tommy looking at him with concern, until he straightened back up, his eyes streaming. "There's always a way."

Kenny

The rhythm was almost hypnotic, the relentless patter of Kenny's gloves on the speed bag, his hands a blur as he gradually increased the speed, faster and faster, lost in his own world.

When he was training, everything else just vanished. His mum with her sixty fags a day habit and her emphysema, his brother inside for the second time, his girlfriend who couldn't understand his obsession, always nagging him to go out and party with her - all of it vanished when he was training.

Whether he was running, skipping, doing weights, or working the bags, Kenny could get completely lost in what he was doing. He loved the work, the pain, the sweat running down his face and covering his body, loved the progress he felt week by week, month by month, and loved, more than anything, being in the ring.

That was when he truly came alive. In the ring he was an artist, a surgeon, in control of his craft, able to analyze an opponent, detect their strengths and weaknesses inside the first round, then carefully and methodically take them apart.

Kenny wasn't a big puncher, though he hit hard enough. He was a pure boxer, wearing an opponent down by sheer number of punches, by dissecting them, countering everything they did so that they felt weak, helpless, and little by little they came to realize that no matter what they did, those lightning fast gloves were going to keep flicking out, keep stinging them, keep finding a way through their defenses, while their own punches only seemed to find thin air.

Mickey had hand-picked Kenny's opponents, Kenny knew that, but they were no mugs he had fought, and each one had been worn down by Kenny's speed and relentless style. Some fights were stopped by the referee, a few had suffered cuts, there had even been a couple of knockouts. Kenny didn't care how he won, only how he fought. Had he controlled the fight? Had he stayed out of trouble? Had he sucked the life out of his opponent like an anaconda squeezing its prey to death? That was what satisfied him.

His hands moved faster and faster, almost caressing the speed bag, until with a final flourish he finished, reached up and stilled the bag, his breathing scorching against his lungs.

He slumped down on a stool, towelled his face, sucked on a bottle of water, looking around the gym for the first time in an hour or more. Most of the time he was so oblivious to what was going on around him that he had no idea who else was even in there. But there was one person he was looking for, and now he'd found him.

Tommy strolled across the floor of the gym with his cocky strut. And why not? He was a talented fighter himself, a good coach, and now he owned the gym and was the rising force in the Taylor family. Why wouldn't he strut?

Tommy was heading towards Kenny, who stood up, wiped his face once more, then began peeling the tape off his wrists with his teeth.

"All right, Kenny?" Tommy gave him an appraising look. "You were really working that speed bag. You're looking sharp."

Kenny gave a shy grin. As confident as he was in the ring, he was not comfortable outside it, especially around someone as confident and powerful as Tommy. "Thanks."

"I just need to tie up some details, but looks like we're set with Luke Watson next month."

"That would be good, really good," said Kenny softly. Watson already had a couple of ABA belts to his name. He would be a big scalp, a real boost for Kenny if he could beat him. "I'm ready."

"Course you are!" Tommy patted him on the back and started to turn away.

"Tommy? Can I talk to you about something?"

Tommy turned back, a quizzical look on his face. Kenny was like a Victorian kid and normally only spoke when he was spoken to. For him to ask to talk to Tommy was almost unheard of. "Yeah, what's up? Is it your mum? If you need anything for her…"

"No. It's not that." Kenny took a deep breath. "It's the Olympics."

Tommy grinned. "Don't worry, they'll be here soon enough, and we'll make sure you're ready."

Kenny nodded. "I know. And I appreciate everything you do for me. But I'm going to win, I'm going to win a gold medal." The words spilled out of him. "And when I do, I'm going to dedicate it to Mickey. He did so much for me, for all of us, and what happened to him wasn't right." He finally came to a halt, looked almost shocked by how much he had said, how much he had revealed.

Tommy looked at him with a curious expression on his face. He had often wondered how much that night – the night Mickey died – had affected Kenny.

Not only had Kenny been at the fight, seen Mickey defeat Frankie Junior, he had also been at the pub, had been the one to find Mickey's body on the floor of the toilet. Tommy had tried several times to talk to him about it, but Kenny couldn't even speak about it, clammed up completely whenever it was brought up. Tommy reached out and squeezed Kenny's arm. "It wasn't right. It wasn't fucking right at all, and something needs to be done about it." He started to turn away, then glanced back at Kenny. "But I appreciate what you said. He'd be proud of you."

Tommy slumped in the chair in front of Martin's desk, a cocky grin on his face, looking from Martin to Sharon. "So now what do we think?"

Martin shuffled some papers on his desk, saying nothing.

Sharon grinned. "I'd say you were on the money - literally!"

Tommy sat up. "No fucking shit! Over a hundred large last week unless I was mistaken."

Martin finally met Tommy's eyes. "One hundred and seventeen and change," he said softly.

Tommy clapped his hands together. "I think that calls for a celebration! Isn't there a bottle of bubbly around here somewhere?"

Sharon stood up. "I think there's one in the fridge. Your dad always kept a couple of bottles on ice for special occasions."

"I don't think we should be celebrating yet," said Martin softly. The room became very still. Tommy looked from Martin to Sharon.

Sharon had paused by the door. "Come on Marty, give Tommy some credit. He was right. The money from the fags is rolling in, it's becoming our biggest earner."

"So far so good," said Martin. "But we all know that things like this can fluctuate. There will be good weeks and bad weeks."

Tommy shook his head in exasperation. "Fuck! What more do you want from me!"

"I want you to take fewer risks."

"What the hell is that supposed to mean?"

"You were out on a job again last night."

"So?"

"So you don't need to take that risk."

Sharon frowned. "Are you being careful, Tommy?"

"Course I'm being careful. But in case you hadn't noticed, we are running a criminal organization. We make money from booze and cigarettes, nightclubs, illegal gambling, protection, you fucking name it, we do it! And sometimes we need to get our hands dirty!"

Martin looked unconvinced.   "You don't need to be out there on the front line. You're just satisfying your need for cheap thrills."

"Don't need to be out there on the front line? In case you hadn't noticed, this business, this little empire of ours recently lost its emperor. I'm trying to fill Mickey's shoes, get people believing in us, and that means getting out there, showing my face, showing that I'm not afraid to work hard and get blood on my hands if need be."

Martin narrowed his eyes. "And there it is. You think you're the new Mickey Taylor, that you're your dad!"

Tommy jumped to his feet, advanced towards Martin, jabbing a finger at him. "And you fucking hate that, don't you!   You lived in his shadow for your whole fucking lifetime, and now you can see yourself living in my shadow, and you don't like it!" He moved round the desk and stood very close to Martin, their faces almost touching. "So here's my advice to you. If you don't like it, then just fuck off!"

Silence filled the room, thick and heavy, the only sound coming from Tommy and Martin's heavy breathing as they eyeballed each other, neither one flinching, neither one blinking, neither one backing down.

Sharon stared at both of them, wondering what she was seeing, what would happen. She had seen Mickey and Martin go at it a few times, but never like this, never such a raw and naked showdown. In the past, Martin had always given in, always backed down when Mickey got fired up. And now?

It was indeed Martin who broke first, turning away, looking down at his desk. For a moment he said nothing, just stared, then he gave a deep sigh, picked up his car keys and eased past Tommy towards the door. He stopped there, looked at Sharon, then back at Tommy. "You're right," he said softly. And then he was gone.

As the door closed behind Martin, Tommy let out a deep pent up breath, glanced at Sharon. "What the fuck," he grumbled.

But Sharon had a big grin on her face. "I reckon that's it then."

Tommy frowned. "What's that supposed to mean?"

"It always happens sooner or later. Just like lions. The two dominant males have a showdown, eventually the younger one wins and the old one leaves."

"You've been watching too many nature programmes."

Sharon shook her head. "We're all just animals under our clothes. It had to happen." She gave a short laugh. "Congratulations. You're the new guvnor."

Tommy started to say something, but Sharon was already heading out the door. "Take a seat guvnor, I'll get that champagne…"

Martin

As Martin closed the front door of his flat, his senses were on full alert. Someone was there. He paused, just listening. Nothing. But still he was convinced that he was not alone.

"Are you going to stand in the hallway all day, or are you going to come in and say hello?" Graham's voice echoed through the spacious flat.

Martin let out a deep breath, relieved that it wasn't an intruder, but not in the mood to deal with Graham. He'd just walked out of a row at the gym, the last thing he needed - or wanted – right now was another of Graham's tantrums.

He walked slowly into the living room. Graham was sprawled out on the couch, shoes off, feet on the coffee table, leafing through a large format book of fine art prints. "Fancy yourself as a bit of an art connoisseur, don't you?" he said, without looking up.

"I like art, like beautiful things," said Martin evenly. He was still trying to gauge Graham's mood. Confrontational or conciliatory?

"And am I one of your beautiful things?" Graham closed the book, turned and looked up at Martin.

Martin gave a gentle laugh. "You know what I think of you."

Graham patted the couch beside him. "So why don't you come sit here and show me?"

Martin walked around to stand in front of Graham. "Give me a few minutes to unwind - I've had a tough day at work, need to clear my head."

Graham gave a coquettish smile. "I'll clear your head - and a lot more besides…" He reached out, grabbed Martin's belt and started to unzip his trousers.

Martin pulled away. "Not now, just give me a while - "

" - Give you a while? I'm done giving you a while, that's all I ever seem to do! What about me? I've got my bitch of a wife nagging at me, wants to know where I go, what I do, she's always on at me about something. Then I come over here to see you and you push me away, tell me to wait, not now, later, tomorrow!" His cheeks were flushed, eyes wide, emotion pouring out of him. "Well I'm done waiting!"

Martin's eyes strayed to the table, noticed the glass, the bottle of whisky. "I think you need to calm down, take a deep breath - "

" - And relax, yeah, yeah, I've heard that before." Graham leaned forward, poured himself a double shot and drained it in one. He wiped his mouth on the back of his hand and looked up defiantly at Martin. "So here's the way it is."

Martin looked at him quizzically. "What the fuck is that supposed to mean?"

"I'm done waiting, done being something secret, hiding from my wife, from the world, feeling like you're embarrassed by me - "

" - That's not true!"

"Well that's the way it feels. So here's what's going to happen." He lifted his glass again, realized it was empty, set it back down. "Either we run away together now - you've got the money, you know we could do it - or I tell my wife, tell everyone, let the chips fall where they may. Maybe you'll see me again, maybe you won't." He looked up at Martin with his hungry, angry eyes. "It's time to choose, Martin!"

Martin looked into Graham's deep brown eyes. That was what he had fallen in love with, those eyes. Sometimes they were soulful and sad, and then at others joyous, excited. But right now they looked pitiful, defiant. Martin lowered himself onto the couch beside Graham, reached out to touch his leg, but Graham brushed him off.

"I'm not going to back down, I can't, I won't. You'll do what I say, or else."

Martin scowled. "What the hell is that supposed to mean?"

Graham reached for a bag at his feet, lifted it into his lap. As Martin looked on, he pulled out a large envelope. "I've got it all here…" He opened the envelope, pulled out a stack of photos, some videos. "Remember when we made these? Remember what's on them?"

Martin reached for the videos, but Graham pulled them back. "Uh uh, you don't get them - they're my bargaining chip, my ticket out. Run away with me and you'll never see them again. Try and screw with me and I'll send them to my wife, to lots of people."

Martin tilted his head to one side. "If you expose me, you expose yourself."

Graham shoved the videos back in the bag. "I don't care. I can't go on living like this, can't go on living this lie. I would rather everyone knew than continue the way it's been, with these secrets, this false life." He peered at Martin, questioning, hopeful. "What do you say? Can we do it? Do you love me?"

Martin said nothing for a moment, just looked at Graham with a sad expression on his face. "You know I love you," he said finally.

Graham looked at him pleadingly. "Then show me!"

Martin stood up, holding out his hand to Graham. "Of course."

Graham took his hand, stood slowly, uncertain. "So it's OK?"

Martin led him towards the bedroom. "Of course. I just never really knew how you felt, what ends you would go to in order to convince me." He pushed the bedroom door open and followed Graham inside. "Now I know, know how far you will go, there's only one answer I can give you."

As they reached the bed, Graham turned around, reached up and touched Martin's face. "I knew it, knew you loved me."

"I do love you."

They locked in a passionate embrace, a hard breathless kiss that went on and on, all their emotion coming to the surface, tears streaming down Martin's face.

When they finally broke apart, Graham reached up, wiping away the tears and kissed Martin's salty cheeks. "Thank you."

Martin said nothing, suddenly pushing Graham down onto the bed.

Graham laughed, excited, aroused. "So that's the way it is, huh? You know I like it rough." He scooted back on the bed as Martin knelt beside him, looking up with love in his eyes as they kissed again, Martin trapping Graham with his body, pinning him down.

Graham groaned in pleasure at the weight of Martin's body on top of him. He closed his eyes, lost himself in the moment.

He didn't see the sad look in Martin's eyes, didn't see as Martin reached for a pillow, didn't see as the pillow suddenly covered his face.

He started to struggle, but Martin was too strong, too certain, held the pillow tight to Graham's face as he struggled and writhed, tried to throw Martin off, but it was to no avail.

Martin knelt on his arms, his weight on Graham's chest, the pillow completely covering his face and turned his head to look out the window. The skyscrapers of Canary Wharf glinted in the late afternoon sunshine, but Martin didn't see them. His thoughts were elsewhere - Graham the first time he had seen him, the sunshine on his fair hair, the light in his eyes. Graham kissing him, holding him tight, clinging to him like a lifeboat on a stormy sea. The two of them in bed together, naked, moving as one, Martin feeling united, fulfilled for perhaps the only time in his life. And finally, Graham sitting on the couch, the videos in his hand; weak, pleading, pitiful, scheming.

Finally Martin looked back down. Graham was still, no movement, no struggle, no life. For a long time Martin looked at the pillow, not wanting to lift it, not wanting to see what he had done, wanting instead to remember Graham when they had been happy, before the alcohol had taken over, before the tantrums and threats and ultimatums had started.

Finally Martin set the pillow aside. Graham looked peaceful, his eyes closed, his face remarkably calm, passive even. Martin brushed a stray hair from his face, caressed his cheek, then slowly bent down and kissed his soft lips for the last time.

He stood up, straightened his shirt and looked around the apartment. He knew exactly what he needed to do, had been planning it for months. He had just needed the catalyst to put his plan into effect. And now, now the time was right. His phone was already in his hand as he marched from the room.

Bernie

Nurse Madison marched down the long hallway in her soft-soled shoes, making hardly a sound as she approached the ward. Her uniform was crisp, as always, her clipboard in her hand, a freshly sharpened pencil tucked behind her ear. There was a right and a wrong way to do things, and Nurse Madison insisted that everything on her ward was done the right way.

She turned briskly into the ward, surveyed the two rows of identical beds. All elderly men, all terminal, but that didn't mean they didn't deserve the best treatment she could give them.

She moved slowly down the row of beds, the morning sun angling through the window into her eyes. She hated to wake them, but breakfast was coming in ten minutes, and she wanted them all to be up and ready when their food arrived. They may be terminal patients, but a schedule was as vital for them as for anyone else, and getting a good breakfast at the start of each day was important.

She reached the last bed, paused, a frown on her face. It was empty. Where was Bernie? She looked around. No sign of him. Must be in the bathroom. She padded across to the bathroom, rapped lightly on the door.

No reply. She knocked again. "Bernie? You in there?"

Still no reply. Again she knocked. "Bernie? You OK, love?"

When there was still no reply she frowned. She hated disorder, changes to schedule. If Bernie had collapsed or even died in the bathroom, it would disrupt the whole morning.

Nurse Madison reached for the keys hanging from her belt, went to unlock the bathroom door, then paused - it wasn't locked. She slowly opened the door, peering inside. The bathroom was empty.

She turned back to the ward, looking around. If he wasn't in his bed, wasn't in the bathroom, where on Earth was he?

The taxi pulled up on the quiet street, the cabby turned to his passenger. "You sure this is it?"

Bernie nodded, saving his breath. Without his oxygen he was feeling tired, breathless. It had been a long day, getting all the supplies and information that he needed, and it had really taken its toll. Two weeks the doctors had said - after his efforts today, he'd be lucky to last another two days.

He leaned forward, shoved a handful of twenties through the glass to the driver. "Keep the change," he gasped.

The cabby looked in surprise at the money, then grinned. "Cheers, mate!" He jumped out, opened the door and helped Bernie to his feet.

Bernie's face was ashen, a sickly sheen to it as he peered up at the bright sun, pulling his coat tight around him.

"You sure you're going to be all right?"

Bernie nodded, straightened up and waved the cabby away. He climbed back into his cab, pulling away in a cloud of diesel. Bernie watched until the car was out of sight, then turned and looked around.

The Vietnamese restaurant was across the street, about twenty yards away. Right now there were a couple of punters inside, so Bernie leaned back against the wall, the sunshine on his pale face and pulled a pack of cigarettes out of the pocket of his coat. He studied the cigarette as he slid it out of the packet, felt it between his fingertips, sniffed it, finally placing it between his lips. How could something that had brought him so much pleasure also have brought him so much pain and misery? He lifted the lighter with shaking hands, watched the flame as it flared to life and sucked deeply as he lit the cigarette.

Bliss! The smoke filled his lungs, soothed his nerves, curled up around his face. Bernie smiled to himself. Doctors had said that smoking would kill him. Shows how little they knew! He closed his eyes, allowing himself a quiet moment of pure pleasure, nothing existing but the cigarette, the sun on his face.

With each breath the moment grew closer, but for now Bernie wasn't concerned with that, wasn't concerned with what happened next. He was simply living in the moment, enjoying every last second until his cigarette was finished.

With a deep breath he finished the cigarette, dropped it at his feet and ground it out with his heel, before coughing vigorously. As he leaned forwards, his hands resting on his knees, he couldn't help but laugh at himself. Silly old sod, to think he could enjoy a fag with no repercussions! He should know better than that by now, life never gives you something without demanding something in return.

Slowly, slowly, he got his breath back and straightened up. The restaurant was empty, no customers, just a waiter standing by the door looking bored. This was his moment.

Bernie looked both ways and slowly crossed the street. He was tired, beyond tired, but all his work, all the planning, all the effort was about to pay off. Tired didn't matter now, there was just the job in hand, and after that was done he could rest for as long as he wanted.

He lifted a weary leg and stepped into the cool, dark exterior of the restaurant. The waiter gave him a cursory glance and picked up a menu from the table by the door.

"Table for one, sir?"

Bernie nodded. "Away from the window, please."

"Of course." The waiter headed towards the back of the restaurant, Bernie following slowly, looking around as he did.

The waiter reached a table in the back corner. "This good?"

"Yeah, fine," gasped Bernie. "Where's your loo?"

The waiter laid the menu on the table and pointed towards a door. "Past the kitchen."

Bernie shuffled in the direction indicated, while the waiter returned to his station by the door. The restaurant smelled good, Bernie had to admit that. He'd been so busy today that he had completely forgotten to eat. For a moment he was tempted to eat dinner first, draw things out, enjoy himself a bit, but he dismissed that idea as quickly as it came to him. He needed the place to be empty - by the time he sat and ate, who knows how many people might be there? No, for what he had planned, now was the best time.

He paused by the kitchen door, peered through the glass panel into the steamy interior. Two cooks were at work, chopping, preparing. A manager stood at the far side of the room, reviewing some paperwork. Were they going to be surprised!

Bernie pushed the door open and stepped inside.

For a moment no one saw him, and he stood simply looking around.

Then one of the cooks looked up, spotted him, gabbled something at him in Vietnamese.

That got the attention of the manager. With a scowl he pulled himself away from his paperwork and hurried over towards Bernie. "Not the toilet!" he shouted. "Down the hall, next door!"

Bernie said nothing and looked around.

The manager got closer to him. "You can't be here. This is kitchen. Customers not allowed in kitchen!" He pointed towards the door. "You go now!"

A slow smile crossed Bernie's face. "I'm not a customer."

The manager had stopped a couple of feet from him and peered at him, puzzled. "You not customer? Who are you?"

Bernie reached down, unbuttoned his coat, spreading it wide. "I'm a messenger."

The manager stared at him wide eyed, not quite believing what he was seeing. Finally he found his voice. "You fucking crazy!" His eyes were still glued to Bernie, to what was strapped to his body.

It had taken a lot of work, a lot of money, a lot of old favours called in, but Bernie had done it. He had turned himself to a human bomb, the explosives strapped to his body, the trigger in his hand. He met the manager's scared eyes and slowly smiled. "This is for my mate, for Mickey Taylor," he announced quietly. And then he pressed the button. The effect was instantaneous. The manager, the cooks, none of them even had time to move. And Bernie? He had a huge smile on his face. He died with a feeling of complete and utter happiness, knowing that his death was nothing compared to the satisfaction he was getting from revenging his friend.

From outside the explosion was massive, ripping through the restaurant, the flat above where the Vietnamese ran their drug business, through the warehouse at the back where they processed and packaged the goods. The windows exploded outwards, the roof lifted off the building, two cars parked outside were hurled across the street. In an instant their business was wiped out, half their leaders killed. In an instant, Mickey Taylor was revenged.

Tommy

Tommy slowly opened his eyes. It took him a moment to remember where he was. He looked around the room - it was a right fucking mess. Empty champagne bottles littered the floor, there was a mess of coke powder on the coffee table, a bundle of cash on the beside.

He pulled back the silk sheet and peered at the three hookers curled up beside him. Not bad, a nice mix - one blonde with pneumatic tits, a skinny brunette with an arse to die for, and a foxy looking black chick. Tommy smiled as the memories of the previous night came back to him. A proper celebration, a real bender, the kind of night people talked about his old man having. And now, well, now he was the boss, the guvnor, it was only right that he should follow in his dad's footsteps.

He reached over, grabbed a bottle of champagne from the bedside and took a swig. Not bad, even though it was flat. He lifted the bottle to take a second gulp but stopped as his phone began to ring. For a moment he was inclined to ignore it, but then he glanced over - Sharon. He clamped the phone to his ear as he drank deep from the bottle. "What's up?"

"Haven't you heard?"

Tommy put the bottle down, instantly alerted by her tone of voice. "Heard what?"

"Someone hit the Vietnamese last night. Wiped out their base near Brick Lane."

"Fuck me!"

"I thought it might be you," admitted Sharon.

Tommy grinned. "Wish it was, but no, nothing to do with me."

"Well whether we did it or not, they will certainly be looking our way. You should keep your head down for a few days while I see if I can find out what happened."

Tommy looked over at the girls, starting to stir beside him. "Yeah. I think I can keep out of sight for a few days."

"All right. Talk soon."

Tommy dropped the phone back on the bedside, a huge grin plastered across his face. Whoever had hit the Vietnamese, he was grateful. As long as no fingers pointed towards the Taylors, they could have their cake and eat it too. People close to them would assume they had found a way to do it, but to the outside world - including, hopefully, the Vietnamese - they would be innocent.

Within the past twenty four hours the world had become a much better place, everything Tommy had dared to dream of coming true at one time.

He felt a stirring as the blonde moved against his leg. He knew exactly how to keep himself busy for a few days. He reached down, wrapped his fingers in her hair, guided her mouth towards his stiff cock. As she engulfed him he lay back, enjoying the sensation, and gave the brunette a nudge. "Get us a snort, darling'." The girl opened her eyes, leaned over and kissed Tommy, before walking naked to the table and began to prepare a line.

You know, thought Tommy, I could get used to this…

Sharon

"Martin?" Sharon pushed the door open and stepped into Martin's flat, her high heels echoing on the wooden floor.

"Martin?" Her voice was the only sound.

Normally Sharon left Martin alone, but with the Vietnamese on high alert and Tommy laying low, she needed to talk to him - and that was exactly when he had chosen to go silent. For two days she had been ringing him with no reply. Now she had to know where he was, what he was doing.

Sharon marched into the living room and looked around. Everything seemed normal. She continued on into Martin's bedroom and stopped cold as she looked into the room. What the fuck was going on? The wardrobes were open, empty. She strode across to the dresser, threw open a drawer - empty. One by one she opened all the drawers, found each and every one empty.

Finally her eyes rested on the bed.

It was made, of course, but that wasn't what she noticed - it was the note, laid neatly on the pillow, waiting to be found, waiting to be read.

Sharon snatched it up, instantly recognizing Martin's angular handwriting. The note was brief - Martin never wasted words.

"I'm gone. Don't bother trying to find me. M."

Suddenly Sharon felt old, tired, weary, all her usual poise and resolve deserting her as she sat heavily on the bed. She looked at the note again. "I'm gone. Don't bother trying to find me. M."

Mickey gone. Martin gone. She looked around the room at the empty wardrobes, each one reminding her of how empty her own life was. And as she looked around, one question ran through her mind, over and over again.

What the hell was going to happen next?

The End

Books by Sandra Prior

Dangerous – published 2012

Diamond Geezer – published 2014

Mickey's War – published 2014

www.SandraPrior.co.uk

http://www.facebook.com/sandrapriorauthor

http://twitter.com/Sandra_Prior

About the Author Sandra Prior

Today, Sandra lives in Clacton with her youngest son, and her dog, Dylan -- who lets her write in peace as long as she takes him for walks on the beach when she's done! Following the success of her first 3 books, *Dangerous, Diamond Geezer and Mickey's War*, she continues to write full time.

Printed in Great Britain
by Amazon